continued . . .

SHROUDS OF HOLLY

KATE KINGSBURY

BERKLEY PRIME CRIME, NEW YORK

THE BERKLEY PUBLISHING GROUP
Published by the Penguin Group
Penguin Group (USA) Inc.
375 Hudson Street, New York, New York 10014, USA
Penguin Group (Canada), 90 Eglinton Avenue East, Suite 700, Toronto, Ontario M4P 2Y3, Canada
(a division of Pearson Penguin Canada Inc.)
Penguin Books Ltd., 80 Strand, London WC2R 0RL, England
Penguin Group Ireland, 25 St. Stephen's Green, Dublin 2, Ireland (a division of Penguin Books Ltd.)
Penguin Group (Australia), 250 Camberwell Road, Camberwell, Victoria 3124, Australia
(a division of Pearson Australia Group Pty. Ltd.)
Penguin Books India Pvt. Ltd., 11 Community Centre, Panchsheel Park, New Delhi—110 017, India
Penguin Group (NZ), 67 Apollo Drive, Rosedale, North Shore 0632, New Zealand
(a division of Pearson New Zealand Ltd.)
Penguin Books (South Africa) (Pty.) Ltd., 24 Sturdee Avenue, Rosebank, Johannesburg 2196,
South Africa

Penguin Books Ltd., Registered Offices: 80 Strand, London WC2R 0RL, England

This is a work of fiction. Names, characters, places, and incidents either are the product of the author's imagination or are used fictitiously, and any resemblance to actual persons, living or dead, business establishments, events, or locales is entirely coincidental. The publisher does not have any control over and does not assume any responsibility for author or third-party websites or their content.

SHROUDS OF HOLLY

A Berkley Prime Crime Book / published by arrangement with the author

PRINTING HISTORY
Berkley Prime Crime trade paperback edition / November 2007
Berkley Prime Crime mass-market edition / October 2008

ISBN: 978-0-425-22431-1

BERKLEY® PRIME CRIME
Berkley Prime Crime Books are published by The Berkley Publishing Group,
a division of Penguin Group (USA) Inc.,
375 Hudson Street, New York, New York 10014.
BERKLEY PRIME CRIME and the BERKLEY PRIME CRIME design are trademarks belonging to
Penguin Group (USA) Inc.

PRINTED IN THE UNITED STATES OF AMERICA

10 9 8 7 6 5 4 3 2 1

To Bill,
for still singing me love songs.

ACKNOWLEDGMENTS

I am indebted to my esteemed editor, Sandra Harding, whose opinions and judgment I value and respect. My sincere gratitude to the art department, who worked so diligently and swiftly on my beautiful cover. To my astute agent, Paige Wheeler, for all the enthusiasm and guidance. To all who worked so hard to get this book into production. To my readers, for their unwavering support and their wonderful letters. And to my husband, who never fails to inspire me.

CHAPTER

🐝 1 🐝

"Madeline, you've achieved wonders with the ballroom this year!" Cecily Sinclair Baxter gazed with satisfaction at the green and red banners swooping in huge loops along the upper balconies of the vast room.

Above them, bountiful bunches of mistletoe adorned the heads of the smiling cherubs that graced the walls, while enormous red velvet bows clung to thick garlands of fir.

Cecily turned to her friend with a smile. "Those wreaths are magnificent. The red apples and gilded walnuts are such a lovely contrast."

With a careless hand Madeline Pengrath swept her long black hair back from her shoulder. "It will all look so much better once I get the holly up there. I do hate waiting until the last minute for that."

"Yes, well, the berries tend to fall if we cut it any earlier. We can't have the guests trampling them underfoot and staining their gowns."

"I suppose not, but it's a shame it won't be up in time for the welcoming reception this afternoon. Though I can't imagine why all these people would want to spend their Christmas holiday in a cold, windy seaside town. Badgers End can be so miserable in the winter, especially now that it has snowed this afternoon."

"It does look rather pretty though, don't you think?" Cecily glanced out of the window, where lawns white with snow rolled down to the frosted trees.

"Pretty, but cold." Madeline shivered in her wispy floral gown. "I'll be glad when it warms up."

Up on the stage, the musicians took their places with a good deal of shuffling amidst a chorus of discordant chords. Cecily never could understand why the tuning of musical instruments had to sound so much like a horde of alley cats on the prowl.

Shuddering, she turned back to Madeline. "Samuel should be back with the freshly cut holly in an hour or two. I had to send Baxter with him. Gerald was supposed to go, but he has fallen ill and all the other footmen are fully occupied."

Madeline's tinkling laughter echoed across the sprung parquet floor. "I can imagine Baxter was less than pleased to be pressed into such undignified service. It must have reminded him of those early days when he was under your employ as your manager."

Cecily wrinkled her nose. Madeline meant well, but there were times when she could be extremely tactless. "My husband knows quite well that no one will regard him with any less respect for assisting me in an emergency."

"Of course not. Nevertheless, I simply can't imagine him tramping around the woods to cut holly." Madeline headed toward the tables lining the walls. "Baxter is not one to willingly take part in such a grubby business. Besides, he's a good many years older than Samuel. He'll be hard-pressed to keep up with him."

Following her, Cecily wasn't about to admit that Baxter had indeed protested with vehemence when she'd made the request.

It wasn't often she asked her husband for assistance. Having assured him on many an occasion that the trials and tribulations of managing the Pennyfoot Country Club were of no consequence, she was reluctant to admit that sometimes the task could be a trifle overwhelming.

After all, more than ten years of the new century had now passed, and this was the era of women's emancipation. Asking Baxter for help was tantamount to admitting that she wasn't as independent as she'd have him believe.

Nevertheless, she felt compelled to defend him. "It was good of him to step in," she said, "and fortunate for me that he'd closed his office in London for the Christmas season. I really don't know what I would have done without him."

"We would have had to make do without the holly I suppose." Madeline paused at a table and studied it with a critical eye. In the center of the white linen tablecloth, a small silver candelabra nestled in a tiny garland of holly and fir. Nudging it over an inch, she murmured, "It must be nearly time to light the candles."

As if in answer, the ballroom doors opened and Gertie, the Pennyfoot's robust chief housemaid, rushed through them like a steam engine charging into the station. In her afternoon black dress and white apron, she looked remarkably tidy for a change. Even her cap, usually askew, now sat carefully pinned into place in her dark hair.

She paused, making an obvious effort to catch her breath before blurting out, "The guests are arriving in the lobby, m'm. Shall I start showing them in?"

Cecily sent one last glance around the room. "Yes, Gertie, if you will. First send in the maids with the refreshments and then show in the guests. Be sure to give me time to greet each one before you send in the next."

"Yes, m'm." Gertie bobbed her head then scurried back through the doors.

"It always amazes me how that young woman can move so quickly." Madeline gazed after Gertie's retreating form. "Considering she has the build of a bull, she's remarkably light on her feet."

Cecily had to bite her tongue. Madeline was as thin as a willow stick and could use some of Gertie's weight, but it was not her place to say so. "Perhaps you should light the candles," she said instead. "Do you have the matches?"

Madeline produced a small box from the folds of her gown and held it up. "Right here."

Cecily watched her strike a match and hold it to the wicks of the candles. The flickering light gleamed on the long-stemmed crystal glasses, and she was most pleased with the charming effect.

Madeline might be a trifle annoying at times with her

blunt comments, but her talents as a decorator could not be denied. She had done her work well, as usual.

Leaving her friend to light the rest of the candles at the tables, Cecily headed toward the stage. The conductor, looking most elegant in his black frock coat and starched white shirt, nodded when she raised her hand in a signal. He immediately turned back to his orchestra, raised his baton and tapped it on the music stand.

As the mellow strains of a waltz filled the room, the doors opened once more, allowing the maids to enter. They carried large oval silver trays bearing tiny mince pies, sausage rolls, swiss tarts, and fluffy cream puffs. As they passed by Cecily, she could smell the delectable aroma of Michel's wonderful bacon-wrapped chestnuts. Her chef had surpassed himself.

Across the room, the Pennyfoot's newest and youngest maid, Pansy, circled the tables, filling wineglasses with their best claret. Well satisfied, Cecily took up her place close to the doors, and made ready to welcome the guests.

All that was needed now was for Samuel and Baxter to come back with the trap loaded with holly, and the preparations for yet another memorable Pennyfoot Christmas would be complete. Now she could relax a little and enjoy the traditional welcoming reception.

Down in the kitchen, things were not quite so serene. Michel stormed about as usual, waving his hands and screaming French phrases that no one understood.

His tall chef's hat bobbed to and fro as he circled the

large kitchen table, and Mrs. Chubb, the Pennyfoot's stalwart housekeeper, had to dodge out of his way to avoid being swept aside.

"For heaven's sake, Michel," she cried, as a dish crashed to the floor and splintered into a dozen pieces. "Look what you've gone and done now! That will cost you a pretty penny to replace."

"It is not my fault we have no eggs!" Michel picked up a large wooden spoon and waved it at her. "How am I to make ze custard tarts without ze eggs? *Mon Dieu!* When there is so much to do, is it not *tres mauvais* that I do not have ze supplies that I need?"

"Screaming about it isn't helping much, either." Mrs. Chubb wiped her hands on her apron, leaving a smear of flour.

"You're the housekeeper. You must do something. Send Gertie or Pansy to get ze eggs!" Michel slammed his hand down on the table, sending a rolling pin tumbling to the floor.

"Pansy and Gertie are busy. All the maids are in the ballroom waiting on the guests."

Michel leaned his head back and let out a howl of rage. "Sacre bleu! How am I supposed to make ze custard tarts?"

Mrs. Chubb pursed her lips. "All right, all right." She bent down to pick up her rolling pin. Panting a little from the exertion, she muttered, "If it'll stop your caterwauling, I'll go and get the eggs myself."

Michel stopped yelling and looked at her in surprise. "You will?"

"Yes, I will. We are short of help, what with this nasty

cold going around the staff, and sometimes some of us have to make sacrifices."

She glared at Michel, who grinned back at her. "I make ze tarts. I leave sacrifices to everyone else."

"So I noticed." Turning her back on him she reached for her shawl, then headed for the kitchen door. The heels of her sturdy black shoes clicked on the brick floor, and she stamped a little harder, hoping the chef would take notice of her resentment.

There were times when she felt like slapping him. "I shall expect a nice drop of your special brandy when I get back," she told him as she opened the door. "It's cold out there."

Without waiting for him to answer, she stepped out into the icy wind. The sun shone in her eyes as she scrunched across the yard, ankles freezing in the crisp, cold snow. The henhouse was on the other side of the garden sheds, and by the time she reached it she couldn't feel her toes.

She was getting too old to be prancing around in this weather, she thought with a flash of resentment. Good job she had plenty of fat on her to help keep the cold out of her aching bones.

Chickens strutted about when she entered the henhouse, protesting with a loud cackling and clucking that made her ears ring. In spite of the heavy shawl about her shoulders, her fingers shook so hard she had trouble holding the eggs when she fished them out of the straw.

Carefully she placed each egg in the bucket someone had left near the coops, and breathed a sigh of relief when she'd rescued the last one. Just as she was about to open the door, she heard the thudding of a horse's hooves in the yard outside. That had to be Samuel and Mr. Baxter back with the holly.

They'd picked it in record time, she thought, as she let herself out of the henhouse. It usually took most of the afternoon to load up the trap with the prickly stuff.

Hurrying across the yard she saw the chestnut stamping his feet and snorting steam from his nostrils. There was no sign of the men. As she drew closer the horse tossed his head and looked in her direction. His eyes rolled wildly at her. The reins hung loose, and she could see his sides heaving, as if he'd run hard and fast.

Something was wrong. She could feel it in her bones. Samuel would never leave the horse out in the yard in that condition. The young man had been stable manager at the Pennyfoot for years. The horses were like his children, and he treated them as such.

Even now, when the guests brought their shiny new motorcars to be sheltered in the stables, Samuel was always saying he'd rather have a horse any day. A lot less trouble, he'd say.

In any case, there hadn't been time for both men to cross the yard. Mr. Baxter never used the kitchen entrance, and he would have been halfway across the lawn on his way to the front doors.

Her heart started to thump uncomfortably as she hurried toward the trap. The chestnut backed away, and she slowed her pace, talking softly to the frightened animal. "Whoa, boy. Whoa, there. It's all right. I won't hurt you. Where's Samuel, then?"

Noticing the small amount of holly in the trap, she felt even more worried. Slowly she put down her bucket and reached out to grab hold of the reins. The horse shivered, but stood still as she ran a hand over its flanks. "Whoa, boy. What's the matter, then? We'll soon have you inside in the warm."

Still murmuring soft words, she moved closer to the trap and peered inside. At first, she thought it was Samuel lying there, so still and cold. Looking closer, she saw that the man was a stranger. His dark eyes were open and staring right at her. In the next instant she realized something else. The stranger was as dead as a plucked chicken.

Without stopping to think, Mrs. Chubb let out a scream, turned tail and leapt toward the kitchen. Her foot caught the bucket and it overturned, spilling the precious eggs out into the snow. The horse reared back and whinnied, but she didn't wait to see if it settled down again. Sliding and slipping, she ran for the back door nearly colliding with Gertie in her haste.

Cecily watched the dancers circling the floor and wished Baxter were there to see them. The ladies looked so graceful in their pastel gowns, their partners equally dashing in black morning coats and gray trousers.

She had taken great care with her own attire for the event, choosing a pale pink tea gown edged with lace at the neck and cuffs. Tiny pink pearls dotted the bodice, and the gleaming pearl necklace circling her throat had been one of last year's Christmas gifts from Baxter.

Gazing longingly at the swirling dancers, she wished she could join them on the arm of her handsome husband. How she loved to dance with him—moving together in time to the music—totally as one. She remembered so well the first time they'd danced together . . . on this very floor.

That was when she'd owned the Pennyfoot, and he was her manager. They had only just begun to acknowledge the bond growing between them. All the uncertainty, the anticipation—such a precious time—and so fleeting.

Lost in her reverie, she failed to notice Gertie until she stood directly in front of her. One look at the young woman's flushed face and pinched mouth, and Cecily knew at once that something was seriously amiss.

Taking Gertie's arm, she pulled her farther away from the group of chattering ladies nearby. "What is it? What's happened?"

Gertie's eyes stared in every direction but at Cecily's face. "Mrs. Chubb sent me to tell you. The t-trap, m'm. It came back."

"Which trap is that?"

"The one with the holly, m'm."

Cecily was beginning to get a nasty feeling in the pit of her stomach. "Oh, you mean Baxter and Samuel are back?"

Gertie visibly swallowed. "No, m'm. That's not what I meant."

Cecily frowned. "I don't understand."

"The trap came back . . . on its own."

"On its own?"

"Yes, m'm. Well, the horse were pulling it, of course. Must have found his own way back. Mr. Baxter and Samuel weren't in it." Her face puckered up like a child's, ready to burst into tears. "We don't know where they are, m'm."

Cecily stared at her, trying to make sense of the confusing words. The trap had returned without Baxter or Samuel. No, that couldn't be.

"That's not all, m'm."

Gertie's voice wavered so badly Cecily was afraid to hear the rest of it. "Go on," she said quietly.

"There's a dead body in the trap."

At first she was too stunned to answer.

Gertie looked even more frightened. "M'm?"

Cecily shook her head to clear the fog. "Dear God." For a dreadful moment she thought the worst. "It's not . . . ?" She couldn't bring herself to voice the horrible thought.

It took a second for Gertie to understand, then she shook her head so violently her cap slid sideways. She seemed not to notice. "Oh, no, m'm. It's not Samuel nor Mr. Baxter. Mrs. Chubb doesn't know who he is."

"Mrs. Chubb?"

"She were the one what found him. Lying in the trap he is. Dead as a doorknob."

For a few dizzying seconds the ballroom seemed to spin slowly around her, then settle once more. Cecily dragged in a deep breath. "Thank you, Gertie. Please don't mention any of this to anyone. I'll call the constable right away, and then I'll come down to the kitchen and talk to Mrs. Chubb."

"Yes, m'm. Thank you, m'm. Right upset, she is. She's had a bloody nasty shock. She's down there now having a drop of Michel's brandy."

She could do with a drop of brandy herself, Cecily thought,

as she watched Gertie hurry away. Doing her best not to let her concern get the better of her, she made her way to the library. It took only a moment or two for the operator to put her through to the police station.

Seconds later the gruff voice of Police Constable Northcott announced, "Badgers End Constabulary."

"Sam, this is Cecily Sinclair." She heard the tremble in her voice and cleared her throat. "I'm afraid we're going to need your assistance." Quickly she gave him the scant information she'd heard from Gertie.

"No," she said, in answer to his question. "I haven't seen the body. Gertie assures me, however, that the gentleman is dead."

"Well, I certainly 'ope so," Northcott said, sounding put out. "I'd hate to come h'up there and find out he's sleeping off an overindulgence, if you get my meaning."

"I think I can trust Mrs. Chubb's judgment on that," Cecily said crisply. She decided not to mention the fact that Baxter and Samuel had not yet returned home. Until she found out what had happened to them, it seemed prudent to keep that information to herself.

Nevertheless, she felt sick with anxiety. A dead man, and her husband missing. What could possibly be more frightening?

CHAPTER
❀ 2 ❀

Hurrying down to the kitchen, Cecily ran several scenarios through her head. The most likely was that the horse had bolted while the men were loading up the trap. But how did that explain the presence of a dead body? Her galloping imagination painted some ugly pictures, and she had to make an effort to regain her composure.

There was no point in borrowing trouble. She would simply have to wait until the men returned home to get the answers to her questions.

She found the kitchen in a state of turmoil when she pushed open the door. Mrs. Chubb sat on a chair, rocking back and forth while she pressed a large handkerchief over her eyes. Michel seemed to be attempting to drown out her sobbing with an uproar of his own as he barked orders at the scurrying maids to an accompaniment of crashing saucepan lids.

Pansy, looking terrified as usual, rushed to and fro between the sink and the stove, while Gertie stood over the housekeeper and patted the wailing woman's trembling shoulders.

Michel noticed Cecily first, and burst into a torrent of garbled words, mingling French and English, that made no sense at all. Obviously he'd joined Mrs. Chubb in downing a generous dose of brandy.

Gertie looked up as Cecily hurried over to the housekeeper. "She's still all of a dither," she said, giving the housekeeper a hefty slap on the back that sent her forward with a gasp. "The brandy doesn't seem to be helping her that much."

More likely it was fueling the awful noise coming out of Mrs. Chubb's mouth, Cecily thought, as she bent over the woman. "I need you to calm down, Altheda," she said sternly. "I need to know exactly what happened."

Mrs. Chubb coughed and spluttered, but mercifully ceased her wailing.

"Pitiful *enfant*!" Michel waved a large saucepan at the housekeeper. "You make enough noise to take off the roof, *non*? How you expect me to work in pandemonium like this? No eggs for the tarts, and all this crying and weeping . . . zis is too much. *Trop* much!"

"Put a bloody sock in it, Michel." Gertie glared at him. "You're only making things flipping worse."

"Gertie!" Mrs. Chubb lowered her handkerchief and sat up straight. "Please do not use that dreadful language in front of madam."

Well accustomed to Gertie's colorful language, unfortunate

as it may be, Cecily shook her head. "It's all right, Altheda. Gertie, why don't you and Pansy go back to the ballroom and make sure the maids have enough hors d'oeuvres to hand out."

Nodding, Gertie slipped past her and made for the door, with Pansy hot on her heels.

"Now tell me exactly what happened." Cecily pulled up a chair next to the housekeeper and sat down.

Michel, muttering and cursing under his breath, moved back to the stove and began stirring a large pot of heavenly smelling soup.

Mrs. Chubb's voice faltered now and then, but she managed to get the words out. "Well, there I was, coming back from the henhouse—"

"With my eggs," Michel butted in.

"—when I saw the trap," Mrs. Chubb continued, ignoring the chef's rudeness. "I couldn't see Samuel or Mr. Baxter anywhere, and so I looked inside the trap and that's when I saw . . ." She drew a shuddering breath. "That's when I saw . . . *it*."

"And dropped ze eggs," Michel muttered.

"He was dead," Mrs. Chubb said, her voice hushed.

"So were ze eggs." Michel smacked a lid down onto the table. "Smashed to pulp."

"Oh, shut up about the eggs, Michel." The housekeeper sounded much stronger as she turned on the chef. "What's a few custard tarts when a man's lying dead outside?"

Cecily also had bigger concerns than custard tarts. "You say you didn't see Samuel or Baxter?"

"No, m'm. I didn't."

"Perhaps they had already gone inside to call the constable."

"No, m'm. I surely would have seen them. They didn't have time to go nowhere. Besides, Samuel would never leave one of his precious horses wandering around like that in the yard." She retreated behind her handkerchief again. "Oh, wherever can they be?"

Cecily was asking herself the same question. The dead body of a stranger was sinister enough, but the fact that Baxter and Samuel had failed to return with the trap really worried her. It was an ominous beginning to the Christmas festivities, indeed.

Determined not to indulge in her darkest fears, she rose to her feet. "I imagine that having lost the trap, they are walking back from the woods. I'll send one of the footmen back there to fetch them. They can tell us what happened when they get here."

"Yes, m'm." Mrs. Chubb blew her nose soundly into the handkerchief. "I wonder who that poor devil is, lying dead out there."

"He was a vagabond, *non*?" Michel said. "Perhaps a gypsy. I think he lie by the side of the road. Then Mr. Baxter, he pick him up and drop him in ze trap. Then poof! Ze horse, he run off, leaving Mr. Baxter and Samuel stranded, *oui*?"

Cecily nodded. "Certainly a possibility worth considering. We'll know more when the men get back here." She peered down at the housekeeper. "Are you feeling any better, Altheda?"

"Yes, m'm. Thank you." Mrs. Chubb got unsteadily to her feet. "I'll get back to work now." She tucked her handkerchief into the pocket of her apron. "If you want to see the dead man, he's still outside in the trap."

"I think I'll leave that for the constable." Cecily moved quickly to the door. "I'll have someone take care of the horse, though."

Mrs. Chubb nodded. "I know Samuel will be grateful for that, m'm."

Cecily closed the door behind her and hurried up to the lobby. Most of the guests had arrived now, and she could manage without a couple of the footmen.

Having decided on one she could trust, she drew the young lad aside and quickly explained about the dead body. "Please stable the horse, then cover up the trap and leave it right where it is," she told him. "And do not mention a word of what happened to anyone. The fewer people who know about this, the better."

"Yes, m'm. Right away, m'm." The footman touched his forehead and sped off.

Cecily sent an anxious glance toward the window. The clouds had rolled in from the ocean, dark and ominous. It looked as if it might snow any minute, and already the daylight was slipping fast away.

Quickly she summoned another footman and ordered him to take a trap out to the woods. By now the men should be tramping along the main road, and no doubt the footman would meet them on the way.

Just as the young man left to do her bidding, a tall, slender man briskly entered the lobby.

Recognizing Dr. Prestwick, Cecily hurried toward him. "Kevin! I'm so glad to see you. I suppose you have seen the dead man?"

"Yes." The doctor removed his hat and smoothed back

17

his graying fair hair. His eyes, usually twinkling with humor, now regarded her gravely. "P.C. Northcott requested my assistance on his way out here. I brought him in my carriage."

"Ah, I thought he might." Cecily gazed up at the doctor's face—a handsome face that had quickened many of his patients' hearts, including hers at one time. "So what do you think happened to the poor man?"

Kevin pursed his lips. "I'd like to know how he came to be in the trap."

"So would I." Once more Cecily felt a sense of foreboding. She could tell from Kevin's expression that he was avoiding a direct answer. "Samuel and Baxter took the trap to pick some holly, but the horse came back on his own without the men. I can only imagine that they are somewhere on the road walking home."

"The constable will want to speak with them when they arrive."

Cecily didn't like his expression. "What is it, Kevin? What aren't you telling me?"

His pause seemed to go on for an eternity. At last he spoke. "I'm sorry to tell you, Cecily, that the man in the trap did not die from natural causes. He was strangled. P.C. Northcott is now investigating a murder and he's assuming Baxter and Samuel are involved in some way."

"That's utter piffle." Cecily suppressed a wave of apprehension. "How on earth could Sam Northcott possibly think such a dreadful thing?"

Kevin shrugged. "You know the constable. Always jumping to conclusions. Invariably the wrong one, I might add.

In any case, as soon as he has spoken with Samuel and your husband, I'm sure everything will be straightened out."

"I certainly hope so." Cecily glanced at the grandfather clock ticking away in the corner of the lobby. It was almost obscured by the Christmas tree standing next to it.

Madeline had covered the branches with white lace angels and white sugar bells tied with red ribbons. The tree looked beautiful, but at that moment Cecily was in no mood to appreciate the pleasing effect.

"I can understand the constable's anxiety to solve this case," Kevin said. "The victim is well known to him. His name is Gavin Hargrove."

Cecily frowned. "That name sounds familiar."

"So it should. He's the son of Charles Hargrove."

"Heavens! Isn't he the owner of Whitfield Manor?"

"He was. He passed away just recently. Extremely prosperous man. He made his money in imports, so I understand. Gavin Hargrove was his sole heir."

"How tragic for the family." Cecily shook her head. "To lose father and son so close together."

"Rather providential for the remaining heir, though, wouldn't you say?"

Something in his tone caught her attention. "What are you saying?"

He looked around, apparently wary of being overheard. Philip, the desk clerk, was busy at his ledger and two footmen were disappearing down the hallway.

Seemingly reassured, Kevin turned back to her. "I understand that a cousin, Randall Thorpe, will now inherit the Hargrove fortune. Apparently the elder Hargrove raised him as his own when Thorpe lost his parents at a young age. A very wealthy and, may I say, fortunate young man."

Cecily caught her breath. "Are you, by any chance, suggesting that this Mr. Thorpe killed his cousin for the family fortune?"

Again Kevin shrugged. "It certainly wouldn't be the first time someone has killed out of greed. Of course, it's not my place to conjecture one way or another. I just thought I'd allay your fears for your husband and Samuel. It seems to me that once P.C. Northcott has spoken to them, he will eventually arrive at another possible conclusion, such as I have mentioned."

Cecily let out her breath on a sigh. "I certainly hope so. The very idea of him suspecting either Baxter or Samuel is ludicrous. Though I do have to wonder how that poor man ended up in their trap."

"I'm sure the constable will want to know that, too. By the way, is Madeline here, by some chance?" Kevin looked about the lobby as if expecting to see the willowy figure floating across the carpet.

Madeline always appeared as if she were gliding effortlessly an inch or two off the ground, her simple gowns managing to look the epitome of elegance as they flowed around her often bare feet. It was that ethereal image that fueled speculation among the villagers about Madeline's mysterious powers. Though normally pragmatic about such things, Cecily had to admit that at times Madeline's ability to see things beyond normal perception could be quite unsettling.

"She was in the ballroom the last time I saw her." Noticing Kevin avoided her gaze, she added lightly, "I'm sure she'd be most happy to see you."

Madeline and Kevin's relationship had fluctuated from cozy to tepid to downright hostile at times. Cecily had long ago given up any idea of her two friends ever agreeing to a permanent arrangement. Sadly. Never were two people more destined to be together. Unless it were she and Baxter.

Thinking of her husband aroused her uneasiness again. "Will you wait here until Baxter and Samuel return? I'd really like you to be present, just in case the long walk in such cold weather has some ill effects on either of them."

"I suppose I could." Kevin's gaze strayed to the grandfather clock. "P.C. Northcott has taken charge of the body. I'll ask him to take it to the morgue in my carriage. If you can spare someone to take me home later?"

"Of course."

"Then, if I may wander into the ballroom for a peek at the decorations? Madeline always creates such a magnificent display."

In spite of her concern, Cecily had to laugh. "You are fooling no one, my dear Kevin. Please, do go along to the ballroom and find your Madeline. While you are there, try one of Michel's bacon rolls. They are simply delicious."

Kevin's eyes lit up. "Ah, I remember from last year. Wonderful. Let me know when the men are here. I'll come at once."

Cecily watched him hurry off, feeling a tinge of envy. Surely there could be nothing more exciting than the fresh bloom of romance. Not that she didn't adore Baxter, of course, and she was confident he returned her affections. It was simply that they now shared a deeper, more comfortable love. Certainly satisfying, but there were times when she missed the tantalizing expectations and delicious suspense of a growing attachment. Ah, what it was to be newly in love.

Sighing, she made her way down the hallway to the library. She had some accounting to take care of, and it might very well help keep her mind off the plight of her husband and her stable manager.

"Are you feeling better now?" Gertie dumped the pile of dishes onto the kitchen table and peered anxiously at the housekeeper. "You still look a little pasty."

Mrs. Chubb nodded. "I'm all right. It's not every day I see a dead body. I just can't get the vision out of my head. Staring he was, his face all pinched and white as the snow under my feet. Gave me quite a turn, it did. I know I'll have nightmares all night."

"No you won't. Just think about Christmas and all the baking you have to do. That'll help you forget."

"Speaking of which, where is Pansy? I sent her to fetch the clean tablecloths for the dining room. She should have been back ages ago."

"Probably chatting up the other maids." Gertie hauled a huge black cauldron up to the sink and began filling it with water. "She does like to blinking talk, that one. She—" Her words were cut off by a sudden rapping on the back door.

Mrs. Chubb dropped her rolling pin and wiped her floury hands on her apron. "Now who could that be?"

Michel, busy at the stove, spoke over his shoulder. "Ze best way to find out who is at ze door is to open it, *oui*?"

Gertie rolled her eyes, while Mrs. Chubb glared at the

chef's back. "One of these days, Michel, that cheeky tongue of yours will get you in trouble."

Michel's retort was lost in renewed pounding.

Gertie turned off the tap. "I'll answer the door. The poor bugger is standing out there in the cold." She rushed over to the door and yanked it open.

A stranger looked back at her—a burly man in a white coat with black curly hair and twinkling brown eyes. "Hello, luv," he greeted her. "I was wondering when someone was going to open the door. Thought you'd all gone to sleep in there." He winked at her in such a way she completely lost her voice for a moment.

Staring at the basket of huge white packages he carried, she croaked, "Who the 'ell are you?"

The man whistled. "Feisty as well as beautiful. I like that, I do."

Gertie lifted her chin. "Here, none of that. I'm a respectable woman, I am."

"Even better." He grinned at her and held up the basket. "Dan Perkins, at your service. I'm the new butcher from Abbitson's. Brought your turkeys for your Christmas dinner, didn't I."

Gertie narrowed her eyes. "Wot, at night? Butchers don't deliver at night."

"They do this time of year. Busy time, it is. Now then, are you going to let me in before my fingers freeze off?"

"Gertie!" Mrs. Chubb's voice rang out behind her. "For heaven's sake let the man in. You're letting all that cold air in with the door open."

Gertie sniffed, but stood aside.

Dan Perkins winked at her again, then stepped into the kitchen. "Hello, luv!" He grinned at the housekeeper. "How's your mother off for dripping, then?"

"Saucy bugger," Gertie muttered, as she closed the door.

"You can put them in the pantry," Mrs. Chubb said, nodding at the door across the room. "Gertie will show you where."

Gertie would rather have eaten coal than be squeezed in that small space with the mouthy Dan Perkins, but she knew better than to say so. Instead, she marched across the floor and pulled open the door.

"Don't mind if I do," Dan said, and followed her into the cold, marble room with its narrow shelves.

Gertie backed away until her spine pressed against the far wall. "There," she said, pointing to an empty shelf near the floor. "You can put them in there."

Dan grunted as he bent his knees and lowered the basket to the floor. Heaving each package onto the shelf, he emptied the basket.

Looking down on him, Gertie couldn't help but notice his brawny shoulders. He looked strong enough to lift an entire cow, she thought, then snatched her gaze away when he looked up and caught her staring.

"That's all of 'em, luv," he said. "Anything else I can do for you?"

"Yes, you can bloody well stop calling me luv." Gertie stalked to the door. "I'm the mother of twins, I am, not a blinking hussy looking for a tumble in the hay."

Dan straightened at once. "Oo, sorry, luv. Didn't mean to offend. Your hubbie's a lucky chap, that he is."

"My husband is dead," Gertie snapped. She marched out into the kitchen just in time to see Michel brush his nose with his finger. "Oo la la! Hoity-toity, aren't we."

"Bugger off," she told him, and earned another disapproving glare from Mrs. Chubb.

"I'll be back tomorrow with the ducks," Dan announced as he headed for the back door. As he passed by Gertie he murmured, "Will you miss me, luv?"

"Like a bad bout of the runs," Gertie assured him.

"Feisty as a firecracker." Dan reached the back door and grinned back at her. "Lovely."

For answer, Gertie turned her back on him. She didn't let out her breath again until she heard the door slam shut behind him.

Her heart had just about settled down when another pounding on the door started it thumping all over again.

"Now what?" Mrs. Chubb murmured.

Gertie started toward the door, determined to put Dan Perkins in his place. "Now look here," she said, as she pulled it open, "if you think . . ." Her voice trailed off at the sight of the two men in front of her.

David, one of the Pennyfoot's young footmen, stared at her with anxious eyes. One arm supported the other man, who seemed hardly able to stand. His chin rested on his chest, and in the darkness outside Gertie didn't recognize him at first. Then he moaned, and raised his head.

Gertie's mouth dropped open, and she felt as if someone had slammed a fist right into her stomach. Samuel's face looked back at her, white as a ghost and covered in blood.

CHAPTER
❀ 3 ❀

"Samuel!" Gertie's shriek rang around the kitchen. "Bloody hell! What's the matter with you?"

"Sacre bleu," Michel muttered, while Mrs. Chubb rushed over to her side.

"What is it, who . . . ? Oh, my lord. Michel! Help this lad in. Something's happened to our Samuel."

Michel dropped the dish he was holding and let it crash to the table. "What's happened?" he demanded, as he leapt to the door. "What the hell is going on?" All traces of his French accent disappeared as he reached for the stricken man. "Strewth, mate, you look bloody terrible."

With David's help he got Samuel stumbling to a chair and sat him down. The young man's eyes were closed and he swayed to one side, causing Michel to grab him before he fell off. Dried blood caked his forehead, and a red rivulet still seeped down one side of his face.

Gertie felt her stomach heave and quickly took a deep, deep breath.

"I found him on the road," David said, panting from exertion. "He was staggering all over the place. I thought at first he were drunk."

"What about Mr. Baxter?" Mrs. Chubb bent down and peered into Samuel's face. "Was he with him?"

"No, he weren't." David sat down heavily on an adjacent chair. "I kept asking him where Mr. Baxter was, but he didn't seem to understand me."

"Did you go and look for him?" Mrs. Chubb faced David with a look that promised death if he said he didn't.

"Of course I did." David rubbed his eyes with a grubby hand. "I got Samuel into the trap and then I went up and down the road looking and calling, all the way to the woods."

He looked at Samuel, his face taut with tension. "I was afraid to take too long in getting him back here with his head bleeding like that and all."

"It's all right. You did the right thing." Mrs. Chubb turned to Gertie. "Go and tell madam what's happened. Michel, boil up some water. I have to clean up that wound."

Samuel groaned again.

"I'll get the brandy and see if I can get some down him." The housekeeper hurried toward the pantry.

Gertie took one last look at Samuel, and fled the kitchen. Halfway down the hallway she almost collided with Pansy coming the other way, her arms full of tablecloths.

"What's yer rush?" Pansy demanded, clutching her load tighter to her chest. "You almost sent these to the floor. Then they'd have to be washed all over again."

"Sorry." Gertie hesitated. She knew Pansy was sweet on Samuel, though the two of them hadn't gone out together, as far as she knew. Still, the young girl got upset easily, and she knew what a shock she'd have at the sight of Samuel's bloody face. "Pansy," she said quietly, "before you go in there, I need to tell you something."

Pansy's expression changed, her face looking even more scrawny than usual in her concern. "What? Has something happened?"

"Samuel's back. He's been hurt. He's—" Gertie never got a chance to finish the sentence. The pure white tablecloths tumbled to the floor as Pansy rushed toward the kitchen door and disappeared inside. A moment later her scream, loud and piercing, echoed down the hallway.

"Bloody hell," Gertie muttered. Leaving the pile of linens where they lay, she dashed up the steps to the lobby.

In the library, Cecily stared at the neat rows of figures in front of her, her mind far away from balancing the books. All she could think about was Baxter and Samuel trudging down a long, cold road in the dark. Hopefully David would find them before they had to walk too far.

She would send Baxter to their boudoir right away, she decided. She'd wrap him in a big fluffy blanket and sit him in front of the fire with a glass of his favorite sherry. Smiling at the thought, she looked up at the sharp tap on the door.

"Come in!" Her smile vanished at the sight of Gertie's face. "What's happened now?"

Gertie seemed to have trouble getting words out. Her chest heaved, and she struggled to catch her breath before managing to gasp, "Samuel. David found him, but—"

"Oh, thank heavens." Cecily stood up so fast she jerked the blotter, and ink slopped out of the inkwell and spread over the corner of her ledger. With the edge of the blotter she quickly dabbed at the stain, managing to stop it from covering up her carefully written figures.

Gertie sounded frightened when she spoke again. "Mr. Baxter weren't with him, m'm. I'm so sorry."

Cecily sharply raised her chin. "What do you mean, he wasn't with him? Where is he, then?"

Gertie shook her head, her dark eyes looking huge in her white face. "We don't know, m'm. We think he's lost."

"Piffle." Cecily scrambled around the side of her desk, hampered by her long skirt. Tugging the hem impatiently, she started for the door. "Samuel must know where he is."

"That's just it, m'm. Samuel's not saying much at all. His head's been bashed about, and I don't think he knows where he's at right now."

Pulling up short, Cecily stared at her. "For heaven's sake! What happened to him?"

Gertie's shoulders shook. "I don't know. He can't tell us."

"Did David look for Mr. Baxter at all?"

"Yes, m'm, he did. He said he looked everywhere, but then he had to get Samuel back here 'cos his head was bleeding that bad."

Cecily made an effort to pull herself together. "It's all

right, Gertie. Don't upset yourself. I'm sure we'll get this all cleared up in no time. I'll come down to the kitchen with you and talk to Samuel myself."

"Yes, m'm." Gertie followed her out into the hallway. "I hope nothing bad has happened to Mr. Baxter."

Cecily sent up a fervent prayer in agreement. Nothing frightened her more than the thought that something terrible might have happened to her beloved husband.

She could not indulge in such fears now, however. She had to be strong, and hold on to the belief that he would come back to her, alive and well. Because if he didn't, there would be absolutely no reason to go on living.

Moments later, she burst through the kitchen door. She found Mrs. Chubb standing over Samuel, a glass in one hand and a brandy bottle in the other.

The housekeeper looked up, relief in her eyes when Cecily rushed in. "Oh, there you are, m'm. Thank goodness."

Pansy stood by the sink, weeping quietly, while Michel hovered in front of the stove, waiting for a kettle to boil.

Cecily bent over Samuel, who sat slumped against the back of the chair, his eyes closed. Shock ran cold through her veins when she saw his gashed forehead. "Gertie," she said quietly, "go at once to the ballroom and find Dr. Prestwick. Be as discreet as you can, but bring him back here right away."

"Yes, m'm."

"And pick up those tablecloths on the way. They'll have to be washed again."

"Yes, m'm."

Gertie retreated through the door, while Cecily laid a

gentle hand on her stable manager's arm. "Samuel," she murmured. "Can you hear me?"

To her relief the young man's eyes opened, and he moaned.

"Keep still," she told him. "We've sent for the doctor and he should be here any minute."

Samuel answered her, his words slurred. "Where am I?"

Cecily exchanged a worried glance with Mrs. Chubb. "You're here in the kitchen with all of us, Samuel. Can you tell us what happened?"

Samuel attempted to shake his head, but let out a groan of agony. "Oo, that hurts!"

"Just keep still," Cecily ordered. "Samuel, do you know where Mr. Baxter is?"

Samuel's eyes closed, then flickered open again. "Mr. Baxter?"

"Yes, he went with you to pick the holly. Can you tell us what happened?"

"I don't know." Samuel mumbled something else Cecily couldn't catch.

She bent closer to his face. "What was that?"

"I don't remember picking no holly."

"Oh, my." Mrs. Chubb clutched her throat. "He sounds really strange. Must have been that bump on the head."

Cecily was about to answer when the door flew open and Dr. Prestwick strode in, followed by Madeline, who sailed at once to Cecily's side.

"What's happened here?" Kevin demanded, unceremoniously pushing Cecily aside.

"We don't know. There seems to have been some sort of accident. Samuel's hurt and no one seems to know what's happened to Baxter." To her dismay, her voice cracked on his name.

"Here, m'm, you need to sit down." Mrs. Chubb looked meaningfully at Michel, who rushed forward and pulled out a chair. "Have a drop of brandy," she added, as Cecily sank onto it. "It does wonders, it does."

"Yes, do drink some." Madeline laid her arm about Cecily's shoulders. "It will give you strength."

"Thank you both, but I'm quite all right." Cecily smiled wearily up a Madeline. "I'll need to keep a clear head."

The housekeeper stared at the half-filled glass in her hand. "I poured this for Samuel but he doesn't seem to want it, either." She hesitated, shrugged, and tipped the glass to her mouth.

Cecily turned her attention back to the doctor, who was busy running his hands over Samuel. Finally he straightened. "He's got a few bruises and a nasty gash on his head, but there doesn't seem to be any serious damage. He's going to be sore for a day or so but I can give him something for the pain."

He looked at Gertie, who hovered white-faced, near the door. "Would you be so good as to fetch my bag? I left it with Philip at the desk."

Gertie nodded and slipped through the door.

Impatient now, Cecily rose to her feet. "I know Samuel is in pain," she said, "but he has to tell us what happened to Baxter and why David couldn't find him."

"David looked everywhere for him," Mrs. Chubb put in. "I sent the lad to his room. Proper shook-up, he was."

Kevin looked grave. "This young man is disoriented

from the bump on the head. I suspect partial amnesia, in which case he might not remember much at all about what happened."

In her desperation, Cecily grasped Kevin's arm. "Can you at least try?"

Kevin sighed. "I'll do what I can." He laid a hand on the stable manager's shoulder. "Samuel? Tell us where you found the dead man. What happened to you and Mr. Baxter?"

Samuel mumbled something.

"What?" Cecily moved closer. "What did he say?"

"He said he doesn't remember." Kevin straightened. "I'm sorry, Cecily."

"No, he has to remember." Cecily bent over the young man, her fear overcoming her restraint. "Samuel, please. Try to remember. Where is Mr. Baxter? What happened to him?"

Samuel made an obvious effort to open his eyes, but only succeeded for a second. "Mr. Baxter," he murmured. "He was lying on the ground."

Cecily's growing anxiety exploded into full blown dread. "Where, Samuel? Where on the ground?"

Samuel swayed. "Mr. Baxter. He was on the ground. I leaned over him. I think he was . . . oh, no, m'm. I'm so sorry, but I think . . . I think he was *dead*."

For several agonizing seconds the silence thickened in the kitchen. Even Pansy was shocked out of her weeping. Everyone seemed frozen, unable to move or speak.

Michel stood absolutely still, with steam rising silently from the kettle in his hand. Mrs. Chubb's mouth hung open, her face paralyzed with shock. Even Madeline seemed struck dumb by Samuel's inconceivable statement.

Cecily tried to move her lips but couldn't form a word. She closed her mouth, afraid that if she did utter a sound, it would be a scream.

Kevin recovered first. "In Samuel's present state, there's no counting on the validity of anything he says. I wouldn't pay attention to any of his words until he's more lucid."

Cecily raised dull eyes to meet his gaze. "We have to find him." With all her might she wanted to believe her beloved husband was alive. Yet a small, insistent doubt made her add, "We can't just leave him lying out there alone on the cold ground."

A sob escaped Mrs. Chubb's lips. The sad sound seemed to pierce the depths of Cecily's heart like a dagger.

Pansy started weeping again, louder now, and Michel swore. Just at that moment Gertie barged through the door, carrying Kevin's black bag.

She stopped short at the sight of their stricken faces. "Oh, crikey, now what?"

"Baxter's dead!" Pansy blurted out, and collapsed in a storm of sobbing.

Gertie stood as still as a stone, clutching Kevin's bag to her chest. "No, no, no! He can't be."

"Of course he can't be." Echoing her, Cecily straightened. "I will not believe he's dead unless I see it for myself. I want every trap available out there looking for him. We'll take lanterns and look all night if we have to . . . and we won't come home without him."

Both Madeline and Kevin uttered a cry of protest.

"Cecily," Kevin said, his voice urgent. "It's starting to snow again. I strongly suggest you let the men go while you wait here."

"No, I'm sorry, Kevin. I must go and help them look."

Samuel started struggling to his feet.

"Wait a minute, young man." Kevin laid a hand on his shoulder and gently pushed him back in the chair. "You're not going anywhere." He signaled to Gertie to bring him his bag.

She did so, passing by Cecily as if she were sleepwalking. As she handed over the bag, she looked at Mrs. Chubb, her eyes pleading.

Mrs. Chubb thrust what was left of the brandy in her hand. "Here, there's more where that came from."

Gertie shook her head. "I want to go with madam and look for Mr. Baxter."

"And I," Madeline added, earning a look of protest from Kevin.

The housekeeper glanced at Cecily, who nodded her head. "Thank you both," she said. "I appreciate your help. Please be sure to wear something warm. It's a cold night out there." With a last look at Samuel, she added, "Take care of him, Kevin. We'll be back just as soon as we find Baxter."

Kevin started forward. "But Madeline—"

She raised her hand to stop him. "I have to go with them, Kevin."

"Then I shall go with you." He glanced back at Samuel. "Just give me a moment or two to patch up this young man."

"We'll meet you in the lobby." Cecily headed for the door, adding, "Gertie, I'll need your help in rounding up the footmen. Mrs. Chubb, you must serve supper as usual. Make excuses for me to the guests. I know you'll think of something. I trust you and Michel can manage?"

"Of course we can, m'm. Good job we took on those extra maids for Christmas. Don't you worry yourself about that. Just find Mr. Baxter and bring him home."

Cecily paused at the door and looked back at her. "I pray that we can." She left the kitchen, with Madeline and Gertie following behind.

"I'm going to get my coat, m'm." Gertie started down the hallway toward her room.

"We'll wait for you in the lobby," Cecily called out after her.

She headed for the stairs, but Madeline stopped her with a hand on her arm. "Wait, Cecily. There's something I need to do. Just take a moment with me and let me concentrate."

Realizing Madeline was about to embark on one of her trances, Cecily tried to pull her hands free. "I appreciate your intentions Madeline, but we simply don't have the time to spare. We must make haste to start the search."

With surprising strength for such a fragile creature, Madeline held on. "Hush, Cecily. Bear with me. This is important. It won't take but a moment."

Cecily found herself unable to do anything but obey.

As the shadows deepened in the darkened hallway, it seemed to her as if the whole world stood still. The hour or so before supper was always a quiet time in the club, but this silence felt different—suffocating in its intensity.

She felt a tingling feeling where their hands were joined. Madeline's eyes closed, and her face took on an eerie glow.

Even her hair seemed illuminated by a thousand tiny lights, odd considering the gas lamps on the walls had not yet been lit.

"I see him," Madeline whispered.

Cecily's heart leapt with ridiculous hope. Afraid to break the spell that appeared to have Madeline in its grip, she waited for her to speak.

"He's alive." Madeline tilted her head back, her long hair reaching to her waist. "He's hurting."

Pain, greater than any Cecily remembered, tore through her. "Where? Where is he?"

Madeline shook her head. "He's . . . no. He's . . . moving. I can't tell where. He's moving from place to place." Her eyes flew open. "That's all I know. I'm sorry, Cecily."

At last Cecily could pull her hands free. "We'll find him," she said firmly. "Come, let us go at once." Her husband needed her, she told herself, as she flew up the steps to the lobby. Nothing could stop her from answering that call.

CHAPTER

❀ 4 ❀

It was snowing again—wet, heavy snow that would make traveling difficult. Cecily gathered the footmen together, and everyone crowded into the three carriages and set off for the woods.

The horses had difficulty finding their footing on the hill, but eventually they reached the riding trail that led through the trees. Once there, however, they were forced to leave the conveyances on the road and search on foot.

Cecily directed the search, sending the footmen in every direction while she joined Madeline, Kevin, and Gertie on the main trail.

After three hours of hunting it was apparent, even to Cecily, that Baxter was nowhere to be found. The searchers had tramped through snowdrifts and trampled over thick underbrush, whistling and shouting until they were hoarse. To no avail. Not only was there no answer, the snow had covered up any sign that Baxter might have left to show them the way.

Twice Madeline called upon her powers to show them where to look, while Kevin did his best to hide his skepticism. Each time she had to admit failure. Exhausted and emotionally drained, Cecily finally felt compelled to call off the search. She simply could not ask her friends to toil any longer for what appeared to be a lost cause.

In any case, she had a country club full of guests expecting to enjoy the Christmas festivities. Baxter would be the first one to tell her she needed to be back there, doing her job. With a heavy heart, she ordered everyone back to the Pennyfoot.

The warmth of the lobby was almost too much after the freezing snow and chill wind she had endured. After dispatching Gertie back to the kitchen, she removed her wet coat and scarf. "Thank you, Madeline. You, too, Kevin." She managed a weak smile for them both. "I could not endure this nightmare without good friends like you. I can't impose on your good nature any longer. I have a footman and carriage outside waiting to take you both home."

"We should contact P.C. Northcott and inform him of Baxter's disappearance," Kevin said. "I'll drop in on him on my way home and let him know what's happened."

Cecily nodded her thanks, too weary to answer.

"And you need to rest," Kevin said briskly. "Here, take these powders. They'll help you sleep tonight." He thrust two small packets into her hand.

"I certainly trust that you will sleep." Madeline's lovely face was filled with concern. "You look dreadful."

As if to confirm her comments, an elderly couple passing by stared at Cecily, unable to contain their shock at her appearance.

She could hardly blame them. She still wore her hat, which had been tied down by the warm scarf. The wide brim flopped dismally onto her shoulders and stray strands of hair floated about her face. Her gloves were torn and grubby, and mud caked her boots.

She groaned as the couple went on their way. "I have no doubt that couple will never spend another Christmas at the Pennyfoot."

"Nonsense. The Pennyfoot's impeccable reputation is not going to be marred by one disheveled appearance of its manager." Madeline took hold of her arm. "Cecily, dear, listen to me. Baxter is in good hands. I don't know where he is—as I said, he appears to be constantly on the move, but someone is taking good care of him. Rest assured of that."

In spite of her best efforts to prevent them, tears pricked Cecily's eyes. She desperately wanted to believe Madeline's words. There had been many times in the past when her friend's predictions had come to pass, sometimes in quite spectacular ways. But her husband's welfare was so vital, how could she trust such an ambiguous assurance?

"Thank you, Madeline." She managed a weary smile. "That's some consolation."

"It's the truth." Madeline's gaze seemed to bore into her. "I would not give you false hope. Believe me, Cecily. Baxter is in good hands."

"I pray that you're right." She glanced up at the doctor. "I'll take the powders and try to sleep. I will see you're both informed if there is any news."

"We'd appreciate that." Madeline patted her arm. "I know this is hard, Cecily. But everything will be as it was. Trust me."

That was all she had, Cecily thought, as she climbed the stairs to her boudoir. Trust in her friend's questionable powers. It wasn't much on which to hang her entire future.

Standing at the kitchen table, Gertie rolled a serviette and tucked it inside a solid silver ring. "I can't believe we searched that long and didn't find nothing."

"Neither can I." Mrs. Chubb spooned mincemeat into tiny round cups of pastry. "Madam must be out of her mind with worry."

"What do you think happened to Mr. Baxter, then?" Gertie reached for another serviette. This wasn't her favorite job and she wanted to get it over with as soon as possible. "Do you think he's dead?"

"I don't know what to think." The housekeeper fitted the lids on the tarts and carried the baking tin to the oven. "I suppose we'll have to wait until Samuel gets his memory back to find out what happened."

"I saw him just now." Relieved that she'd done the last one, Gertie stacked the rolled serviettes onto a tray. "His face is as white as the bandage on his head. Talking daft, he is. Says he saw a swing in the trees. I thought someone had put a swing up there for Christmas, like they do in the summer, but I couldn't see no swing. I told him he were seeing things."

"It's the bump he got on the head. It's making him confused. That's why he can't remember what happened to him." Mrs. Chubb bustled back to the table. "Dr. Prestwick said he might never remember."

"Does that mean they'll never find Mr. Baxter?" Pansy asked from the sink, where she stood peeling potatoes.

Mrs. Chubb turned on her at once. "Of course they'll find him." She wagged a finger at her. "Don't you ever say that again."

"Unless he ended up in Deep Willow Pond," Gertie said mournfully. She met Mrs. Chubb's worried gaze. "They'll never find him, then, will they."

"It's not going to be a very good Christmas, is it," Pansy said, in a small voice.

"Of course it is. We'll just have to make the best of it, that's all." Mrs. Chubb looked up at the clock on the shelf. "Better get a move on, you two. It's getting late and the dining room tables need to be laid for breakfast tomorrow."

Gertie sighed. "I feel sorry for madam. What will she do without Mr. Baxter? He's her whole life."

"Well, let's hope it doesn't come to that." The housekeeper picked up the lid to the mincemeat and slammed it on top of the jar. "Now enough of this talk. The sooner you get this done the sooner you can get to bed. Those twins of yours will be wondering what happened to you."

"Daisy's looking after them." Gertie picked up the tray. "She tells them stories until they fall asleep. I don't know what I'd do without her, really I don't."

"Well, you're lucky to have a nanny, that's for sure." Mrs. Chubb started cutting more rounds of pastry. "Let's hope the twins don't hear nothing about what's going on. We don't want to spoil their Christmas."

Gertie nodded in agreement, though her heart was heavy as she left the kitchen. If something terrible had happened to Mr. Baxter, everyone's Christmas would be spoiled. There was nothing anyone could do about that.

Cecily awoke the next morning with a start, memory flooding back the moment she opened her eyes. The empty space in the bed next to her seemed to mock her. How foolish she'd been, longing for the silly, sentimental dizziness of young love, when everything she had, everything she was, dwelt in the man she loved beyond life itself. How could she go on without him, if he was lost to her forever?

Madeline's words came back to haunt her. *He's in good hands.* Whose hands? And where? The only hands she wanted him in were her own. Now. Even so, she'd wait for however long it took, if it meant he'd eventually be returned to her.

Her thoughts scattered when she heard a light tapping on the door. Stumbling out of bed, she reached for her dressing gown and struggled into it.

Still tying the gold cord at her waist, she sped across the carpet on bare feet. With eager hands she tugged the door open, filled with hope that her husband stood on the other side.

She saw Pansy instead, standing there with a white face

and dark circles under her eyes. "I'm sorry to disturb you, m'm," she mumbled. "The constable is here. He wants to speak to you."

Her disappointment was crushing. Then the significance of Pansy's words sunk in. She didn't know whether to cling to hope or brace herself for the worst. "Is the constable alone?"

Pansy's face mirrored her sympathy. "Yes, m'm. He is."

She didn't know why she'd entertained the hope that Baxter would be with him. "Very well," she said, her weariness dulling her voice. "Show him into the library, please, Pansy. I'll be down in a few minutes."

Hurriedly, she dressed, while trying to block out of her mind all the terrible things Sam Northcott might possibly say. With all the upheaval of searching for Baxter, she'd almost forgotten about the body of Gavin Hargrove. If the constable was here to accuse her husband of being involved in a murder, she'd have something to say to him, and it wouldn't be polite.

Her head throbbed with worry as she made her way down the stairs. Several people greeted her, and she managed to sound cordial enough, though secretly she longed for them all to leave her alone so she could wallow in her misery.

The thought of entertaining a country club full of guests throughout Christmas without Baxter by her side was unbearable. All she could hope was that Sam Northcott did not bring her the news she dreaded to hear. For as long as she had faith that her husband was alive, she could prevail. Without that belief, she was lost.

Entering the library a few minutes later, she was relieved

to see that none of the guests lingered by the fire. Somehow the constable had managed to wheedle a buttered scone out of Mrs. Chubb, the remains of which he held in his hand. Judging from the crumbs clinging around his mouth, he'd captured more than one.

He'd removed his helmet, and the glow from the blazing coals in the fireplace gleamed on his almost bald head. He seemed unperturbed by the recent events, and aroused Cecily's irritation when he greeted her with a cheery "Happy Christmas, Mrs. Baxter!"

She failed to return his smile. "I can hardly be happy when my husband is missing, my stable manager has been assaulted, and a murdered man has been found in my yard."

"Ah, about that." Northcott shoved what was left of the scone in his mouth and wiped his lips with the back of his sleeve. "I believe I've solved the case."

"Really. I trust you are not putting the blame for the murder on my husband's shoulders?"

The constable blinked at her. "Wot? H'oh, no, m'm. Not at all." As if remembering the dilemma of Baxter's disappearance, he added, "I'm sorry to hear he's missing, m'm. Must be a worry for you."

"It is, indeed. In fact, I want you to mount a search for him right away."

"According to one of your footmen, you already searched the woods pretty thoroughly last night." Northcott pulled a notebook from his pocket and started to flip through it.

Resisting the urge to slap him, Cecily said evenly, "He must be somewhere. He's missing, and it's your job to find him. Or must I take a complaint to the inspector?"

Her threat had the desired effect. If there was one person Northcott feared, it was Inspector Cranshaw. For good reason. The man could be insensitive at best and downright cruel at his worst. Cecily's disputes with him were legendary.

Heartily disapproving of the Pennyfoot's game rooms, not to mention its manager, Cranshaw was constantly looking for an excuse to shut down the country club, and at times had come perilously close to doing so. Cecily did her level best to avoid any contact with the man.

Northcott's face had turned pale when he answered her. "There's no need for that, Mrs. Baxter. "No need h'at all. I shall endeavor to send out a search for Mr. Baxter as soon as I return to the police station. We'll more'n likely find him sleeping under a tree somewhere. It's easy to get lost in the woods at night, that it is. Especially with all that snow around. Makes it all the more confusing."

"Thank you." Cecily took a deep breath. "Now, if you've decided that my husband is not to blame for the death of Mr. Hargrove, then whom do you blame?"

Northcott studied his notebook. "According to my notes here, after a thorough search of the dead man's home last night, certain letters were discovered in his bureau that led me to my conclusion."

Cecily frowned. "Letters?"

"Yes, m'm. Threatening letters, they were. Apparently delivered to him by a member of a gambling syndicate residing in London. The notes made it quite clear that if Mr. Hargrove did not pay his debts h'immediately, he would be eliminated. It is my belief that this organization carried out its threat."

46

In spite of the warmth from the fireplace, Cecily's bones chilled. "Are you saying . . . ?"

"Yes, m'm. Looks like the gamblers caught up with 'im, and knocked him off, so to speak."

She stared at him for a long moment. "Are you certain of this? You have proof?"

Northcott closed his notebook with a snap. "I don't need proof, Mrs. Baxter. I'm turning the whole case over to Scotland Yard, since the syndicate resides in their jurisdiction. Let them take care of it, I say, then I can get on with enjoying my Christmas."

"Then how do you suppose Mr. Hargrove came to rest in my trap?"

"Ah, well, I'm inclined to believe that Mr. Baxter found the dead body where it had been hidden by the syndicate, and was endeavoring to bring it back when the horse bolted. Most likely before he could climb back in. Samuel must have fallen from the trap, which is how he got that nasty gash on his head." The constable puffed out his chest. "I deduced all that from information given to me by Dr. Prestwick."

Cecily was more inclined to believe that Northcott had arrived at his deduction after talking to Michel, since it resembled the chef's theory so closely. She kept her judgment to herself, however.

She had no desire to upset the constable. She needed him to conduct the search for Baxter, and in order to secure that, she'd kiss the man's boots if needs be. "I see. Well, if you're no longer pursuing the case, you'll have time to look for my husband, then."

"That I shall, Mrs. Baxter." Northcott picked up his helmet and tucked it under his arm. I'll see to it right away. Right after I've bid farewell to Mrs. Chubb."

And snatched another handful of scones, no doubt, Cecily thought. She waited for him to leave, then wandered over to the bookshelves. Often when she was worried or upset, reading a few pages of her favorite books helped to ease the anguish.

Today, however, even that pleasurable pastime seemed to offer no solace. Giving up the idea, she turned to leave, just as the door opened and Samuel's head appeared in the opening.

Wincing at the sight of his bandages, Cecily hurried forward. "Samuel! Have you remembered anything yet?"

He entered the room, looking pale and unsteady on his feet. "I'm sorry, m'm. I keep trying but when I do me head hurts something awful."

Cecily sighed, and gestured at an armchair. "Here, sit down. Has the doctor given you anything for the pain?"

"Yes, m'm. Thank you." Politely he waited for her to sit before edging onto the chair. "I came to see if there's anything I can do to help find Mr. Baxter. The boys tell me you didn't find any sign of him last night."

"No, we didn't." She stretched out her cold feet toward the fire. "Thank you, Samuel, but I've asked P.C. Northcott to conduct a search. Not that I have any faith in his ability to find Mr. Baxter."

"Well, perhaps the daylight will make it easier to see if he's left a trail somewhere."

"That could be, were it not for the fresh snowfall. It will cover any signs of his presence, I'm afraid."

Samuel looked most unhappy. "I feel it's my fault, somehow. How can I not remember anything what happened yesterday?"

"Sometimes a head injury will do that. Make you forget, I mean." Cecily looked intently at him. "Just how much do you remember, Samuel? Do you remember leaving here in the trap to pick holly?"

"No, m'm, I don't. Last thing I remember is filling the coal buckets for Pansy. I was going to ask her to join me for carol singing this week, and I was that nervous—I could hardly keep me teeth from rattling."

"And did you ask her?"

"I don't know, m'm. I don't remember much at all after that moment. If I did, I don't know what she said. I s'pose I'll have to ask her again."

"So you don't remember how the dead man got into the trap, or how you got hurt?"

"No, m'm. I wish I did. I wish I could tell you what happened to Mr. Baxter. All I can remember is bits and pieces. Just a flash of him lying on the ground and me bending over him. Like bits of a dream coming back, it is."

At least this time he didn't say Baxter was dead. She didn't think she could bear to hear those words again. He was out there somewhere, and all she could do was pray the constables would find him. Beyond that, she couldn't seem to think of anything else at all.

CHAPTER

❀ 5 ❀

"The constable thinks a gambling syndicate is responsible for Mr. Hargrove's demise," Cecily said, when she could compose herself enough to speak.

Samuel gave her a puzzled frown. "Hargrove?"

"Oh, I'm sorry. Did the doctor not tell you the victim was Gavin Hargrove, son of Charles Hargrove, who recently died?"

"No, he didn't, m'm. At least, I don't think he did. To tell the truth, I didn't know nothing about a dead body until Gertie mentioned it this morning. She told me what went on last night. I don't remember nothing about it."

"Well, apparently some threatening letters were found in the dead man's house, and P.C. Northcott is convinced that the victim failed to pay his gambling debts and was strangled to death as a result. He's handing the case over to Scotland Yard."

Samuel uttered a scornful laugh. "I don't know how that twerp ended up a policeman. Proper nitwit, he is."

Cecily studied his face. "You think he's mistaken?"

"That's not how them people work, that's all. A shot in the back of the head—that's how they get rid of someone. They wouldn't take the time to strangle no one."

"You seem to know a lot about these ruffians."

"I do." Samuel fidgeted on the chair. "I spent enough time up in The Smoke to know what goes on in the underworld. Take my word for it, that bloke weren't done in by no bunch of gamblers. I'd stake my life on it."

Cecily was quiet for a moment. "Dr. Prestwick mentioned a cousin, who was apparently raised by Charles Hargrove. He did wonder if perhaps the gentleman disposed of the younger Mr. Hargrove in order to inherit the family fortune."

Samuel eyed her warily. "A lot of money, is there?"

"A great deal."

He nodded, flinching as he did so. "I s'pose that's possible. People have done worse to get rich."

"It also occurs to me that perhaps, if this cousin is responsible for the murder, he might also know where Mr. Baxter might be."

Pure alarm lit up Samuel's eyes. "You're not thinking of talking to this gent, are you, m'm? You know what Mr. Baxter would say to that."

"Yes, well, Mr. Baxter's not here." Cecily stood, causing Samuel to rise to his feet. "Besides, if by talking to this man

I'm reunited with my husband, I hardly see that he has any right to object."

"You should talk to P.C. Northcott first, or Dr. Prestwick. Someone." Samuel looked about to cry.

"I appreciate your concern, Samuel, but my mind is made up. I shall go immediately after I've eaten something. Not that I have any appetite, but one must keep up one's strength in times like this." She headed for the door. "Please see that I have a carriage and a driver waiting for me in forty minutes."

Samuel sounded desperate when he blurted out, "I'll go with you, m'm!"

She turned to shake her head at him. "No, Samuel. You must rest. I need you to get well as soon as possible."

He came toward her, his hand outstretched in a plea. "I can't rest knowing you're going out there all by yourself. Besides, I feel a lot better already. I really do think I should come with you. Please, m'm?"

She hesitated. Next to her husband, in a perilous situation she trusted Samuel more than anyone. He had shared many an adventure with her, and had proved his worth on more than one occasion. If she were honest with herself, she had to admit she'd feel a great deal more comfortable with him at her side.

"Very well," she said slowly. "Only if you're quite certain you feel well enough to come with me. I don't want to be responsible for causing you more harm."

"I'm feeling a lot better, m'm. Honest. My head hardly aches at all now."

"Then I shall be very glad of your company. Thank you, Samuel."

Samuel let out an audible sigh of relief. "Thank goodness. Mr. Baxter would have my guts for garters if I let you go there without me."

She tried to contain the surge of hope. "Samuel, you sound as though you don't think he's dead, after all."

He looked as miserable as she felt. "I honestly don't know, m'm. I wish I did. Like I said, I keep getting flashes, that's all. It's hard to tell."

She sighed. "Well, I suppose we'll find out eventually. I'll be ready to leave in forty minutes." Leaving him to follow, she went out into the hallway and headed for the kitchen. She would not dwell on Baxter's condition, she told herself. She would concentrate instead on finding him, and pray that he was still alive when she did.

"Darling Cecily! What awful, awful news!" The woman hurrying across the lobby stretched out her arms. "I can hardly believe my ears!"

Cecily halted, one eye on the grandfather clock. Phoebe Carter-Holmes Fortescue was one of her best friends, but right now she wished she had chosen another time to visit. That wish was intensified when Cecily caught sight of the white-whiskered gentleman ambling along several feet behind Phoebe.

Colonel Fortescue was an amiable fellow who had endured many a battle during the Boer War. Unfortunately his experiences had addled his brain, and any encounter with him was invariably confusing, as well as painfully time wasting. Cecily did not have any time to waste. She could only hope he refrained from rambling on with one of his boring war stories.

"Phoebe," she said brightly, as her petite friend reached her and kissed the air on each side of her cheek. "How nice of you to call."

"Well, my dear, of course I came!" Phoebe shook her lilac parasol and closed it with a snap. The brim of her hat was so loaded down with silk flowers, pale pink ostrich feathers, and a stuffed dove, that she seemed to have trouble holding up her head. "I was absolutely devastated to hear about Baxter." She looked around the lobby. "How utterly awful. I don't suppose he has come home yet?"

Cecily frowned. "No, I'm afraid not. How did you hear the news?"

"Well, it's all over town, of course. After all, Cecily dear, one can hardly have people searching the woods at night without someone learning about it. And to find a dead body in the trap instead of Baxter—well, my dear, Dolly's tea shop was positively agog with speculation this morning."

Northcott, Cecily thought in disgust. Most likely bragging to everyone about his solved murder case. So much for keeping everything a secret from her guests. It would only be a matter of time before word reached their ears.

"We even did a little searching ourselves on our way over here, didn't we, precious." Phoebe gazed fondly up at her husband, who had finally caught up with her. "Since we had to pass by the woods anyway, we just had to do our part.

Well, at least, dear Frederick went searching. He insisted I wait in the carriage, of course. Such a gentleman."

"Not at all, old bean." The colonel gave his wife a hearty slap on the back, sending her hat slipping over her eyes.

With a glare that he missed entirely, she struggled with both hands to straighten it.

Completely ignoring her dilemma, the colonel beamed at Cecily. "What ho, old girl! Sorry we couldn't find Baxter. Don't like to think of the old chap out there in the cold. Did my best, by Jove, but all that snow—made it dashed difficult. Jolly bitter out there today, what? What?"

"Indeed it is, Colonel." Turning to Phoebe, she added, "I'm terribly sorry, but I really must run. I have an urgent appointment—"

"Reminds me of the time I was in Siberia." The colonel stroked his beard. "Hmmm . . . can't remember what year that was, but it was blasted cold. I do remember that. Enough to freeze your—"

"Frederick!" Phoebe's sharp exclamation echoed across the lobby, turning more than one head as guests strolled toward the doors. She glanced at Cecily. "He tends to forget where he is at times," she said, with a smile of apology.

"Never forget where I'm at," the colonel boomed. "Though I sometimes forget where I've been."

"Yes, well," Phoebe muttered darkly, "I sometimes wish you would forget Siberia altogether."

"Ah, yes," Fortescue murmured, "that was it. Siberia. I remember it well. Knee deep in the white stuff we were, stalking a moose . . . or was it a bear? Something like that, anyway."

Cecily raised her voice. "I'm sorry, Colonel, but—"

"Big as a house, it was. Darn thing came right at us. Went to shoot it—blasted gun jammed. Frozen, I suppose."

Cecily looked at Phoebe for help. "I really am in rather a rush—"

"Had to throw it at him."

"Frederick," Phoebe warned sternly.

"Caught it right in its mouth. Damned if the thing didn't go off. Blasted my hat right off my head."

"Frederick, please!" Phoebe tugged at his sleeve.

"First time I've ever been shot at by a blasted bear."

"Fred . . . er . . . *ick*!"

Phoebe's screech did the trick. The colonel blinked, and stared at Cecily. "Sorry, old girl. Don't suppose the bar is open yet, what? What?"

"Not for another hour, I'm afraid." Cecily glanced at the clock again. "You're welcome to wait in the library, if you like. I could have one of the maids bring up a hot toddy."

"Jolly good show!" Without waiting for his wife, the colonel started toward the hallway.

"So sorry about that," Phoebe muttered. She reached up for her pink beaded hat pin, removed it, then stuck it more firmly back in her hat.

Wary of offending her friend, Cecily murmured, "Not at all. I know how much the colonel enjoys telling his stories."

Phoebe tossed her head in annoyance. "I really think he fabricates these things. No one could possibly have done all the things he says he's done. Like yesterday morning, for instance. He came back from his walk in the woods insisting that he chased a fox dressed up in riding clothes. Can you imagine?"

"He was probably dazzled by the sunlight."

"Well, I'm sure. If I didn't love the man so much, I'd wring his neck." She glanced at the hallway, down which the colonel had disappeared. "Heaven's, I'd better be after him, before he wanders into somewhere he shouldn't be. It's quite like taking care of a child at times."

She rushed off, waving a hand in farewell as she went.

Shaking her head, Cecily made for the kitchen. The sooner she got some food inside her, the sooner she could be on her way to talk to Gavin Hargrove's cousin.

Searching in her mind on her way down the steps, she finally remembered the name Kevin had given her. Randall Thorpe, that was it. There was no way of knowing if he had killed his cousin, of course, but if he had any knowledge at all that might lead her to Baxter, she was certainly going to get it out of him. Somehow.

"So, I heard you had quite a bit of excitement here last night." Dan Perkins sat on the edge of the kitchen table, one leg swinging back and forth.

"Where'd you hear that?" Gertie demanded. She was determined not to be dazzled by the butcher's smile, the way she had the night before. He was a lady-killer, all right, and she'd had more than her fill of that type of bloke, thank you very much.

"Oh, I get around in my tea half hour." Dan rubbed his

hands together. "Now that I come to mention it, how about a cuppa char to warm the cockles of my heart?"

Gertie sniffed. "What do you think this is, a bleeding tea shop? Go to Dolly's in the High Street if you want a cup of tea."

"Aw, don't be like that, luv!" Dan grinned at her. "Go on, admit it. I brighten your day, don't I. I brighten all the ladies' days. Little ray of sunshine, that's what I am."

"Full of horse's manure, that's what you are." Gertie picked up the bread knife lying on the breadboard. "You'd better not let Chubby catch you sitting on the table. She'll cut your bloody legs off."

Dan eyed the knife in her hand. "Not threatening me with that, are you, luv?"

"I will if you keep calling me luv." She reached for a loaf of bread and started sawing it into thin slices. "Now be off with you. I have to make some toast and you're in my way."

To her relief he slid off the table, but made no attempt to leave. "So, what's all this about a dead bloke turning up in your yard, then?"

"I don't know nothing about that."

"You were here, weren't you?"

"Yes, I was."

"Well, I heard there was a search party went out last night in the woods. One of your chaps is missing, isn't he? Is he a suspect? Aren't the bobbies looking for him?"

Gertie bit her lip. It was understood among the entire staff that anything going on behind doors remained a secret. The rules were set when the Pennyfoot was a hotel, and the game rooms in the cellars below were illegal. Now that it was a country club it was licensed for the game rooms, but there was enough hanky-panky going on among the guests in the boudoirs to warrant a strict maintenance of the rules.

Still, someone had been talking, that was for sure. Since the word was out, she couldn't see any sense in denying it. "Someone is missing, yes, but he's not a killer and the constables are only looking for him to bring him home, so don't bloody go spreading around lies about him."

"Whoa, all right, hold your horses. I was just wondering if there was any way I could help, that's all. I'm good at hunting things down. If someone's lost in there, I bet I could find him."

"I don't see how." Gertie sliced so hard the knife bit into the board. "We looked for hours last night and didn't see nothing."

"That's because you were looking in the dark. No one's going to find anything at night, are they. You have to look for signs that you can only see in the daylight."

She glanced at him out of the corner of her eye. "Don't you have to work?"

He smiled. "I've got the afternoon off. If you like, I could put in an hour or two before it got dark."

"Why would you do that?"

"Well, one, because I'm a generous, good-hearted chap, and two, I like pleasing a pretty lady."

"Go on with you." Secretly flattered, Gertie put down the knife. "Well, that's very nice of you, I'm sure. Madam would be very grateful for any help she can get. I'll let her know that you're looking."

"I'll do anything you want when you smile at me like

that." Dan put his fingers to his mouth, kissed them and flipped them in her direction.

He was gone before she could respond. Which was just as well, since for once she'd completely lost her tongue. Proper sweet talker that Dan, though she had to admit, he seemed to have his good side. It would be nice if he found Mr. Baxter. Everyone would be all over him for that.

She sighed and picked up the knife again. Not much chance of that, though. Much as they tried to hide it, she knew what was in everyone's mind. Mr. Baxter was a goner. There didn't seem much doubt about that.

Settled in the carriage, Cecily listened to the clip-clop of horses' hooves as they trotted along the Esplanade. The sun had begun to melt the snow, and dirty gray slush sprayed up from the wheels.

The blue sky above the ocean promised a warmer day. Perhaps if the snow melted the constables would have better luck searching for Baxter.

It hurt her too much to think about him, so she concentrated instead on her visit with Randall Thorpe. It wouldn't be easy to get information out of him, especially if he was responsible for Gavin Hargrove's death. She would have to tread with care, and try not to reveal that she suspected him of murdering his cousin.

Leaning back, she kept her gaze on the countryside speeding by. The journey took them up a steep hill, where again the horses had trouble keeping a foothold and the carriage slid from side to side.

She felt quite relieved when she spied the gray walls of Whitfield Manor on the brow of the hill. All that jostling about upset her stomach.

The carriage jerked to a stop in front of the impressive portals of the manor. Samuel pulled open the door and held out his hand. "It's a little slick, m'm, so watch your step."

"Thank you, Samuel." She allowed him to help her down, though she was quite capable of managing the feat on her own. He followed her up the steps, and stood close by her side as she tugged on the thick bell rope.

Now that she was here she felt a trifle apprehensive. If Randall Thorpe had disposed of his cousin and realized she suspected as much, he could very well attempt to silence her as well. Thank heavens she'd agreed to bring Samuel along.

As if reading her mind, he said quietly, "You will allow me to come in there with you, won't you, m'm?"

She smiled at him, pulling her shawl closer around her shoulders as a draft invaded the back of her neck. "Of course, Samuel. Your presence will be a comfort to me."

"You really think this bloke is a killer?"

"I don't know what to think. It's possible, I suppose, but this whole thing is so confusing. If only we knew how the body came to be in the trap, it might give us some answers."

"I know." Samuel sounded miserable. "I'm sorry, m'm. I'm doing my best."

"It's all right, Samuel." She patted his arm. "I know you are."

Seconds later the door creaked open and a lanky man with sparse gray hair and a sour expression stood on the threshold.

Cecily wasted no time with unnecessary formalities. "We are here to see Mr. Randall Thorpe." Normally she would have sent a calling card before arriving in person unannounced, but this was no time to observe the rigors of protocol.

The butler's nose lifted a trifle. "Whom shall I say is calling?"

"You can tell Mr. Thorpe that Mrs. Sinclair Baxter from the Pennyfoot Country Club wishes to convey her regrets for the sudden death of his cousin."

She saw a flicker of contention in the man's eyes as he murmured, "I will see if Mr. Thorpe is available."

He started to close the door, but Samuel was quick enough to jam his foot in the opening. "We'll wait inside," he said firmly. "It is too cold for madam to wait out here."

For a moment it seemed as if the butler would refuse to open the door again, but then apparently thought better of it. With a look of pure disdain, he stepped back.

Cecily stepped over the threshold, her gaze darting at once to the magnificent staircase that wound its way up to the next floor. Covered in deep red carpet, the stairs split at the top, branching in opposite directions. A brilliant chandelier hung over the landing, its hundreds of crystals gleaming in the sunlight that filtered through a leaded pane window high on the wall.

"Posh," Samuel murmured, as the butler disappeared down the hallway.

"It is indeed." Cecily gazed at a landscape hanging on the wall. She found it exceptionally fascinating and moved closer to read the signature. "Monet," she murmured. "I've heard of him. I believe he lives somewhere near Paris. I thought he only painted water lilies."

"I think I remember something else," Samuel said quietly behind her.

She spun around. "What is it?"

"Well, something's been nagging at me all morning. I think I saw something in the woods. Something swinging from a tree."

"Samuel, do you—"

"The master will see you now."

Startled, Cecily turned to see the butler standing a few feet away. The thick carpet had deadened the sound of his footsteps. Raising her eyebrows at Samuel, she gave him a warning shake of her head, then followed the rigid back of the butler down the hallway.

CHAPTER

❧ 6 ❧

Walking behind the butler, Cecily felt a twinge of sympathy. He moved as if he suffered from rheumatics, a common complaint of the aging in the damp climate of the English coast. The man must be older than he appeared, she thought, as he paused in front of a door on the right.

The butler tapped lightly, waited for a response, then opened the door. "Mrs. Sinclair Baxter and servant," he announced.

Samuel pinched his lips together but made no comment as they stepped inside the room.

Randall Thorpe was a big man, tall and muscular, with a florid face that suggested a fondness for spirits. He stood by a brocade armchair, which had been placed in front of a blazing fire. Above it the mantelpiece had been decorated with thick boughs of fir and holly, with sprigs of mistletoe tucked in here and there.

A matching armchair sat on the other side of the fireplace, occupied by a slender young woman with startling red hair. She wore a simple afternoon frock of blue silk, and managed to seem as elegant and grandiose as if she were royalty.

"Thank you, Wilmot." Randall Thorpe moved forward, his face alive with curiosity. "I must say I'm delighted to meet you, Mrs. Baxter."

"Likewise." Cecily held out her hand and allowed it to be swallowed up in Randall's huge paw.

He lifted her fingers to his mouth and brushed them lightly with his lips. "Charmed, I'm sure."

"My manager, Samuel," Cecily murmured, determined that he should not be ignored.

Randall nodded at him, then turned to the woman. "May I present Miss Naomi Kendall, the late Gavin Hargrove's fiancé."

"Oh, my dear." Cecily hurried forward to take the woman's hands. "I'm so sorry. You must be utterly devastated."

Naomi's hands felt cold and limp, and her expression was completely devoid of emotion. "Thank you," she murmured. "You're so very kind."

Withdrawing from her, Cecily looked back at Randall. "My sympathies to you as well. This must have been such a terrible shock for you."

"It was indeed. I must confess I am curious, however." He gestured at the chair he'd obviously just vacated. "Please, take a seat." He waited for her to seat herself before adding, "I have to say I find it immensely odd that my cousin's body was found on your premises."

Cecily met his gaze squarely. If he had been responsible for the murder, he certainly hid it well. She could see no guilt or uneasiness lurking behind his pleasing features. "Indeed," she assured him, "I am curious about that myself. I don't know how much you have been told, but my husband and Samuel here left to pick holly yesterday afternoon. The trap returned without them, carrying the body of your cousin."

"So I understand. Has your husband returned home yet?"

She paused, waiting for the pain to pass. "I'm afraid not," she said finally. "The constables are searching for him right now."

"Then I must offer my sympathies to you as well, Mrs. Baxter." He bowed his head. "I trust your husband will return home safe and well."

"Thank you." *Very smooth*, she thought. *Maybe a little too smooth.*

Randall turned to Samuel and addressed him directly. "You appear to have met some kind of accident. Surely you must be able to shed some light on the puzzle?"

Cecily answered for him. "The injury to Samuel's head has erased all memory of yesterday's events."

"Well, not quite," Samuel said.

Randall stared at him for a moment or two longer. "How very distressing for you," he murmured.

Cecily decided it was time to come to the point. "I understand that your cousin owed a considerable amount of money to a gambling syndicate in London."

"M'm—" Samuel began, but she shook her head at him and he closed his mouth.

Randall raised his eyebrows, then exchanged a quick glance with Naomi. It was the first time he'd shown any sign of discomfort. Cecily found that interesting.

"I see P.C. Northcott has wasted no time in informing you of my cousin's personal business."

"In view of the fact your late cousin was discovered in my yard and my husband was nearly considered a suspect in his death, the constable saw fit to inform me of his deductions. He now believes the syndicate was responsible for your cousin's death, however. He intends to hand the matter over to Scotland Yard."

There was no mistaking the uneasiness on Randall's face. "Does he, indeed. I think that would be a mistake."

"Why would that be?"

Randall seemed at a loss for a moment, while Naomi sat silently watching him.

"I'd like to say something, m'm," Samuel said, his voice urgent.

Cecily frowned. "What is it, Samuel?"

"I've remembered something."

Alarmed that he might say something to put them in danger, Cecily shook her head. "Not now, Samuel."

"Let him speak," Randall said. He moved to Samuel's side. "He may be able to shed some light on this dreadful business, after all."

Samuel seemed undecided whether to continue or not, glancing from Cecily to Randall and back again.

She had to trust him to use discretion, Cecily decided.

Obviously he felt it important to tell what he knew. Hoping she wasn't making a mistake, she said quietly, "It's all right, Samuel. Tell us what you remembered."

"He was hanging from a tree," Samuel said, looking directly into Cecily's face. "That's where we found him. The dead bloke. He was hanging in a tree. Mr. Baxter and I cut him down."

"Good Lord," Randall said softly.

With a surge of hope, Cecily demanded, "Can you tell us what happened after that?"

Samuel stared at her for an interminable moment, then shook his head. "I don't remember, m'm. I'm sorry. But it's starting to come back. I'll keep trying."

"Do, please, Samuel." Disappointed, Cecily turned back to Randall.

"Well, there you are, then," he said, with an air of relief. "That explains everything!"

Cecily frowned. "Then perhaps you will enlighten me?"

"It's quite obvious to me that my cousin's death was an accident." Randall sent a triumphant glance at Naomi, though not a muscle in her face so much as twitched. "Gavin was in the habit of riding through the woods every morning after breakfast. When he failed to return yesterday we assumed at first he had ridden into town, as he sometimes did."

"To do some Christmas shopping," Naomi offered.

"Right." Randall looked at her for a moment longer, then turned back to Cecily. "Yes, well, Wilmot had offered to drive Mrs. Trumble into town for supplies, and we thought perhaps

Gavin had ridden in with them. Needless to say, we were terribly shocked when the constable informed us of his death."

"But I don't understand why you are so certain it was an accident."

"Ah." Randall reached for a pipe that lay smoldering in an ashtray on the arm of his chair. "Unfortunately it's happened to him before, you see. Several months ago he was knocked off his horse by a low-lying branch."

He puffed at the pipe, sending up a cloud of blue smoke around his head before continuing. "The horse came home without him. When we found him he was unconscious and took days to recover."

"We thought he would never wake up," Naomi said.

Randall nodded. "Indeed we did. Anyway, yesterday Gavin was in rather a temper when he left here. He tends to ride hard when he's out of sorts. He must have been caught up by another low lying branch, but this time he simply hung there. I imagine he was strangled by his own clothing." Again he exchanged a glance with Naomi and his voice softened. "Gavin has always been rather reckless."

For the first time Cecily saw the young woman's face change. Her eyes filled with warmth, and her lips softened, as if greeting a lover. "You're right of course, Randall. How clever of you. Of course that must be what happened!" She smiled at Cecily. "I imagine the constable will want to hear about this, before he involves Scotland Yard with an unnecessary investigation."

Faced with such conviction, Cecily found herself wavering. It all sounded so logical when Randall explained it.

Until something else occurred to her. "But then how did his body end up in my trap?"

"I would venture that your husband intended to bring the body back to the Pennyfoot. Perhaps having a dead body dumped in the trap spooked the horse and he bolted."

"Then where is my husband?"

Randall shrugged. "Ah, that I have no answer for, I'm afraid."

"It's so easy to lose one's way in the woods," Naomi put in. "Especially when the snow is deep. I'm sure your husband will find his way back before long."

Cecily heard again Madeline's words. *He's alive. He's hurting.*

"You must have some tea." Randall reached for a bell rope at the side of the brick fireplace.

A second or two later the door opened and the stone-faced butler appeared in the doorway—so fast Cecily knew he had to have been lurking right outside the door. "You rang, sir?"

"Yes, Wilmot. Please have Mrs. Trumble bring up a tray of tea and scones for our guests."

"As you wish, sir." The butler withdrew, leaving an uneasy silence behind.

Cecily would just as soon not partake of tea. She could accept Randall's assumption that his cousin's death was an accident. It certainly seemed feasible.

However, much as she wanted to believe everyone's theory that the horse had bolted leaving Baxter and Samuel behind, she couldn't rid herself of the feeling that something was not right with that scenario.

Another thing—accident or not, neither Randall nor

Naomi seemed to be grieving over Gavin Hargrove's death. Randall had, in the past month, lost not only his cousin, but the uncle who had raised him. Apparently the inheritance meant more to him than his family.

As for Naomi, having so recently lost the man whom she had hoped to marry, her lack of distress seemed unforgivable. Even her dress was inappropriate. The reason for that soon became clear when Cecily saw Naomi's gaze following Randall as he crossed the room to a small writing desk. Just for a second or two passion blazed in her pale blue eyes, then was gone again when she noticed Cecily observing her.

She set her gaze on the fire instead, perhaps in the futile hope of convincing Cecily she was in mourning.

At Randall's bidding, Samuel retreated to the corner of the room and sat on a brocade Queen Anne armchair. He looked uncomfortable, and Cecily knew he felt even more unsettled than she did.

The arrival of the housekeeper interrupted the conversation. The wiry woman flitted around the living room, speaking in a low nervous voice that was difficult to understand. The keys that hung from her belt jingled constantly, and a large pendant swung to and fro across her chest as she moved this way and that.

She served the tea with a deft enough hand, though a spoon rattled in the saucer when she set a cup in front of Randall.

There was an awkward moment when she apparently failed to notice Samuel sitting in the corner. She was most apologetic, however, when Randall pointed out her oversight. Seemingly anxious to make amends she overfilled Samuel's cup, allowing a few drops to run down the side and into the saucer.

He pretended not to notice, earning a smile of approval from Cecily. Obviously the poor woman was distressed by the upheaval of Hargrove's death—the only one who showed any anguish thus far.

After she left the room, the tension seemed to ease a little. "It isn't often," Randall said, after he'd settled himself in a captain's chair, "that one meets a lady managing a large establishment. Rather a taxing profession, I would think."

"At times, yes, but certainly one most women could manage." Cecily sipped the steaming hot tea and put down her cup. "Rather like running a household on a grand scale."

"I greatly admire you, Mrs. Baxter," Naomi said, surprising her. "I'm quite sure I could never find the stamina to cope with such an arduous undertaking."

Cecily regarded her with skepticism. The young woman was quite tall and too muscular to be considered frail. Obviously she underestimated her own strength. "I really am sorry for your loss," she said quietly. "How long were you and Mr. Hargrove engaged?"

"Six months." Naomi sighed. "I shall miss him."

"I'm sure you both will." Cecily looked meaningfully at Randall.

"Oh, indeed!" Randall hurriedly agreed. "It's a great shock, of course, coming so soon after my uncle's death. Two funerals in as many months. So depressing. Especially hard this time of year."

"Yes." Naomi wiped the corner of her eye with the corner

of a delicate handkerchief. "There will be no Christmas for us this year, I'm afraid."

Seated across from her, Cecily could see no tears on the thick lashes. "A sad time for you all," she murmured.

Randall turned to Samuel, who sat quietly in the corner, nibbling on a scone. "I must thank you, sir, for clearing up the mystery of my cousin's death. Knowing it was an accident is a great comfort to us all."

Samuel nodded, looking as if he wasn't sure if he should smile or not. Apparently being addressed as sir had frozen his tongue.

Deciding it was time to take her leave, Cecily stood. "Thank you both for your hospitality," she said, ignoring Randall's murmured protest, "but I really must get back to the Pennyfoot." She looked at Naomi. "I'm happy we had this opportunity to meet, and I trust we shall meet again in the near future."

Naomi smiled, though her expression clearly suggested she was in no hurry to repeat the experience.

Samuel had leapt to his feet the moment Cecily rose. Crossing the room, his gaze lingered on Naomi but she appeared not to notice. He reached the door just as it opened.

The butler stood in the entrance, staring at nothing in particular.

"Ah, there you are, Wilmot." Randall smiled at Cecily. "I swear the man has a sixth sense. I was about to ring for him."

More like an ear pressed to the door, Cecily thought, as she allowed Randall to once more molest her hand.

"My deepest gratitude for taking the time to call on us at this grievous time," Randall said, his voice belatedly somber. "I do hope your husband returns swiftly and unharmed."

"Thank you." The little knot of worry tightened in Cecily's chest. "And I hope you both soon recover from your tragic loss."

If either Randall or Naomi detected a note of irony in her voice, neither gave a sign.

Escorting her out to the carriage, Samuel shivered. "I'm glad we're out of there. That butler gives me the willies. Like a blinking ghost he is, appearing out of nowhere like that."

Cecily glanced at him. "What did you think of Randall Thorpe and Naomi?"

"He doesn't look like a murderer, but then it's hard to say, really. She's a looker, but she didn't seem too cut up about losing her fiancé, did she."

"Exactly what I thought." Cecily climbed up into the carriage. "Do you think it was an accident?"

Samuel shrugged. "Could have been, I suppose. He could have strangled to death on that branch before we cut him down." He stared down at his feet, and shoveled the melting snow with the toe of his boot. "I just wish I could remember. It's sort of like shadows in the night—I can see them moving but I can't see what they are."

"The good news is that you're beginning to remember." Cecily settled herself more comfortably on the seat. "Soon you'll remember everything and perhaps then all this will be cleared up."

"I just hope it's not too late." He shut the door, and she

sat for a long time staring out the window. She knew what he meant. Every hour that Baxter was missing could bring him closer to disaster. *He's alive. He's hurting.* Madeline had also said that he was in good hands. She had to cling to that hope, no matter how small. It was all she had.

CHAPTER

❃ 7 ❃

The minute Cecily arrived back at the Pennyfoot she asked Philip if there was news of Baxter.

The puny desk clerk swept a fringe of gray hair back from his forehead with his thumb. "Not a peep, m'm, I'm afraid to say."

It was no more than she'd expected. Even so, she found it hard to suppress the rush of disappointment and fear. "Thank you, Philip. I shall be in my office if you need me."

"Yes, m'm." As she turned away, he added, "I'm so sorry, m'm. Mr. Baxter was a proper gentleman. Not many like him out there."

"He's not dead, Philip," she said sharply. "He's simply missing, that's all."

"Oh, yes, m'm, indeed, m'm. I only meant—"

Relenting, she forced a smile. "Never mind, Philip. I know you meant to be kind."

Philip's thin face twitched. "He'll be back, m'm, you'll see."

"I hope and pray for that." She left, before the threatening tears had a chance to fall.

Once inside her office, she allowed herself the luxury of shedding a few tears, but only for a moment or two. After dabbing her moist cheeks with a handkerchief, she picked up the telephone and asked the operator to put in a call to Kevin Prestwick.

Fortunately he was between patients, and before long she heard his calming voice on the phone. "Cecily? Has Baxter returned?"

"Oh, how I wish." She paused to steady her voice before adding, "I have a question for you." Quickly she recounted her visit to Whitfield Manor and the conversation that took place. "Is it possible," she asked at length, "that Mr. Hargrove could have been hung by his collar on a tree by accident?"

"There is no question in my mind," Kevin answered. "The bruises around the victim's throat are consistent with pressure from someone's fingers. Gavin Hargrove was deliberately strangled." His voice became stern. "What, may I ask, were you doing by yourself at Whitfield Manor? All things considered, that could have been extremely dangerous."

"I wasn't alone," Cecily assured him. "Samuel was by my side the whole time."

"Samuel should not be gallivanting around the countryside with that head injury. Neither should you be taking

77

such extraordinary risks. I'm quite sure if Baxter were there he would have absolutely forbidden you to go."

"No doubt," Cecily said tartly. "And it would have done him no good at all. For heaven's sake, Kevin. You are being just as tiresome as my husband."

"For good reason, apparently." Kevin's sigh echoed down the line. "Please, Cecily, do try to use some common sense. Losing one of you is quite enough for the present."

"I do wish everyone would stop talking about Baxter as if he were dead! As I keep telling everyone . . ." She caught back the sob, but Kevin must have heard it anyway.

"Cecily."

When she didn't answer he repeated her name more urgently. "Cecily, please, try to remain calm. I never meant to imply that Baxter is dead. Your husband is a strong and resourceful man, and I'm quite sure that he will return to you in due time."

How she wished she could be so positive. "Thank you, Kevin. You will be among the first to know when that happens."

"I certainly hope so." He hesitated, then added, "Is there anything I can do for you? Perhaps another powder to help you rest?"

"Thank you, but no." She let out her breath. "I have work to do and I need a clear head." Bidding him good-bye, she replaced the phone on its hook.

After staring at rows of figures that seemed determined to run into each other, she gave up her attempts to balance the books. Slamming the heavy ledger closed, she sat back in her chair.

She'd been too easily swayed by the affable Randall Thorpe and Naomi. Now that she thought about it, they had been remarkably eager to convince her that Gavin Hargrove's death was an accident.

She remembered the look they had exchanged when she'd mentioned the gambling debts and Northcott's intention to hand the case over to Scotland Yard. She'd assumed at the time that they would prefer that the sordid details didn't come to light, thus protecting Gavin's reputation.

Then again, since neither of them seemed to be mourning his death, why would they worry about his reputation?

She'd left too soon, she decided. There were questions still unanswered. Remembering the nervous little housekeeper, she wondered if perhaps she would learn more from her. There was only one way to find out. Reaching for the bell pull, she tugged it.

Seconds later, Pansy answered her summons.

"Please tell Samuel I'll need the carriage again," she told the maid. "As soon as possible. Advise me as soon as it's ready."

"Yes, m'm."

Pansy disappeared, and Cecily glanced at the clock. The hours were speeding by and still no sign of Baxter. "Where are you, Hugh?" she whispered out loud. "You must come back to me. You simply must."

She needed something to eat. It would help keep up her spirits. She had enough time to pay a visit to the kitchen before Samuel would have the carriage ready again.

Reaching the top of the kitchen stairs, she was about to descend when a familiar voice hailed her.

"Cecily, dear! I had no idea you were back!"

Curbing her impatience, she turned to greet Phoebe. Colonel Fortescue hovered behind his wife, his red nose bearing testimony to the amount of spirits he'd consumed.

"Tally ho, old girl!" he roared. "Off to the woodsh again, what? What? We're going to hunt for another silver fox, aren't we, my little pet?"

Phoebe rolled her eyes at Cecily. "Dressed up in riding clothes, I suppose." Turning to her husband she shouted, "Don't be ridiculous, Frederick. You're not going back to those woods, so please stop talking about your silly foxes!"

Fortescue's white whiskers bristled. "No need to shriek like a banshee. I'm not blashted deaf." He started muttering, and Cecily caught just a word here and there. "Blashted fellow . . . singing out there in the trees . . . rude chap. Never answered me."

Phoebe faced Cecily again, the pink feathers on her hat trembling with her agitation. "Really, he gets worse every day. I don't know what I'm going to do with him, really I don't."

It was Cecily's considered opinion that if the colonel's good wife prevented him from downing a pint of brandy a day he might have a little better control of his mind. Afraid that he'd launch into one of his endless stories, she said hurriedly, "I'm so sorry, Phoebe, but I'm in a dreadful rush. Perhaps we can visit with each other later?"

Phoebe looked surprised. "Well, of course we will, Cecily dear. Are we not invited to the carol singing ceremony this evening?" Apparently noticing her friend's blank expression, her face filled with concern. "It is this evening, isn't it?

I know you always used to have it on Christmas Eve, but I thought this year you'd decided to hold it early so that the staff would have more time to prepare for the Grand Ball on Christmas Eve. Or am I wrong in thinking that?"

Before Cecily could answer, Phoebe slapped a hand over her mouth. "Oh, my dear, how thoughtless of me. Baxter's still missing, isn't he. Of course you will be canceling the carol singing."

"Not at all." Cecily made a valiant effort to smile. "We will carry on with the Christmas season at the Pennyfoot as usual. Baxter would have wanted it that way."

Tears brimmed in Phoebe's blue eyes. "How very brave of you, my dear. Then we most certainly shall be there." She glanced back at her husband, who had wandered off across the lobby and appeared to be engaged in an imaginary sword fight with the grandfather clock. "At least," she amended with a sigh, "I shall be there."

"Then I shall see you tonight." Exchanging kisses in the air with Phoebe, Cecily sent up a prayer that she would be able to keep that appointment.

Pansy skipped down the front steps of the hotel, her heart thudding in her chest. Anytime she had an excuse to see Samuel was a moment crackling with anticipation. To actually have the chance to talk to him in the stables, out of sight of Mrs. Chubb's eagle eyes—well, that was pure bliss.

Instead of going back through the kitchen, she'd chosen to take the long way around to the stables. That way she didn't have to explain to Mrs. Chubb where she was going until after she'd been, and then the housekeeper couldn't watch the clock every minute she was gone.

Picking up her skirts, Pansy flew through the rose gardens, past the ballroom doors, around the back of the hotel and across the courtyards.

The milder ocean breezes had melted all the snow, and only wet puddles were left to dry out in the sun. Pansy picked her way across to the stables, where she could hear Samuel whistling as he tended to the horses.

Her excitement was so intense she could hardly breathe. Quietly she crept up to the main doors and peered inside. At first she couldn't see him in the sudden contrast from sunlight to shade, but then she spied him down in one of the stalls.

He had his back to her, smoothing a brush over a chestnut's gleaming coat. She crept closer, trying not to breathe too deeply as the stink of horses intensified.

Samuel stopped whistling, just before she reached him, and swung around, the brush held aloft in his hand. For a moment she saw an odd look in his eyes, almost as if he was scared, but then it was gone. "Oh," he said, turning back to the horse. "It's only you."

Piqued at the lukewarm welcome, Pansy lifted her chin. "Who were you expecting, then? One of them flighty maids we took on for Christmas, I s'pose."

He grinned. "Jealous?"

"Course not." She moved closer to run her hand over the horse's silky hide. Its coat felt warm and smooth under her fingers, and she felt a shiver run through the horse's back. She wrinkled her nose at Samuel. "It's smelly in here."

"It's a stable. What do you expect?" He started brushing the chestnut's coat again. "What're you doing in here, anyway?"

Reluctant for her big moment to be over too soon, she smiled at him. How dashing he looked with that bandage on his head! Like a pirate, or something. "I came to see you, didn't I. I never did thank you for filling the coal buckets for me yesterday."

"Oh." He seemed tongue-tied for some reason, and frowned at the brush as it moved in smooth strokes down the chestnut's sides. "Well, it was my pleasure."

"While you were filling them you said you were going to ask me something, remember?"

His cheeks turned red, and he turned his face away from her. "Not really. I can't remember much about what went on yesterday."

Spying a bucket, she overturned it and sat down on it. "Well, you said you had something you wanted to ask me, but then Mrs. Chubb called you and said madam wanted to talk to you and you never did ask me. Don't suppose you remember it now." She didn't tell him that she'd been awake half the night wondering what it was he hadn't had time to say.

"Well," Samuel said, his voice sounding strange, "as a matter of fact I do remember. I was going to ask you if you wanted to go out with me."

She jumped up so fast she overturned the bucket. It clattered and rattled along the ground, then rolled under the feet of the chestnut. The horse reared back on its hind legs, whinnying in fright.

Pansy darted out of the stall, leaving Samuel to struggle with the startled animal. "Whoa there, Major! Calm down, then. Whoa there, boy."

She watched in awe as he coaxed the rearing animal to gradually quiet down, then eventually still its quivering body and swishing tail.

"Goodness, that was clever." She gazed at him in genuine admiration. "I could never have done that. I—" She broke off at the sight of his face. His eyes stared right at her, yet she knew he wasn't seeing her. She could see his throat working, but no sound came out of his mouth.

Frightened, she wondered if the bump on his head had damaged his mind. "I'm sorry," she stammered. "I didn't mean to knock the bucket into the horse. I only—"

Samuel dropped the brush and swung out of the stall. "I've got to see madam right away," he muttered, and rushed past her, out the doors.

It was only when she was on her way back to the kitchen that she remembered she hadn't given him madam's message. Now she was in for it. She could only hope that whatever was so important he had to tell madam, it would be enough to make them forget what it was she'd forgotten.

Cecily looked up in surprise when Samuel burst unceremoniously into her office. "Well," she said, laying down her pen, "that was quick. I only sent Pansy out there a few moments ago."

For a moment he seemed confused, then he stepped

closer and laid both his hands on the desk. Leaning forward he said hoarsely, "I remembered."

She shot up in her chair, afraid to hope for too much. "Do you know where Baxter is?"

Once more she felt the crushing disappointment when he shook his head. "I do know he wasn't dead when I left him."

"Well, that's something, at least. Where did you leave him?"

He frowned in his effort to recall the details. "On the trail. I'd started loading holly in the trap when I heard Mr. Baxter yell. He was farther down the trail, and I went running to see what was up. I found him staring up at a tree, and when I looked where he was pointing . . ." He shuddered.

"You saw the dead body of Gavin Hargrove," Cecily finished for him.

"Yeah. We didn't know for sure if he was dead, but once we cut him down, we could see he was a goner. Mr. Baxter says as how we should bring him back to the Pennyfoot and call the constable, so I went back to get the trap."

He paused, appearing to struggle with his thoughts, and for a moment Cecily was afraid he'd lost track of them again. Then he lifted his head, his eyes bright with excitement. "I heard horses in the distance coming down the trail. When I brought the trap back, there was Mr. Baxter, lying on the ground. I bent over him to see if he was breathing, because I couldn't see any movement from him at all. I thought at first he was dead, but then I saw his chest moving up and down."

"He was unconscious?"

"Yes, m'm. He was. I remember that clearly now. I remember wondering what happened to him and that I had to get him home somehow. Then all of a sudden a trap came out of nowhere, driving right at me." He shuddered again. "I can still hear the horses hooves, and the harness jingling. Like a nightmare, it was. That's all I remember until I woke up with a terrible headache, all alone in the woods and not knowing what the blazes I was doing there."

"Did you see who was driving the trap?"

"No, m'm, I didn't. At least, if I did see him, I don't remember. It all happened so fast it's a blur."

"And so you started walking home."

"Yes, m'm. That's it. Then David came along and that's all I remember."

Looking at the young man's stricken face, Cecily felt sorry for him. "So you still don't know what happened to Baxter?"

"No, m'm. He wasn't with me when I woke up. I kept calling out but no one answered me. I went back to the trail where I'd last seen him but he was gone. Whoever was driving that other trap must have taken him."

"I suppose so." Cecily stared at her desk for a long time. She didn't know whether to feel relief or even more worried. At least Baxter was alive when Samuel had last seen him, but who had taken him, and to where? Was he a prisoner somewhere?

"Don't worry, m'm. He'll turn up, I'm sure of it."

She sighed. "Dr. Prestwick assures me that Mr. Hargrove's death was not an accident. Perhaps the theory that members of a syndicate were involved is true after all. They could have taken Baxter prisoner to keep him from talking to the police."

Samuel's face changed. "I do hope that's not the case, m'm."

She felt cold when she realized what he implied. *He's in good hands.* Dear God, make that so. "Samuel," she said sharply, "we must go back to Whitfield Manor. I need to find out as much as I can about this gambling syndicate and Gavin Hargrove's involvement with them."

"If you don't mind me saying so, m'm, I don't think that's a good idea. I think we should talk to P.C. Northcott."

"We're wasting far too much valuable time as it is." She rose. "Please get the carriage ready at once."

"I've just this minute put the carriage away—" Samuel began, then closed his mouth when Cecily raised her eyebrows. "Very well, m'm." He turned and headed for the door, muttering quietly, "We're going to pay for this, I know we are."

For a moment Cecily felt guilty. Kevin's warning echoed in her head. It was one thing to put herself in harm's way, but Samuel was not well, and she was being most inconsiderate to expose him to what could be a dangerous mission.

Not that it would prevent her from carrying out her plan. She was convinced the answers to Baxter's disappearance lay at Whitfield Manor, and she would risk everything to find him. Everything.

CHAPTER

❈ 8 ❈

The journey back to the manor took less time than earlier. Although patches of snow still dotted the open grassland on the cliffs, the roads were merely wet and fairly comfortable to navigate.

Arriving at their destination, she accepted Samuel's guiding hand and descended from the carriage. "No doubt they will be surprised to see us back so soon," she said, as she made her way to the steps.

"I hope you've got a good explanation for coming back," Samuel muttered.

Alerted by his sullen tone, Cecily looked at him in concern. "Is your head hurting you, Samuel? Did you take the medicine Dr. Prestwick gave you?"

"It's not me head, m'm." Samuel looked most unhappy.

"Though it does ache a bit. It's more us being here without a good excuse. They're bound to know something's up, and that could get us in a lot of trouble."

"Don't worry, Samuel. I'll think of something." Lifting her skirts, Cecily mounted the steps. She reached the top and tugged purposefully on the bell rope.

Samuel stood silent and fidgeted at her side as they waited for the summons to be answered. At last the door creaked open, and Wilmot's cold eyes peered over their heads.

"I regret having to disturb you again," Cecily said, with her brightest smile. "I seem to have lost my necklace. The clasp must have broken. It's nowhere in the carriage so I assume it must be here. If you don't mind, I should like to come in and look for it."

The butler's dark gaze descended just long enough to flick across her face. Without a word he stepped back and allowed them to enter.

Standing once more inside the sumptuous entrance hall, Cecily made a pretense of scrutinizing the carpet. "I don't see it anywhere. I wonder if I might have a word with Mrs. Trumble. She might have picked it up."

Wilmot's forbidding expression didn't look promising. He opened his mouth to speak, but the clang of the doorbell silenced him.

Cecily waited while he stalked stiffly to the front door and pulled it open once more.

Naomi's voice echoed shrilly across the vast hall. "I saw a trap outside, Wilmot. Do we have more visitors?" She appeared in the doorway, dressed in a dark blue coat. A blue wooly muffler, one end embroidered with a coat of arms and tied under her chin, anchored her hat to her head.

Her shocked expression seemed almost comical as she came forward. "Mrs. Baxter!" Her glance skimmed over Samuel. "Are you looking for Randall? He's outside, working on his motorcar."

"Actually I was hoping to speak with your housekeeper." Cecily repeated her story about a lost necklace. "It was a gift from my husband," she added. "It has great sentimental value for me."

"Well, then, we shall have to look for it." Naomi turned to Wilmot. "Please have Mrs. Trumble come up here at once."

The butler looked as if he would refuse, then with a sniff that clearly conveyed his displeasure, he stalked awkwardly off down the hallway and out of sight.

"I hope you will excuse me," Naomi said, moving toward the hallstand. "I have something rather pressing to attend to this afternoon." She slipped out of her coat and hung it alongside the other coats that hung there. "I'm sure Mrs. Trumble can help you find your necklace." She paused, then added slyly, "If it's here, that is."

Cecily hoped the woman didn't notice Samuel's guilty face. "Oh, I'm sure it must be. I've looked everywhere else."

Naomi pulled off her scarf and hooked it over her coat. "Then I hope you find it."

She started to leave, but halted when Cecily called out, "By the way, I received a report from Dr. Prestwick this afternoon. He tells me that without a shadow of a doubt, Gavin Hargrove was murdered."

Naomi stood for several seconds before slowly turning

back. Her expression was hard to read, but her voice was high with tension when she answered. "How positively awful. I wonder who could have done such a dreadful deed?"

"I think we'd all like the answer to that, Miss Kendall," Cecily said meaningfully.

Naomi hesitated, sent a nervous glance in Samuel's direction, then said quickly, "Mrs. Baxter, may I be frank?"

"By all means."

"Privately?"

Cecily looked at Samuel.

She thought he might resist, but after staring hard at Naomi, he muttered, "I'll go and check on the horses." He gave the young woman another meaningful stare. "I'll be back in a tick."

Naomi waited until he'd left, than after looking around, she drew closer to Cecily. She spoke low and so fast her words tumbled over each other. "I'm not altogether surprised someone wanted Gavin dead. He was not a nice man, you know."

Cecily raised her eyebrows. "Rather an odd thing to say about one's fiancé," she murmured.

"Well, nobody liked him. He was horrible to the staff, especially after his father died and left him in charge. He was going to get rid of some of them. He told me they were mean to him when he was growing up."

"You must have liked him well enough to agree to marry him," Cecily pointed out.

Naomi pursed her lips. "Yes, well, that was before I found out what he was up to."

"Oh? And what was that?"

91

"I found out that Gavin had been—ah—dallying with someone else, to put it delicately."

Cecily studied the anxious face. "I'm so sorry."

Naomi shrugged. "I always suspected he couldn't be faithful to one woman, but when I found out it was Emily Gower . . . well, that was going a little too far."

"Emily Gower?"

Naomi nodded, and leaned closer. "She's the gardener's wife. Mind you, I can see why she fell for Gavin. Silas, that's her husband, he's such a boorish man. He treats Emily as if she's a worm beneath his feet. Horrible. He has a violent temper, too." Her eyes opened wide. "You don't suppose he found out about it and killed Gavin, do you?"

Cecily continued to study her for a moment. "It's possible," she said at last. "It's also possible that members of the gambling syndicate killed your fiancé in retaliation for refusing to pay his debts."

She saw a flash of alarm leap into Naomi's eyes, then it was gone. "I certainly hope not," she mumbled. "What if they come after me, too? This is all so disturbing."

"Well, it seems as if Samuel might be starting to regain his memory, in which case, we might find out before too long who was responsible for your fiancé's death."

The clinking of keys sounded behind her, and Naomi's gaze slid to the passageway. "I have to go," she added abruptly. "I hope you find your necklace."

She made for the stairs, and Cecily turned to see Wilmot and the jittery housekeeper standing a few feet away.

Advancing toward the butler and his companion, she wondered how much of Naomi's disclosure the couple had overheard. "I'm sorry to bother you," she said to the house-keeper. "Mrs. Trumble, isn't it?"

The woman nodded and started to curtsey, then thought better of it. "I'm sorry to hear about your lost necklace," she said, in her thin, low voice. "Wilmot says you lost it some-where in here?"

"Either here or in the drawing room." Cecily smiled to put the woman at ease. "I'd appreciate it if you would help me look for it."

Wilmot spoke, startling them both. "The servants will look for the necklace, madam. If and when they find it, I will see that it is returned to you."

"Oh, I don't want to put anyone to all that trouble." Cecily turned her smile on the butler's stoic face. "Mrs. Trum-ble and I can look for it ourselves, can't we?"

"No, madam, that is a servant's duty. The master would be most displeased if I allowed a guest to do servants' work."

In other words, Randall Thorpe would not want her snooping around. Cecily stared at the butler in frustration. It seemed as if she would be thwarted in her attempt to talk to the housekeeper alone. "Very well. I shall return at a later date to see if my necklace is found."

The clang of the doorbell cut off Wilmot's reply. Once more he limped to the door and opened it, then turned to gaze above Cecily's head. "Your servant is here," he announced.

Behind him, Samuel made a rude gesture with his thumb to his nose.

Cecily decided it was time to leave. She would have to find an opportunity later to speak with Mrs. Trumble. Meanwhile, she had other fish to fry. With someone who just might be more promising than the skittish house-keeper.

"I'm going to talk to the gardener," Cecily announced, as she followed Samuel down the steps to the carriage. "He must be somewhere about."

"The gardener?" Samuel paused at the foot of the steps and peered up at her.

"Yes." She told him the story Naomi had given her. "It all sounds a little too pat to me. I have an idea that Naomi might have made the whole thing up in order to throw me off the scent."

Samuel looked puzzled. "Off what scent?"

"She could be protecting Randall, or even herself."

Samuel stared at her for a moment, then uttered an incredulous laugh. "That woman a killer? I'm sorry, m'm, but I just can't see her putting her hands around a bloke's throat and squeezing the life out of him."

"Never underestimate a scorned woman." Cecily marched down the last of the steps. "Besides, look at it this way. Considering Naomi's poor opinion of her late fiancé, why would she want a man like that, unless it was his fortune she was after? Apparently she's living at the manor. Suppose she found herself attracted to Randall—a much more desirable prospect—except he was entirely dependent on Gavin for his living."

Samuel's eyebrows shot up his forehead. "So you think she might have bumped Gavin off so that Randall would get the money instead?"

"Something like that." Cecily stepped down onto the path and proceeded to follow it around the back of the building.

Stumbling after her, Samuel said breathlessly, "So why are we talking to the gardener?"

"I want to know if what she said about Mr. Hargrove's interest in the gardener's wife is true."

"And you think he's likely to tell you that?"

"I'm hoping he'll give something away, yes." She reached the edge of the back lawns and shaded her eyes with her hand. "Can you see him?"

Samuel stared into the shrubs that lined the edge of the lawn. "There's someone moving about back there. Want me to go and see, m'm?"

"No. We'll go together." She set off across the lawn at a brisk pace, followed by her reluctant stable manager.

Samuel was right, the gardener was on the other side of the shrubs, cutting sprays from a fragrant cedar of Lebanon. He looked up as Cecily approached, a scowl on his leathery face. He reminded Cecily of the tree in front of him— strong and sinewy, though twisted with age. What was left of his gray hair hung down to his stubbled chin, and his eyes almost disappeared beneath his heavy lids.

"Good afternoon, Mr. Gower," Cecily called out. "My, that cedar does smell heavenly."

The gardener straightened, the shears grasped in one gnarled hand. "You were looking for me?"

"I was." She stepped closer, making sure that Samuel was not too far behind her. "I'm Mrs. Baxter, and I wanted to talk to you about Mr. Hargrove's death."

Silas Gower's eyes narrowed even more. He lifted a knee and planted his foot firmly on the pure white stones of a small rockery. "Which Mr. Hargrove would that be?"

"Mr. Gavin Hargrove." She waited, and when there was no response, added, "His body was found in my trap in the yard of the Pennyfoot Country Club."

"Ah," Silas Gower said, as if her words explained everything.

Cecily tried again. "I was wondering if you had any idea who might have killed him?"

Apart from a blinking of the eyes, the gardener appeared to have no reaction to her blunt question.

Cecily took a deep breath. "I understand your wife knew the deceased quite well."

The sudden rage on the man's face took her by surprise, and she stepped back as he raised the shears in the air.

Behind her she heard Samuel swear, but she kept her gaze steadily on Silas Gower's face.

"You don't talk about my wife like that," the gardener roared. "I'm not talking to you about nothing. Get out of my garden. Go!"

He shook the shears at her, and Samuel stepped up by her side. She gave him a swift shake of her head, then addressed the irate man in front of her. "I'm sorry if I upset you, Mr. Gower. I wasn't accusing your wife, if that's what you thought."

"I don't know who killed 'im." Silas took a step toward her, causing Samuel to step between them. "What's more, I don't care. Gavin Hargrove were an evil man, not fit to lick his father's boots. Someone did us all a favor, and that's all I'm saying. Now get out. Both of you!" Once more he waved the shears at them.

"We're going," Samuel said firmly. He turned and looked beseechingly at Cecily. "Aren't we, m'm?"

"Very well." Cecily nodded at Silas. "Good day, to you, Mr. Gower. Thank you for your time." Lifting her skirts, she hurried back across the lawn to the carriage.

"Well, that was nearly a blooming disaster," Samuel said, panting as he scrambled to keep up with her.

"Well, it tells us one thing." Cecily waited for him to open the door of the carriage. "It appears Naomi might have been telling the truth about Mr. Hargrove's attachment to the gardener's wife. It's clearly a sensitive subject for Mr. Gower."

"I can see that gardener bloke strangling someone. Much more likely than Miss Kendall." Samuel handed her up to her seat. "He's got a nasty temper, all right."

"Yes, he does." Cecily sighed as she settled herself down. The bad thing is that we're no closer to finding out what happened to Mr. Baxter."

"I've been thinking about that, m'm." Samuel leaned into the carriage. "Now that I remember where I last saw him, why don't I go back there on the way back to the Pennyfoot. P'raps if I'm standing in the exact same spot as where it all happened, I might remember something else that could help. Like the driver of that trap, for instance."

"Can you find the exact spot again?"

"Yes, I think so, m'm. It were right where the trail takes a sharp turn. That's why I couldn't see the trap until it was on top of me."

Cecily thought about it for a moment. "Very well, Samuel,

but only for a moment. I'm anxious to get back to the Pennyfoot to find out if there's any news of Mr. Baxter. P.C. Northcott must have conducted his search by now. In any case, I'd like to return before it gets dark."

"Don't worry, m'm. I'll get us back there in record time." He shut the door, and a moment later climbed up into the driver's seat. With a flick of the reins they were off, clattering down the driveway to the road.

Cecily tried to curb her impatience as they turned off the main thoroughfare at the top of the hill and headed for the woods. She didn't hold out much hope of Samuel remembering anything else that could be useful, but she was willing to try anything if it would bring her beloved back home.

The ache in her heart was an ever-present reminder that she had lost what was most precious to her, and there was no way of knowing if she would ever have him back.

The rustling trees cast shadows all around as the carriage came to a halt on the riding trail. Samuel jumped down and tethered the horses before opening the door. "Did you want to step out with me, m'm?"

Cecily shivered as a cold draft invaded the interior. The thought of gazing upon the site where her husband had lain distressed her beyond belief. "I think it better if you do this alone," she told him, and leaned back in her seat as he nodded, and closed the door.

The seconds ticked by, lengthening into minutes, until her impatience grew intolerable. Leaning forward again she opened the door and peered out.

Dusk had begun to cloak the trees, silencing the forest. Where was Samuel? Why hadn't he returned?

Fearing the worst, Cecily climbed down onto the chilled ground. Snow still lay around in patches, though moisture from the branches above her head splashed on the logs that lay at her feet.

Cupping her hands to her mouth, she called out, "Samuel? Where are you? We must go home now! Samuel?"

Only a faint rustling in the undergrowth answered her call. Somewhere in the distance she heard the mournful hooting of an owl. It was the loneliest sound she had ever heard.

The cold, damp smell of the forest seemed overwhelming. Unsettled now, she once more cupped her hands to her mouth. Just as she gathered breath to shout, another sound broke the silence. The sound of wheels rattling along the trail. Someone was coming, and at a fast clip.

Samuel had pulled the carriage alongside the trail, and the horses shifted uneasily as the thunder of hooves drew closer. Thoroughly unnerved, Cecily stepped behind a tree and peered anxiously in the direction of the noise.

Suddenly she heard a shout above the clattering wheels, and then another. Seconds later a horse and trap hurtled into view. To her horror she saw they were headed straight for the carriage. There seemed no way they could avoid crashing into it.

For a terrifying instant she thought the driver had no head, until she realized he wore a scarf over his face. He whipped his horse as they approached, and certain the carriage would be smashed to pieces and the horses horribly maimed, Cecily closed her eyes and prayed.

CHAPTER

❀ 9 ❀

With her eyes shut tightly, Cecily clung to the tree as the contraption roared past in a flurry of thudding hooves and jingling harness. She heard her own horses whinnying, their hooves thrashing the ground as they fought the bindings tethering them to the tree.

Then the intruder was gone, trap and horse disappearing down the trail and into the dusky depths beyond. As the rattling faded away, Cecily stumbled out from her refuge.

Dear God, what has happened to Samuel?

It took her several seconds to soothe the horses enough so that she felt she could leave them. Then she started down the trail, dreading what she would find. It was darker now, the night overtaking the shadows in the silent trees. Something scurried away into the blackness, and she shivered. "Samuel?" she called out, her voice barely carrying beyond the closest tree.

Then, as if in answer to her plea, she heard the thudding of running feet. Heart racing, she peered down the trail. She could see nothing beyond a few yards now, with only the blackness surrounding her. Her voice trembled with fear when she called out again. "Samuel? Is that you?"

He came running, bursting out of the darkness and charging toward her. For a moment terror gripped her when she couldn't recognize him in the murky shadows. Then she heard his voice.

"Are you all right, m'm?"

"Samuel!" She put out a hand to steady herself against a sturdy trunk. "What a scare you gave me. Did you see the trap?"

"See it?" Samuel halted in front of her, his chest heaving with the effort to catch his breath. "It almost bloody well run me over." He pressed his fingers against his mouth. "Sorry, m'm, didn't mean to swear."

"That's quite all right, Samuel. Under the circumstances it's quite understandable." She started walking with him back to the carriage. "You're not hurt, are you?"

"No, m'm." He coughed, then added a little breathlessly, "I jumped out of the way just in time. I didn't even hear it until it was almost on me. He must have been waiting for me to come out on the trail."

Cecily came to a standstill. "Gracious. Are you saying he deliberately tried to run you down?"

"Yes, m'm, I am." Samuel's expression was hard to read

in the darkness, but his voice betrayed his anger. "Just like yesterday."

Cecily caught her breath. "You remember? It's the same man? I saw him when he passed by me. His face was covered by a scarf. How terribly disappointing. Neither one of us could possibly recognize him."

"Yes, m'm. I mean, no, m'm. I'm sorry."

"Well, I suppose we shall have to think of something else. Though I tell you, Samuel, I'm becoming quite discouraged." She resumed walking back to where they'd left the carriage.

Samuel was quiet as they approached the horses that now stood calmly waiting for them. He opened the carriage door and thankfully, Cecily climbed in.

He sounded odd when he spoke. "I think someone out there wants to finish me off."

Afraid for his safety, she peered at him through the gloom. "I think you're right. Gavin Hargrove's killer must know you are regaining your memory and is afraid you'll remember something that will lead to his arrest. You are in danger, Samuel. I think it's obvious that someone at Whitfield Manor is responsible. We must inform the constable at once."

"Fat lot of good that'll do," Samuel mumbled.

"You will have to be extremely careful and keep your wits about you until this case is solved."

"Yes, m'm. I think I will. Oh, I nearly forgot. With all the excitement, and all." He pulled something out from inside his jacket and held it up. "Look what I found. If those bobbies searched the woods this afternoon, they missed this."

She stared at the muddy object in confusion. "What on earth is that?"

"Half a mo, m'm." He searched in his pocket. A moment later she heard the scrape of a match and then a flash of light flared, revealing his face. Sheltering the flickering flame in his cupped hand, he moved to the rear of the carriage. Before long, the glow of lanterns made the shadows dance among the trees.

In the light they cast, Samuel held up the object he'd found. Cecily reached for it, her breath catching when she saw what it was. "Baxter's shoe. Where did you find it?"

"I remembered where I'd come out on the trail yesterday. After I woke up, I mean. I recognized the fallen tree I'd climbed over." He pointed back down into the trees. "I went back in there for a closer look and my foot kicked something. I recognized it right away."

"It must have been covered up by the snow last night." Cecily turned it over in her hand. "I'm not surprised the searchers missed it. It would be like looking for a needle in a haystack. If you hadn't remembered exactly where you'd been standing when you were attacked, I doubt very much if you would have found this, either."

"Well, I don't know how much help it will be." He shook his head. "I still can't remember anything after the trap hit me, until I woke up again somewhere else."

She leaned forward to look more closely into his face. "Can you remember anything about that trap? Or the horse? Any markings, the color? Anything at all about the driver?"

Samuel appeared to be thinking hard, but then he shook his head. "Sorry, m'm, it were all a blur. Just like just now.

I was so busy trying to get out of his way I didn't have time to take much notice. And it were dark tonight, not like yesterday. It's funny, though . . ."

His voice trailed off and impatiently Cecily prompted him. "What is it?"

"I'm almost remembering something, but then it keeps slipping away. Something important, I think." He rubbed a hand across his bandaged forehead. "It just hurts when I try to grab hold of it in my mind."

Disappointed, Cecily leaned back on her seat. "All right, Samuel. Perhaps if you stop trying to remember, it will pop back in your mind. In any case, we must get home now. I'm anxious to see if P.C. Northcott has word for us."

As the carriage jolted and swayed down the hill to the Esplanade, she recalled the events of the day in the hopes of gleaning something from them that might help find her husband. All the possibilities ran through her head.

Had Gavin Hargrove been killed by the men to whom he owed money? Or had Randall Thorpe eliminated his cousin so that he might inherit the family fortune? Could Naomi have killed her fiancé so that her new love would have the means to provide her with the luxuries she craved? Or had Silas Gower killed his employer in a fit of jealous rage?

Anything and everything was possible, and she was no nearer to finding her husband than she had been that dreadful moment when she'd first heard he was missing.

And now she must go back to the Pennyfoot and appear as if she were enjoying the singing of Christmas carols. How could she possibly celebrate such a joyous occasion, when she was dying inside?

The moment the carriage halted in the courtyard she had the door open. Without waiting for Samuel, she hopped down the step and took the shortcut to the kitchen door.

Flinging it open, she stepped inside the warm room. The enticing aroma of spicy, fruity plum puddings greeted her. Michel had begun his Christmas dinner preparations.

Hot on the heels of that thought came the realization that everyone in the kitchen stood staring at her.

Mrs. Chubb's cheeks glowed beneath a smear of flour as her mouth dropped open. Michel stood frozen at the stove, one hand holding a wooden spoon suspended in midair, while Gertie leaned against the sink, next to a dark-haired man Cecily didn't recognize at all.

"Pay no attention to me," she called out as she sailed past them all to the door. "I'm in rather a hurry." With that she pushed open the door and fled into the hallway.

Several seconds passed before everyone in the kitchen recovered. Mrs. Chubb went back to rolling out her pastry, while Michel turned back to the stove to stir his gravy.

Gertie shoved herself away from the sink. "Blimey, what got into her? She never comes in through the kitchen."

"Who was that?" Dan Perkins helped himself to a sausage roll and got a slap on the hand from Gertie.

"That was madam. Mrs. Baxter to you, and leave them sausage rolls bloody well alone. They're for the guests at the carol singing tonight."

"Gertie's right," Mrs. Chubb said, after a worried glance at the door that had just closed. It was none of her business, of course, but madam could not be thinking straight to come through the kitchen like that. After all, she was always the first one to remind everybody how important it was to observe protocol at all times.

Recovering from her shock, she glared at Dan. "Anyhow, young man, you're not supposed to visit the staff in the kitchen. It's better you leave, so Gertie can get on with her work."

She transferred the glare to Gertie, who raised her chin. "Here, it's not my bleeding fault. I didn't ask him to come here."

"All right, all right, I'm going." Dan shoved the rest of the roll in his mouth. "These are very good, Mrs. Chubb. Very good, indeed."

The compliment brought an even deeper flush to Mrs. Chubb's cheeks. Softening a little, she muttered, "Go on with you. All that sweet talk is not going to get you anywhere. This is our busy time and you're in the way, so off you go."

"Fair enough." Dan sauntered over to the back door. "I just came to tell Gertie what I found in the woods this afternoon, but if you're not interested—"

His last words were drowned out by a squeal from Gertie, the crashing of Michel's saucepan on the stove and Mrs. Chubb's howl of protest. All of them spoke at once.

"Why didn't you bloody say so! What was it you found? Does it have anything to do with Mr. Baxter?"

Dan turned back with a grin. "Thought you'd want to know. I don't know if it has anything to do with the missing chap, but I can tell you one thing. There's been gypsies in the woods, and they only just left."

Mrs. Chubb gasped, while Gertie frowned at him.

"Gypsies? How'd you know?"

"Sacre bleu," Michel muttered, and crossed himself.

"I found wheel tracks leading out of the woods, and a place where they'd built a fire. The ashes were still warm." Dan shook his head. "Amazes me how they get their caravans through the trees like that."

"We should tell madam," Mrs. Chubb said, hurriedly wiping her hands on her apron. "They might have seen something that could help find Mr. Baxter."

"Do you want me to go?" Gertie was already halfway across the kitchen when Mrs. Chubb stopped her.

"No, you have to load the trays for the carol singing. Tell Pansy to help you." She left the kitchen and hurried down the hallway to the stairs.

As she crossed the lobby, the Christmas tree in the corner seemed to mock her with its lacy angels and glittery bells. So much anguish going on right now, and here they were, all done up for Christmas.

In a few minutes the carol singing would begin in the library, and the country club would ring with the sacred choruses. It didn't seem right, somehow, celebrating like that with Mr. Baxter missing and God knows what happened to him.

Puffing and panting as she climbed the main stairs, she finally reached the landing. Hoping she'd find madam in her boudoir, dressing for the gathering in the library, she sped down the hallway as fast as her feet would carry her.

* * *

107

Cecily sat at her desk, impatiently waiting for the telephone operator to put her through to the constabulary. The second hand on the wall clock seemed to race around the numerals at breakneck speed, the loud ticking reminding her of time wasting away.

She should be dressing for the festivities right now, instead of tapping her fingers in her office, waiting for Sam Northcott to find the time to answer his telephone.

At long last she heard a gruff male voice, and knew at once it wasn't P.C. Northcott.

"He's in London," the voice informed her, when she inquired as to his whereabouts. "He's taken the murder case to Scotland Yard."

She did her best to keep her voice civil when she demanded, "When did he leave?"

"On the afternoon train, m'm. He won't be back until tomorrow night."

Her anger made her throat hurt. "Did he, by any chance, organize a search of the woods for my husband before he left for the city?"

"I believe he sent a couple of blokes out there, but they didn't find nothing."

"I see." She took a calming breath. "Well, I wish to report another attack on my stable manager this afternoon." She gave him as many details as she could. After extracting a promise that he would inform P.C. Northcott the moment he returned, she hung the telephone back on its hook.

Not that she expected him to do anything about it. Once he'd handed the case over to Scotland Yard, he would not pursue it any further.

Given the flimsy evidence upon which the constable had based his deductions, it was doubtful Scotland Yard would be in any hurry to pursue it, either. Meanwhile, Baxter's life could hang in the balance.

She couldn't just sit there and wait for someone to do something. Someone, somewhere, knew where he was. It was up to her now to find out who that someone was and get the truth out of him.

She looked up as a tap on the door interrupted her thoughts. "Come in?"

Try as she might, that little flare of hope sprung to life, only to be dashed again when Mrs. Chubb put her head around the door.

"Oh, there you are, m'm." She edged into the room and closed the door behind her. "I thought you should know. Dan Perkins went looking in the woods this afternoon, to see if he could see something that might help find Mr. Baxter."

Cecily frowned. "Dan who?"

"Oh, sorry, m'm. The young gentleman who was in the kitchen when you came in just now. He's working at Abbitson's, the butcher's."

"Oh." Cecily pushed her chair back and stood. "Well, that was very nice of him."

"Yes, m'm. He said as how he saw a gypsy camp in there. Well, the gyspies had gone, but he said he could tell they'd been there until this morning. We was wondering if they might have seen what happened to Mr. Baxter."

Cecily sighed. "It's a possibility, I suppose. Thank you, Mrs. Chubb. Please tell Mr. Perkins I appreciate his help."

"Yes, m'm." The housekeeper narrowed her eyes. "Are

you all right, m'm? I mean, I know all this business is upsetting you, but is there anything I can do to help?"

Cecily forced a smile. "Thank you, Mrs. Chubb, but I'm quite all right. Is everything going well downstairs?"

"Yes, m'm. We're ready for the carol singing in the library. Gertie's taking the hot chestnuts and cider up there now."

"Very well. I will be there just as soon as I am properly dressed."

"Yes, m'm." With a worried frown still on her face, Mrs. Chubb left the room.

The next hour raced by as Cecily hurriedly dressed in a lilac tea gown, then ran down the stairs to the library. There she stationed herself at the door, ready to greet the guests as they arrived.

Her smile felt permanently fixed on her face, like the false mouth painted on a clown. She had a strange feeling of standing outside her body, watching herself going through the motions of the congenial hostess, while her true self writhed in unspeakable frustration.

The news Mrs. Chubb had given her had raised a small hope after all. Other people had been in the woods. Other people who might have seen something that could lead her to Baxter.

The fact that these other people were gypsies was not entirely comforting, though she knew from experience that by and large the Romanies were not the ruffians most people thought them to be. If she could ask for their help, they might consider searching the woods for Baxter.

But for now, she was forced to stand there, smiling and

nodding, while people she hardly knew crowded into the library expecting to be entertained.

"Cecily!"

Startled, Cecily blinked at the woman standing in front of her. Madeline wore a cream muslin gown, caught becomingly at the waist by a band of silk flowers. A crown of mistletoe nestled in her hair, which no doubt would arouse the wrath of Phoebe, who regarded her as somewhat lacking in morals and never missed an opportunity to subtly chastise her.

"I've spoken your name three times," Madeline complained, her beautiful eyes clouded with concern. "I assume there's no word of Baxter?"

Cecily's smile wavered. "None at all."

"My dear, I'm so sorry." Madeline laid a delicate hand on Cecily's arm. "Try to look upon it as good news. If he were . . . if something really nasty had happened to him, we'd surely know it by now."

"Would we?" Cecily's faint hold on her optimism collapsed. "What if he's buried somewhere? Or tossed into the ocean? Taken to a place far away where we'll never find him?"

"Hush." Madeline looked around, and smiled at a group of guests who glanced their way. "You have been so brave so far, Cecily. You must hold on to your belief. Baxter is in good hands. I'm sure of it. I would know if he were not."

"Then where is he?" Cecily lowered her voice to a harsh whisper. "What has happened to him? What will I do without him if he doesn't return?"

"He will return. I swear it."

Cecily shook her head. "I'm no longer certain of that, Madeline. As the time goes by, I feel him slipping farther and farther away from me. If he isn't found soon, I shall give up all hope. I shall no longer be able to manage the Pennyfoot, or my life. And that's all there is to it."

CHAPTER

❀ 10 ❀

Hating herself for her weakness just when she needed to be so strong, Cecily struggled to regain her composure. She even managed a smile when a gentleman paused in front of her with an elegant woman at his aide. "Mrs. Baxter! I have yet to see your husband, this year. I do hope he is well?"

Cecily hesitated a little too long. A discreet nudge from Madeline helped loosen her tongue. "Quite well, as far as I know, Sir Randolph."

"Ah, good, good." The elderly gentleman twirled one end of his mustache in his fingers. "I trust he will be joining us before too long?"

"I certainly hope so." Apparently word of his disappearance had not reached the guests as yet, she thought thankfully. A testament to the closed lips of her admirable staff.

"Yes, well, we really must commend you on the decorations." Sir Randolph eyed the Christmas tree in the corner. "You have surpassed yourself this year."

"Thank you." Cecily drew Madeline closer. "May I present Madeline Pengrath. She is responsible for our wonderful displays. She has worked hard to make the Pennyfoot as festive as possible."

Sir Randolph's gaze flicked over Madeline. "Indeed."

Well used to people's reaction to her primitive appearance, the gentleman's disdain appeared not to faze Madeline one bit. Instead, she ignored him and turned to his wife. "Your ladyship, that gown is utterly adorable. Paris, I assume?"

The woman tapped her chin with her fan and treated Madeline to a smile. "Why, Miss Pengrath, how very astute of you. It is, indeed."

"Ah, I thought so." Madeline glanced up at the woman's glowering husband. "So nice to know someone in your family has good taste."

Cecily winced, but thankfully just then Phoebe arrived with her usual fanfare of waving arms and a shrieking welcome.

"Baxter?" she asked, when Sir Randolph and his wife were out of earshot.

Cecily shook her head. "Nothing, I'm afraid."

"Oh, bosh. I'm sorry, Cecily. I was hoping he'd be found by now."

"We did find his shoe this afternoon," Cecily said, keeping her voice low as more people filed past her. "Samuel found it in the woods."

"Do you have it?" Madeline grasped Cecily's arm. "I might be able to locate him with it."

Phoebe shook her head. "Really, Madeline, must you always pretend you can solve the ills of the world with all that mumbo jumbo? Cecily is in quite enough pain, without you raising false hopes."

Cecily saw a familiar gleam in Madeline's eyes, and hurried to intervene before one of their constant spats erupted. "I'd be willing to try anything at this point. In fact, I plan to talk to the gypsies about it."

"Gypsies?" Madeline's face lit up, while Phoebe looked aghast.

"Good Lord, Cecily," she said, fanning her face with her gloved hand, "don't tell me you actually believe all that crystal ball nonsense? I thought you were far too practical to be misled by such chicanery."

Even Madeline looked doubtful. "I have the utmost respect for gypsy power," she said, earning a derisive sniff from Phoebe, "but I must warn you they do not take kindly to outsiders invading their camps."

"Which is why I would like you to accompany me." Cecily raised her voice as the string quartet began to tune their instruments. "I have word that gypsies were possibly in the woods during the time Baxter and Samuel were attacked. I would like to have a word with them tomorrow, and ask for their help in finding my husband."

"No, no, no," Phoebe said, violently shaking her head. "That is far too dangerous."

Madeline looked at Cecily in surprise. "Baxter and Samuel were attacked?"

"Samuel remembers being deliberately run down by a trap. We think whoever it was might have taken Baxter with him."

Madeline shook her head in confusion. "But why would he take Baxter and leave Samuel behind?"

"I wish I knew." Cecily lowered her voice again as the discordant tuning ended. "Samuel was again attacked by the same man in a trap this afternoon."

Phoebe gasped in shock. "The dear boy! He's not hurt again, I trust?"

"He managed to jump out of the way." Cecily looked appealingly at Madeline. "Something very dangerous is afoot. We have to find Baxter as soon as possible."

"What about the constables?" Phoebe demanded. "What are they doing about it?"

"P.C. Northcott is handing the case over to Scotland Yard. He's convinced a London gambling syndicate is responsible. Apparently Gavin Hargrove owed them money."

Madeline studied her face. "And what do you think?"

"I don't know what to think." Cecily blinked hard. "All I know is that someone killed Hargrove and somehow Baxter got involved. We must find him." She appealed once more to Madeline. "The gypsies know those woods better than anyone. I need their help."

"Tomorrow morning, then. But they might not be easy to find."

"If anyone can find them, it would be you." Cecily gave Madeline a grateful smile, then turned to look at the quartet, who appeared ready to begin the first carol.

Usually she loved this part of the Christmas traditions at

the Pennyfoot. Madeline had hung all sorts of ornaments on the thick branches of the Christmas tree, from gilded walnuts and iced biscuits to beautiful glass baubles imported all the way from Germany.

She had also placed tiny white candles on the end of each branch, although Cecily no longer allowed them to be lit, ever since the year a Christmas fire almost destroyed the library and had come close to taking her life.

In spite of the festive scene and the inspiring sound of voices joined in a chorus of "The Holly and the Ivy," she could not find the will to sing. She made a pretense instead, moving her lips though no sound emerged.

Neither Madeline nor Phoebe were fooled, of course, but it was comforting to have her good friends stand by her side. She needed their support more now than ever before.

Cecily dozed fitfully throughout the night, and awoke the next morning in a fever of impatience. She had arranged for Samuel to fetch Madeline and bring her back to the country club, while she performed the necessary duties that could not be ignored.

After discussing the menu for the following day's meals with Mrs. Chubb, she returned to her office to finish the paperwork she had neglected the day before.

By the time Samuel returned with his passenger, Cecily could hardly contain herself. The minute she saw them enter the lobby she rushed to meet them.

She could tell right away that something had happened. Samuel's face was flushed, his eyes wide with excitement, while Madeline, who rarely showed emotion, looked as if she were ready to burst.

"I remembered something else, madam!" Samuel called out, before Cecily could reach them.

Mindful of the people milling about the lobby, Cecily hushed him with a finger to her lips. "Wait until we're outside," she said, as she led the way to the front doors.

Once outside, the clean salty air seemed to clear her head. Eagerly she turned to Samuel. "What have you remembered?"

Madeline gave him an impatient nudge of her arm. "Go on, Samuel, tell her."

"Well," Samuel began, "remember yesterday, m'm, when I said something kept slipping away before I could hold on to it? I was driving along the Esplanade just now when it popped into my mind. Just like that."

"Oh, do get on with it," Madeline cried. She looked at Cecily. "He won't tell me what it is until he's told you."

"I knew I'd seen it somewhere before," Samuel said, ignoring Madeline, "when I first saw it, but then I forgot when I saw it again, but now I remember where I saw it—"

Cecily put a halt to the rush of words with a raised hand. "You're not making one bit of sense, Samuel. Slow down and tell us what you are talking about."

Samuel took a deep breath. "The scarf. The one the bloke in the trap had wrapped around his face. It's the same one Miss Kendall was wearing when she came into the manor yesterday afternoon."

Cecily stared at him. "Are you quite sure?"

"As sure as a chicken lays eggs, m'm. It had a coat of

arms on one end, and when I saw that trap I remembered seeing the end of that scarf flapping in the wind."

Madeline looked from one to the other. "What are you talking about? Who is Miss Kendall?"

"Gavin Hargrove's fiancée," Cecily said shortly. "And she has some explaining to do. Come, Samuel, we'll go there right away."

"But what about the gypsies?" Madeline cried. "I thought you wanted to ask them to help."

"We may not need their help." Cecily was already striding toward the carriage that waited in the courtyard. "If Naomi Kendall is responsible for attempting to silence Samuel, then she could very well be the cause of Baxter's disappearance. He might even be right there at the manor."

"Blimey," Samuel muttered. "Don't tell me he was right under our noses all the time."

"I just hope I'm right." She clambered up into the carriage, then looked back at Madeline hovering a few feet away. "Aren't you coming with us?"

Madeline drew her shawl closer around her shoulders. "I'm not accustomed to visiting the aristocracy."

"We're not exactly visiting," Cecily reminded her. "We're looking for Baxter, are we not?"

Madeline came forward and climbed up next to Cecily. "I'll wait in the carriage while you pay this woman a visit."

"You will not." Cecily settled herself comfortably on the seat. "I would feel a great deal more comfortable with you by my side."

"Yeah," Samuel said, just before he shut the door, "there's safety in numbers."

"He sounds as if he's expecting trouble," Madeline said, looking worried.

"Which is one of the reasons I'm happy to have you along." Cecily glanced at her friend out of the corner of her eye. "You have rescued me from dire peril more than once."

"More by luck than judgment." Madeline's serene smile smoothed the worry lines from her face. "My powers can be, shall we say, unpredictable. As you well know. I'd hate to change the honorable Miss Kendall into a toad by mistake."

"I'm not so sure she is honorable. That's what I hope to find out this morning." Cecily glanced out of the window and surveyed the calm ocean and cloudless sky. If Baxter was, as she feared, still facing the elements, at least the weather had turned in his favor. It was small consolation, but all she had right now.

Madeline said little on the journey to the manor, but sat huddled in the corner, lost in her own thoughts. Or so Cecily assumed.

It wasn't until the carriage had turned into the driveway of Whitfield Manor that she spoke. "I don't think he's at the manor," she said. "He's moving from place to place."

Cecily turned to her. "Baxter?"

Madeline nodded.

"He's on foot?"

"I can't tell. I can feel his strength slowly returning, though."

Cecily's surge of relief was quickly tempered. Much as she wanted to believe her friend, she had to remind herself of Madeline's limitations.

She was well known for her potions and salves—made from herbs and plants—which according to her customers were highly effective. There were, however, many who believed Madeline to be a witch.

While Cecily knew quite well that Madeline possessed strange powers that could not be explained, she also knew her friend was more a dabbler than an expert in such matters. When it came to magic, for want of a better word, the less one knew, the more danger one invited. Madeline had sometimes had her share of disasters. Cecily could only hope this was one time she would manage to avoid them.

The carriage halted in front of the manor steps, and once more Cecily climbed them, with Madeline at her side and Samuel close behind.

Wilmot's haughty gaze, as usual, swept the sky above their heads when he opened the door to her summons.

Without giving him a chance to speak, she announced, "I wish to speak with Miss Naomi Kendall."

The butler lifted his nose a fraction. "I shall ask milady if she cares to respond." With a frosty glare he drew back to allow them to enter.

"Goodness," Madeline murmured, as the butler disappeared down the passageway, "a smile would surely crack his face wide open." She flung her long hair back from her shoulders with an impatient hand. "He needs one of my potions. He's much too rigid. Very bad for the liver."

"You sound like Kevin," Cecily murmured. "Could it be that your ideas of herbal remedies are meshing with his scientific theories?"

Madeline snorted. "Hardly. He still maintains that I am

poisoning my customers with weeds. I'm afraid we shall never see eye to eye on that subject."

"More's the pity." Cecily turned as Wilmot's voice spoke from the passageway. "Miss Kendall and Mr. Thorpe will receive you in the drawing room."

Madeline looked wary. "Are you sure you want me to go with you? You might learn more if I were not there to distract them. You know how people like that regard me."

"All the more reason you should be there." Cecily lowered her voice so that Wilmot should not hear. "I had hoped to speak to Miss Kendall alone. She will not be as forthcoming if Mr. Thorpe is present. Perhaps you can tell better than I if she attempts to lie."

Madeline had no chance to answer, as Wilmot had already tapped on the door and opened it. "Mrs. Baxter and servants," he proclaimed.

Seeing the sparks in Madeline's eyes, Cecily coldly stalked past him.

The smell of burning tobacco overpowered the pungent fragrance of pine. Randall Thorpe was in the act of rising from his chair, a cloud of smoke from his pipe hovering above his head.

Cecily addressed him directly. "Good day, Mr. Thorpe. As you can see, my good friend and my stable manager have accompanied me. Neither of them is my servant."

"That will be all, Wilmot." Randall laid his pipe in an ashtray and sauntered toward them, his face arranged in the usual smile.

He wore a maroon velvet smoking jacket and a gold cravat, which gave him a debonair appearance that didn't quite match the expression in his watchful gaze. "Good morning, Mrs. Baxter." He glanced behind her and widened his eyes.

"May I present Miss Madeline Pengrath," Cecily said quickly. "Mr. Randall Thorpe."

Randall looked down at Madeline's feet, where her bare toes peeked out from her sandals below the hem of her cotton frock. She wore a garland of laurel leaves around one ankle, clearly visible when she walked.

He seemed fascinated by this scandalous lack of decorum, his gaze fixed on her feet as she drifted to the center of the room. "Charmed, I'm sure," he murmured.

A sharp movement from the fireplace brought Naomi to Cecily's attention. "This is becoming something of a habit," Naomi said, her scowl directed at Madeline, who stood smiling up at Randall's handsome features.

Cecily stepped forward. "Good morning, Miss Kendall. I trust you are well."

Naomi's gaze slid past Cecily to where Samuel stood near the door. "As well as can be expected. All this upheaval with funerals is extremely taxing."

"Gavin's funeral will be held tomorrow," Randall said, addressing Cecily. "At St. Bartholomew's Church. Will you be attending?" His gaze wandered to Madeline's face. "We should be most honored to see you there."

"I regret that will not be possible," Cecily said firmly.

"Of course," Naomi said, hurrying forward. "Really, Randall, we can't expect everyone in the village to mourn Gavin's passing."

"Funerals can be so moving," Madeline said, her mellow voice just above a whisper.

Randall seemed hypnotized by her eyes. "Indeed they are," he murmured.

Naomi made a sound of disgust. "Thoroughly depressing, if you ask me. All that sobbing and weeping. Quite, quite devastating."

Neither Randall nor Madeline appeared to have heard a word she said.

Watching her friend's face, Cecily wondered uneasily what she had in mind. A moment later she was enlightened.

"You have such a magnificent home here, Mr. Thorpe," Madeline purred. "I am a decorator of sorts, and beautiful homes like this fascinate me. I'm sure this one would give me some wonderful ideas for my little hobby. Would it be too much trouble to ask that you conduct a short personal tour?"

Randall fell over himself to oblige. "Why, not at all, my dear. Not at all." He took hold of her arm. "May I escort you?"

"Please do." Madeline sent one swift, meaningful look at Cecily, then bestowed her gorgeous smile on the somewhat dazed Randall Thorpe. "Shall we?"

Naomi uttered a sound of protest. "Randall! We have other guests!"

"I'm sure you can manage to entertain them," Randall murmured, his gaze permanently fixed on Madeline's face. Without taking his eyes off her, he opened the door and ushered her through.

Cecily silently thanked her friend. She had deliberately removed Randall Thorpe from the room, leaving her and Samuel to question Naomi alone. Now, perhaps at long last, she could get some answers.

CHAPTER
❀ 11 ❀

"Well, there you are, sunshine!" Dan Perkins stepped into the kitchen, his brown eyes alight with mischief as he smiled at Gertie. "I was hoping you'd be here this morning." He carried his loaded basket over to the table and dropped it. Looking back at her, he tapped his cheek with his finger. "How about a kiss then?"

"Cheeky bugger." Gertie flounced past him and grabbed a large orange china jar off the table. "Nearly knocked me marmalade on the ground, you did. You should watch what you're bloody doing."

"I'd rather watch you." He glanced around the empty kitchen. "Where is everyone, then?"

"The maids are cleaning the bedrooms, Mrs. Chubb is in

the laundry room and Michel is taking a stroll outside. Anything else you want to know?"

"Yeah." He slid one hip on the corner of the table and leaned in close to her. "Come out with me."

Gertie felt her stomach flip right over. "What? Go out with you? What for?" She twisted the lid off the marmalade then pulled open the drawer under the table. Taking out a spoon, she dipped it into the marmalade and scooped up a generous amount.

"I could show you a good time."

She slid a glance at him under her lashes. "I bet you could. Well, I'm not that sort of girl, so you're out of bloody luck."

Dan pretended to be offended. "Here, what kind of chap do you think I am?"

Gertie dropped the spoonful of marmalade into one of the small silver dishes lined up in front of her. Unfortunately, thanks to Dan's comments, her hand was none too steady.

The sticky jam oozed over the side of the dish and onto the table. "Now look what you made me do." She scooped the mess up with her finger and stuck it in her mouth. After licking it clean, she wiped her finger on her apron.

For some reason, Dan seemed to find all this fascinating. With his gaze riveted on her mouth, he murmured, "I'd really like to take you out. We could go play darts at the pub."

She nearly dropped the spoon. "What! Ladies don't go in the public bar!"

"Of course not." Dan slid off the table. "They've got a dartboard in the lounge bar now. I've seen ladies playing darts in there."

"Yeah?" Gertie dug the spoon in the marmalade. She didn't want to admit she was tempted. "I played darts down there once. A long time ago." She shut her mouth, wondering what on earth had prompted her to tell him that.

"Go on." Dan leaned his back against the sink. "I thought ladies didn't go in the public bar."

"Well, they don't. This was different."

"How was it different?"

"Never mind."

"Go on, I dare you to tell me."

She gave him another sly glance. "What's it worth?"

"I'll take you out in my new motorcar."

That got her attention. "You got a motorcar?"

"Yeah. So tell me about the darts."

For a ride in a motorcar, she'd tell him her life history. "Well, it was when me and my friend, Ethel, went on a women's lib protest. We marched into the public bar and started throwing darts at the board."

Dan laughed—a really deep chuckle that seemed to rumble in his chest. It made Gertie feel warm all over. "What happened?"

"All the men started yelling at us. We got flipping scared, didn't we, and ran right out of there. I don't think we were cut out to be suffragettes."

"I should hope not." He shook his head. "Real violent lot they are."

"Yeah? Well, they got a lot to be angry about." Deciding she didn't want to get into that particular argument, she shut her mouth.

"So when are you coming out with me, then?" Dan

looked at the clock above the stove. "I've got to get going. You coming out with me or not?"

She wavered. A motorcar. She'd never ridden in one. "I'm off Christmas Eve, after I get everything ready for the ball," she said quickly, before she could lose her nerve.

Dan's face changed. "Can't do it Christmas Eve, luv. Sorry."

Her disappointment surprised her. "What, got someone else you're taking out?"

"No, it's not that." He glanced once more at the clock then headed for the back door. "I'd really, really like to take you out, Gertie, but not then, all right? Some other time."

She shrugged, trying to ignore the little ache under her ribs. "It's all right."

"No, it's not." He sounded upset and she stared at him, trying to understand. "I can't talk about it, Gertie, but I wish I could take you out on Christmas Eve. Let's make it another time, all right? I really mean that."

"All right." She wasn't sure if he meant it or not. One thing she did know. He was up to something on Christmas Eve. Something he didn't want to talk about, and she'd give anything to know exactly what it was, and why it got him so upset.

Naomi stared in disgust as the door closed behind Madeline and Randall Thorpe. She seemed about to erupt in a fiery fit of rage. Digging her fists into her hips she spit out words as if they tasted sour. "How dare that brazen hussy waltz in here like that and manipulate my . . ."

She snapped her mouth shut as Samuel stepped forward. "I think, Miss Kendall, you should watch what you're saying. Miss Pengrath is a very good friend of Mrs. Baxter, and she's a fine lady. Calling her names like that can make me really, really cross."

Naomi tossed her head. "And just who are you to tell me what to do?"

Cecily saw Samuel's mouth tighten and quickly stepped in. "Miss Kendall, Samuel has every right to be angry. Twice he has been attacked by someone in a trap attempting to run him down with the obvious intention of doing him great harm."

Naomi's frown seemed genuine enough. "What does that have to do with me?"

"The driver wore a scarf. A blue scarf embroidered with a coat of arms on one end."

"Yeah," Samuel snarled. "Sound familiar?"

Naomi stared from one to the other. "M-my scarf?"

"The one you were wearing yesterday afternoon," Samuel assured her.

Naomi shook her head. "But I didn't, I haven't . . ." She slapped a hand over her mouth, her eyes wide and staring at Cecily. "I thought I'd lost it again."

Cecily studied her face. "Lost it?"

"Yes." Naomi stumbled over to her armchair and sat down heavily. "Yesterday evening Randall and I went to make final arrangements for Gavin's funeral. When I put on my coat, my scarf wasn't on the hallstand. I didn't have time to look for it, so I went out without it. I thought I must have left it somewhere."

129

"I suppose someone else could have taken it," Samuel said, sounding doubtful.

"That must be it." Naomi looked nervously over her shoulder, as if expecting a murderer to creep up behind her. "Mrs. Baxter, I don't know who killed Gavin, but I do know it wasn't the gambling syndicate."

Narrowing her eyes, Cecily demanded, "How can you be so sure?"

Naomi flicked a frightened glance at the door and lowered her voice. "Please don't tell Randall I told you this, but Gavin didn't have any gambling debts. Those death threats were meant for Randall. That's why he didn't want the constables involved in all this. He was afraid the truth would get out and he'd be in trouble for associating with those criminals."

Cecily frowned. "But I thought the notes were found in Mr. Hargrove's private desk."

"They were. Randall gave them to Gavin. Gavin told me that Randall wanted him to settle the debts for him. He took them and put them in his desk so that Randall would think he was paying them and would stop pestering him about it. He had no intention of paying them. I really think he was hoping the syndicate would carry out their threats and get rid of Randall." She shook her head. "They really hated each other, you know."

"They grew up as brothers, though, didn't they?"

"Not exactly." Naomi stared into the dancing flames of the fire. "Charles Hargrove took Randall in when his mother and father died in a boating accident. Randall was three years old, and barely remembers his parents. His mother was

Charles's sister. The boys grew up in the same house, but were treated very differently."

She looked up at Cecily. "It's sad, really. Charles left everything to Gavin, with the stipulation he provide Randall with a home as long as he wanted it. Only in the event of Gavin's death would Randall inherit anything from the old man."

"That must have been a bitter blow to Mr. Thorpe."

"It was." She stared back at the fire. "He hated the idea of being dependent on Gavin, especially when Gavin made it very clear he resented having to provide his cousin with a living."

"Why didn't Mr. Thorpe leave?" Samuel asked.

Naomi's mouth twisted in a bitter smile. "Randall would find it very difficult to live on his own in the manner to which he's accustomed. He loves this place, and would never leave unless forced to do so. Though I think if Gavin had lived, he might well have made things intolerable for Randall."

"But he didn't live," Cecily said quietly.

Naomi's eyes widened. "You think Randall . . . ? No." She shook her head. "Randall has his faults, but I can't believe he would kill his own cousin."

"People have done far less for a prize such as this." Cecily swept a glance around the sumptuous room. "Tell me, do you think Mr. Thorpe's manner changed at all since your fiancé's death?"

Naomi wrinkled her brow. "Well, of course. Naturally he's saddened by the death of his cousin and concerned as to who was responsible. He is, however, the new heir to the Hargrove fortune. His life has changed full circle. Any man would be heartened by those circumstances, would they not?"

"Absolutely." Cecily felt a moment of despair. She felt as if she were trying to find a way through a maze, encountering one blocked avenue after another. She was no closer to discovering Baxter's whereabouts than she had been two days ago.

Perhaps Madeline could find out something on her tour, though it was doubtful while she was under the watchful eye of Randall Thorpe.

Personally, Cecily didn't share Naomi's conviction of Randall's innocence. Then again, she'd heard nothing to connect him to the murder, either. It was all so terribly frustrating.

Moments later Madeline returned on the arm of her host, her expression carefully guarded. Cecily had to wait until they were outside before her curiosity could be satisfied.

"Did you see anything out of place?" she asked, as they made their way down the steps to the carriage.

"I'm sorry, Cecily." Madeline paused as Samuel hurried ahead to open the door for them. "I saw lots of rooms where Baxter might be but nothing to show he was inside. I tried to listen above Mr. Thorpe's annoying chatter, but I heard no sound from any of those rooms."

Cecily waited for the lump in her throat to subside. After giving instructions to Samuel to drive them back to the woods, she climbed up into the carriage. Once they were seated and on their way, she said dismally, "We're never going to find him, are we."

"Nonsense." Madeline patted her arm. "I feel strongly that Baxter is not in the mansion. As I said, he has been moving from place to place, and I can't see that happening if he's a prisoner in one of those rooms."

"Then I suppose our next step is to find the gypsies and ask for their help."

"Exactly." A strange gleam appeared in Madeline's eyes. "Somehow I feel that we shall have much more success with the Romanies."

"I hope you're right." Cecily gazed out of the window at the hedges floating by. "I only hope we are able to catch up with them."

"I think I know where to find them."

Cecily caught her breath. Turning eagerly to Madeline she asked breathlessly, "You know where they are?"

"I know where they might be. There's a meadow on the other side of the woods, next to a fast-running stream. When I envision the gypsy camp I can hear that stream."

"Then we must go there at once."

"This carriage will not be able to travel through the woods. It's too wide. The riding trail is narrow and the branches are low. Only a trap will be able to get through. Unless we go around by road, which will take a great deal longer."

Cecily stared at her in dismay. "What if we travel on foot?"

"I was going to suggest that." Madeline looked grave. "It is a great deal faster, but an arduous journey. Are you sure you have the stamina?"

"If it will lead me to my husband," Cecily said firmly, "I would climb a mountain if needs be."

Madeline nodded. "Very well." She looked up as the carriage came to a halt. "It might be as well to send Samuel back to the Pennyfoot for a trap. He can meet us at the meadow and take us back."

"An excellent idea." Cecily clambered down from the carriage, barely touching Samuel's proffered hand. "I want you to go back to the country club," she told him, "and return with a trap. Madeline will tell you where to meet us."

She listened to Madeline's directions, which seemed simple enough. Samuel, however, argued strenuously about leaving the women to fend for themselves.

"It's my duty, m'm, to see no harm comes to you," he told Cecily. "I can't just ride off and leave you and Miss Pengrath alone in these woods. Especially with the gypsies about. Gawd knows what might happen to you."

"The most that could happen," Cecily said firmly, "is that I might tear a hole in my skirt. I'll be perfectly safe with Madeline. You know how familiar she is with the outdoors. I trust her completely."

"I'd rather come with you." Samuel got a stubborn look on his face.

"That means we'd have farther to walk," Madeline said, giving Samuel one of her soft smiles. "Whereas, if you meet us at our destination with the trap, we'd only be walking one way. Besides, if we should find Mr. Baxter, he might not be able to walk very far. In which case, we'll need the trap."

Pain sliced through Cecily at the thought of Baxter being incapacitated. "Madeline's right," she said. "Now go, Samuel. We are wasting valuable time talking."

"Yes, m'm." Samuel walked back to the front of the carriage and climbed up on his seat, leaving Cecily in no doubt that he was thoroughly disgruntled.

She had a moment of misgiving as she watched the carriage and horses noisily jostling away from them, and then, with firm resolve, turned her back on him. "Come," she said to Madeline. "We have much to do before darkness falls again."

"Samuel's been acting awfully strange since he got that bump on the head." Pansy shoved her mop into the bucket of soapy water, swished it about, then leaned over to wring out the wet strands with her hands.

Gertie placed a pile of towels in the cupboard and shut the door. This was her favorite room. Edward Sandringham, madam's cousin and owner of the Pennyfoot, had installed the water closet, putting in a gleaming tile floor and fancy bathtub with brass claw-feet. When he'd handed the reins over to madam, she'd moved into the lavish suite.

The blue tiles on the floor had white roses in the center of each one. Delicate blue cornflowers decorated the white wallpaper, and the frieze around the top was a twisted garland of dark green leaves and tiny white rosebuds.

Gertie had never seen anything like it before, and vowed that one day she'd have a house with a water closet in it. Just like this one.

Aware that Pansy had spoken to her, she turned her head. "Whatcha say?"

"I said Sam is acting strange." Pansy sloshed the damp mop over the floor. "What was you thinking about, anyway?"

"I was just thinking that when I have me own house again I'll have a water closet put in it."

Pansy burst out laughing. "Whatcha going to do, marry a rich man?"

Snatched out of her daydream, Gertie glared at her. "What's so bleeding funny about that? Lots of women marry rich men. Like Doris. You remember her? She was here last year. She's my nanny's twin sister. She used to be a maid here and then she went on the stage in London. She's married now, to a bloke what owns a factory. Got a posh house and everything."

Pansy shrugged. "Well, she was in London, weren't she. The likes of us'll never meet no one like that. The only rich blokes we see are guests, and they don't hobnob with the servants."

Gertie smiled. "Sometimes they do."

"Well, the best you can hope for is to end up with some-one like Dan Perkins." She gave Gertie a sly grin. "He fan-cies you, he does."

"Go on with you!" Feeling her cheeks warm, Gertie made a big show of straightening the towels on the shelf above the lavatory.

"He does!" Pansy insisted. "I know by the way he looks at you." She raised her tone until it squeaked. "His eyes are all soft and twinkly!"

"Shut up," Gertie said rudely. "You don't bleeding know what you're talking about."

"I do, too." Pansy pouted. "I've seen that look in a bloke's eyes before. Plenty of times. I know what happens when they get that look."

"Yeah? Well, you can forget about Dan bloody Perkins and me." Gertie grabbed the door and tugged it open. "I've had two husbands already. One was a bleeding bigamist and we weren't married at all. The other one died on me. I ain't going to get mixed up with no more bleeding men, I can tell you that."

"That's what they all say," Pansy said, her smile turning wicked. "I bet you'll fall for Dan's sweet talk, and you'll be going out with him before the winter's over."

"Like bloody hell." Gertie slammed the door and stomped across the plush carpet to the outer door. She wasn't sure why she felt so angry. Pansy was talking nonsense, of course. Dan Perkins was a bloody Casanova, that's what, and she knew better than to fall for that kind of blarney. She'd had a lucky escape, almost agreeing to go out with him. Thank goodness he had something better to do.

Out in the corridor, she headed for the stairs. All right, so she was tempted by the idea of riding in a motorcar. That was stupid. Just because she got a flutter now and then when he talked to her, didn't mean she liked him. She was just lonely, that was all. She missed being married, and having a man to take care of and cuddle up to in bed. Didn't mean she was ready to take on another one.

Besides, she had an idea he was up to no good on Christmas Eve. Why else would he not want to tell her where he was going? No, she was better off staying out of his way, that's what.

Still disturbed by Pansy's remarks, she clomped down the stairs to the lobby. From now on, she vowed, she'd ignore Mr. Honey Mouth Perkins and his twinkly eyes. That'd shut Pansy up all right.

As she reached the bottom of the stairs, one of the front

doors flew open and Samuel barged in, his cap stuck in his back pocket, his hair all ruffled and standing on end.

"Flipping 'eck," Gertie said, staring at him in concern, "what's got you in all of a bloody tiz?"

"David," Samuel said, panting so hard he barely got the word out. "Have you seen 'im?"

"No, I haven't." Gertie felt a stab of concern. "Here, what's up? Not another dead body, is it?"

Samuel shook his head, swallowed, and fought to get his breath. "I have to get back to the woods right away. Find David, will you, and ask him to put the carriage away? I don't have time to do it now."

Certain something was wrong, Gertie stepped closer to him. "What's happened?" she demanded. "Is madam all right? Where is she?"

Samuel had already spun around and was at the door when he flung the words over his shoulder. "In the woods, and if I don't get back there right away, I have a feeling there might be trouble."

"Whatcha mean? What kind of trouble? Is it something to do with Mr. Baxter?" Gertie swore. She was talking to empty air. Samuel had already slammed the door behind him, leaving her with a horrible, nasty feeling in the pit of her stomach.

CHAPTER
❀ 12 ❀

In spite of Madeline's assurances that the gypsies would not harm them, Cecily's qualms remained. During their hike, Madeline had told her about the Romany, as she called them.

Apparently they had arrived in England four hundred years earlier and in spite of modern progress had clung to their traditions and lifestyles in a stubborn resistance to change.

"They are determined to remain self-employed," Madeline had told her. "Their children are taught to be independent and start work very young. They do everything from picking hops and fruit to selling clothes-pegs. They raise horses and collect scrap iron to sell. They work very hard and are a very proud people."

It was obvious to Cecily that Madeline admired and respected the gypsies, unlike most folk, who feared them. But, it was hard to understand a race of people who lived such a primitive life, constantly on the move and never putting down roots.

Madeline had told her that only in the last twenty years or so had the majority of them been able to afford caravans. Before that they had lived in tents. Their only stability came from their fierce loyalty and commitment to their extended families.

All this had aroused Cecily's sympathy, but still she was wary of speaking with them. But as the minutes passed and her steps grew weary, she began to look forward to the journey's end.

A fine sea mist had begun to penetrate the trees, adding a chill that seemed to seep into Cecily's bones. It felt as though she had been tramping across fallen acorns, dried leaves and dead twigs for hours. Her common sense, however, told her it couldn't have been more than forty minutes or so since they had first started out.

While Madeline appeared to float effortlessly ahead, parting tendrils of ferns and networks of shrubs with a careless sweep of her arm, Cecily struggled to keep her feet in the tangle of undergrowth that seemed determined to snatch at her ankles and topple her to the ground.

Madeline had assured her it was the shortest route and she knew which direction to take, though they had left the riding trail far behind. Ahead of them lay the gnarled trunks of ancient beech and oak, clumps of nettles and tall grass, and thick branches that shut out the sky.

The air smelled damp and earthy, and all around she could hear scuffling and shuffling, until she imagined a thousand tiny eyes watched their progress.

The prickling feeling in her back held her so tense she was certain she would break a tooth from clamping her jaw. The ache in her side became more intense as she trudged up a slight incline behind the gliding figure in front of her.

Madeline seemed as at home in the forest as Cecily was in her library. The slender woman appeared not to notice the sharp twigs tugging at her hair, or the wayward branch that sprang back and slapped her cheek. She stepped sure-footedly over fallen logs, across tiny streams, and up the slippery, steep slopes without hesitation.

She seemed to have plenty of breath to spare as she occasionally sang out a warning of a low-lying branch, while Cecily barely had enough breath left to cough an answer.

"The trees are thinning," Madeline called out, as they reached the top of the incline. "We should see the meadow quite soon."

For Cecily it couldn't come soon enough. She gritted her teeth and started down the slope ahead, then stopped, frozen, as the sharp snap rang out behind her.

Madeline stopped, too, pausing to look back at her. "What was that?"

Cecily shook her head. Fearfully she peered back the way they had come, trying to penetrate the shadows. "What do you think it was?"

"Probably a beaver. They bite off small branches to use in their dams. We must be getting closer to the big stream."

Only half reassured, Cecily took a step toward her. Just as

she did so, something large whizzed by her ear, narrowly missing her head. She let out a small scream of fright and bounded forward.

The shock on Madeline's face did nothing to settle her skittering nerves. "What in heaven's name—"

The words were barely out of her mouth before another large white rock sailed through the air and landed with an ominous thud at her feet.

"Oh my God." Cecily clutched at her sleeve. "Someone is trying to kill us."

For answer, Madeline grasped her hand and tugged hard. "Come on! Run!"

The two of them plunged down the incline. Leaping and running, Madeline dragged Cecily after her, dodging in and out of the trees like a rabbit chased by a hungry dog.

Cecily gasped painfully for breath, certain her heart was about to burst as it pounded in her chest. Slipping and sliding, she concentrated on staying on her feet, spurred by the crashing, thudding sounds behind them that told her someone was in hot pursuit.

And drawing closer.

Then, without warning, Madeline stopped in her tracks. Taken by surprise, Cecily smacked into her, sending both of them staggering a few more paces.

Unable to gather enough breath to speak, Cecily merely stared at her friend and made wheezing noises of protest.

Madeline seemed not to hear her. Instead, she slowly raised her hands, her palms flattened as if pressing against an invisible wall. "They are here," she whispered.

Cecily's next wheeze rose in question.

The crashing in the forest behind her had ceased, as if their pursuer waited, listening, for their next move. Quite sure that if either one of them took a step he would be after them again, Cecily stayed as motionless and quiet as her trembling body would allow.

Nothing moved in the forest. It was as if all had gone silent and still, waiting for something to happen. Cecily's shoulders ached with tension. Braced to run, she waited for the next rock to come hurtling out of the dark woods.

Then she heard a rustling, louder than before. A snapping of twigs, a slap of a branch. It seemed to come from all directions, closing them in and trapping them inside the menacing circle.

She whimpered, and Madeline looked at her. The strange gleam was back in her eyes, and her mouth curved in a smile. "They are here," she said again.

Cecily was about to ask to whom she referred, when a shadow detached itself from the trees and came forward. She jumped violently, backing away. Then another shadow moved, and then another.

They came out of the trees. Dark, swarthy men and bright-eyed women. Young and old, all of them strong. The women wore bright clothes, and kerchiefs holding back their long, black hair.

The men wore scarves about their necks, their rough-hewn features tanned and weathered by the sun.

Madeline spoke first, to the tall, sturdy man who appeared to be their leader. "Greetings, Pedro. We meet again."

Cecily let out her breath. Of course. She should have known Madeline was acquainted with gypsies. She waited for Madeline to introduce her.

Instead, Madeline gestured at the woods behind her. "Back there. We are being followed by someone who wishes to do us harm."

The man named Pedro issued harsh commands to his followers in a language Cecily didn't understand. Several men broke away from the group and disappeared among the trees.

Pedro turned back to Madeline. "If he is still there, they will find him." He glanced at Cecily. "What brings you into the woods alone, Madeline?"

He pronounced her name with a faint foreign accent that Cecily found rather charming. She managed a frozen smile as Madeline introduced her.

"We have come to ask for your help," Madeline added, after Pedro had greeted Cecily. "We are searching for someone who may be lost in the woods. A man who is not accustomed to the severe climate of the outdoors in winter."

Pedro's dark eyes rested on Cecily's face for a moment, then switched back to Madeline. "Who is wishing you harm?"

"That we do not know." Madeline hesitated. "Bad things have been happening, Pedro. A man is dead, and we think his killer will do terrible things to prevent us from discovering his identity."

"So I have heard. And the man who is missing? What is his name?"

"Hugh Baxter," Madeline answered. "He is Mrs. Baxter's husband."

Once more Pedro's sharp gaze raked Cecily's face. "Come,"

he said shortly. "We will return to the camp." He beckoned to the rest of the group, then started striding away from them through the trees.

"What will they do if they find the man who chased us?" Cecily asked Madeline in a whisper.

"They will most likely hold him prisoner until we decide what to do about him." Madeline gave her an encouraging smile. "We will let the constables deal with him."

"Not until I have questioned him," Cecily said fiercely. "He must tell us what happened to Baxter."

"I think we can trust Pedro and his men to get the information you need. You have no idea what an honor this is, to be invited into their camp."

"Well, I appreciate the honor, but I trust it isn't too far away." Cecily sighed. "I really don't think I can walk much farther."

As if understanding her weariness, a young woman took hold of her arm. "Lean on me," she said softly. "I will be pleased to help you."

Gratefully, Cecily allowed herself to be supported through the trees.

Soon they emerged from the thicket, where the trees grew farther apart. Between the trunks Cecily glimpsed a grassy area and a patch of cloudy sky. The sound of music drifted toward them on the breeze—fiddles played fast and furiously, and the tinkling beat of tambourines.

As she stumbled out into the meadow, she saw the caravans, painted in startling hues of red, blue, yellow, and green. Lines of wash, strung between the caravans, flapped in the wind.

Children ran about, their feet bare in the cold grass, their cheeks glowing like the embers of the blazing fire around which they frolicked.

A group of musicians played for a lone dancer—a young woman with flowing black hair and flying bare feet. Her yellow and red skirt swirled about her knees as she twirled and leapt to the fiery music, and kept time with a tambourine flashing in her hand.

Several older members, their backs bent with age and some leaning on canes, stood by the colorful doors of their tiny homes, watching warily as Cecily approached.

The music died away and the dancer stood still. Silence settled over the camp, until only the flapping clothes on the line and the faint jingle of iron pots hanging from the sides of the caravans broke the eerie hush.

Fascinated by the scene, Cecily could only stare about her, absorbing all she saw.

Pedro strode forward, one hand held above his head. He called out something in the strange language again, and more heads popped out of the narrow doors.

An elderly woman came forward, her silver hair bound by a long, wispy scarf. Pedro said something to her and she listened intently, then nodded.

Turning back to Cecily, Pedro said quietly, "He who wounds the hunted is wounded himself. A fair exchange."

Cecily gave him a blank look, having understood not one word he'd said. She had no time to ask him to explain, however, as the old woman took hold of her hand and gave it a tug.

"Come," she said, her voice a low croak.

Alarmed, Cecily looked at Madeline, surprised by the excitement she saw in her face.

"Go with her," Madeline said.

Following the woman, Cecily picked her way across the grass. As they passed the caravans, the people nodded and smiled at her, easing her apprehension. Whatever this woman wanted with her, it could not be something to be feared.

At last they reached the caravan farthest from the fire. It was not as colorful as the others, though it seemed larger. The brown paint had faded in the sun, and the wheels looked worn. Assuming this was the woman's home, Cecily hung back.

"Come," the gypsy said again. She reached up and opened the door.

She did not want to go inside. Not without Madeline, anyway. She wasn't sure what awaited her on the other side of that door. On the other hand, if the woman had the power to see into a crystal ball, she wanted to know what the gypsy could tell her.

One thing she did know. Her legs were so weak and trembling she marveled that they still held her weight. If by going through that door it meant she could sit and rest, then she would do it.

Nodding at the woman, Cecily stepped up into the tiny confines of the caravan. The sudden darkness robbed her of sight. She blinked, trying to adjust.

Slowly the room swam into focus, just as the door closed behind her, leaving her alone in the shadows with only the faint light from a candle.

There was barely room to move around in the space between a bed on one side and an armchair on the other. Cautiously she moved forward, wondering why she'd been left alone and more than a little scared. Then, with a shock, she realized someone lay on the bed. The figure moved, and turned over.

Cecily opened her mouth to apologize for her intrusion, but before she could speak a familiar voice muttered her name.

"Cecily? Can that really be you?"

What little strength she had left completely drained from her legs. She went down on her knees, clutching at the bed for support. Tears streamed down her face, and the one word she could utter came out in a sob. "Bax!"

Samuel flicked the reins along the chestnut's back, urging it to run faster. Clouds had gathered over the ocean and a fresh wind promised rain. The thought of madam and Miss Pengrath trudging through the trees terrified him, and the threat of a storm only made matters worse.

Madeline had told him how to get to the meadow, but it meant taking the riding trail if he were to get there in good time to meet them. After the attempts to run him down, he was not relishing the idea of returning to the menacing shadows of the woods.

He reached the top of the hill and urged the chestnut into a full gallop. The trap swayed from side to side, the wheels groaning in protest as they hit a bump in the road.

Samuel's teeth rattled as he was jolted out of his seat and

crashed down again with a bone-jarring thud. Still he would not allow the horse to let up, and entered the riding trail at breakneck speed.

The next few minutes were a nightmare of grasping branches that threatened to snatch him from the trap, and loose stones thrown up by the chestnut's flying hooves. On and on they thudded, down slopes and over ridges, turning the bend on one wheel while Samuel's heart jumped to his throat.

Deeper into the woods they plunged, farther than Samuel had ever been before. The trail narrowed even more, until he was afraid the trap would become jammed between the trees. He reined in the sweating horse, coaxing it to a trot and then slowed to a walk.

Just as he did so, he heard a sound of twigs snapping. Nerves twisting, he lifted the reins to press the horse back into a gallop. Then, from out of the darkness, someone stepped in front of him. With a lurch of apprehension, he jerked the reins and halted the trap.

"Come," the man said, his harsh voice echoing through the trees. "They are waiting for you."

Tingling with alarm, Samuel grasped the reins tighter. "Who's waiting for me?"

"Your friends. Miss Pengrath. Mrs. Baxter."

Samuel narrowed his eyes, and demanded, "Are you one of them gypsy folk?"

"I am Romany." The man beckoned, and still uncertain, Samuel nudged the chestnut forward.

The man guided them through the rest of the trees, until at last they came out into the wide-open meadow. At first

Samuel's attention focused on the young woman dancing by the fire. Dusk had already settled over the camp, and the leaping flames bathed the dancer in their fiery glow.

Enthralled by the lithe body twisting and bending to the music, he failed to see Madeline approach until she spoke at his side.

"It's about time you got here. Mrs. Baxter is impatient to get back to the Pennyfoot."

Samuel jumped, and stared down into Madeline's green eyes. "Did the gypsies agree to help look for Mr. Baxter?"

"There's no need." Madeline signaled at a couple who moved slowly toward them, the man limping heavily and leaning on the woman at his side.

Samuel blinked, and blinked again. "I don't believe it," he murmured. "They found him."

"Yes," Madeline said, her voice warm with satisfaction. "They did. They've been taking care of him. But now we're taking him home."

CHAPTER
❀ 13 ❀

"Will you stop fussing around me," Baxter said peevishly. "I'm not an invalid."

"You have been through a great deal." Cecily tucked the blanket under his knees and plumped up the cushion at his back. "You're going to sit there in that armchair while we wait for Mrs. Chubb to send you up a decent meal. Heaven knows what you've been eating the last day or two."

Baxter gave her a wry smile. "I'm sorry to disappoint you, my dear, but the gypsies are remarkable cooks, even if their taste in meals is somewhat strange."

Cecily shuddered. "I can imagine."

"Their rabbit stew was delicious. Quite an imaginative use of spices and herbs, I must say. Michel could well take a lesson from them."

Cecily gaped at him in horror. "For heaven's sake, Bax, don't you dare mention such a thing to anyone. If Michel got so much as a hint that you preferred someone else's cooking, he'd blast a hole right through the roof with his temper."

Baxter actually grinned, which was not something he was apt to do that often. "I was merely teasing you, my dear. I can't tell you how happy I am to be home. The delicious smell of mince pies that invades this place, not to mention Michel's plum puddings, is enough to make me faint from hunger."

Despite her best efforts to prevent them, tears sprang to Cecily's eyes. Angry with herself, she dashed them away with the back of her hand. "We were all so worried about you," she muttered. "We imagined you lying in the woods somewhere, cold and alone, injured or . . ." Even now she could not bring herself to say the word.

Baxter reached for her hand, his fingers warm around her own. "I worried about you, too, my dear one. I couldn't imagine how I would feel if our positions had been reversed. I begged Pedro to get word to you, but he was afraid that the constables would suspect them of having a hand in Hargrove's murder. You know how quick they are to blame misfortune on the gypsies."

"I'm surprised they heard about the murder." Cecily fetched another pillow and carefully propped up Baxter's foot. "But I'm glad they told you. At least you were prepared for the news."

"News travels fast in that community." Baxter winced and shifted on his chair.

She glanced at his face in concern. "Does it hurt very badly?"

"Only when I move my foot." He patted her hand. "You worry far too much, Cecily. As I'm always telling you."

"Yes, well, this time you gave me plenty of reason to worry." She pulled up a chair by his side and sat down. "Do you feel up to discussing all this now? I hesitate to burden you with all my questions. At least until you feel well enough to answer."

"I'm quite well now." He shifted again and grimaced. "At least I will be when I can walk on this dratted foot again."

"So tell me everything that happened to you from the moment you entered the woods to cut the holly."

At last, she thought, as she watched him make himself comfortable. She had waited until this moment, wary of troubling him too soon with her questions. She'd wanted him home, where they could discuss this whole distressing business in the quiet privacy of their boudoir.

Now it was time, and at last she was about to learn who had strangled Gavin Hargrove, put him in the trap, and sent him back to the Pennyfoot for her to find.

Baxter sighed, and leaned back in his chair. "It's all still rather a blur, I'm afraid. I suggested to Samuel that we should go in different directions. I thought we'd have a better chance of finding enough holly in a short amount of time. I had cut a small bundle and put it in the trap, then decided to go farther down the trail, around the bend. That's when I saw the poor blighter."

Cecily leaned forward, clinging to every word. "You saw the body."

"Yes. He was hanging from a branch over the trail. I shouted for Samuel and he came running. We cut him down and saw at once he was dead. I told Samuel we should take him back to the Pennyfoot and send for P.C. Northcott. Samuel went back to fetch the trap. That's the last I remember."

Her cry of dismay raised his eyebrows. "You didn't see who attacked you?"

"I'm afraid not."

"Nothing? You saw *nothing*?"

He shook his head at her. "I'm sorry, Cecily, believe me. I'd give anything to know who was behind this. At least I'm safe and relatively unhurt. After all, that's what's important, isn't it?"

"Of course it is." She buried her disappointment at once. "I'm sorry, my love. Please, go on."

"I suppose whoever it was must have hit me with something. I still have a lump the size of a walnut on the back of my head." Gingerly he raised a hand and touched the back of his head.

"Oh, goodness. Let me look." She jumped up to peer at the spot where his hand had touched. "Oh, my, that's quite a swelling. You were most likely hit with a rock." She sat down again. "Someone threw some at Madeline and me while we were on our way to the gypsy camp."

Baxter looked alarmed. "Why would anyone throw rocks at you?"

Cecily assumed an air of innocence. "I haven't the slightest idea."

"But my dear, I had no idea you had been in such danger. Why didn't you tell me?"

"It didn't seem important." She smiled at him. "The gypsies did chase after the man, but lost sight of him in the woods. They couldn't even tell me what he looked like."

"I don't understand—"

Impatiently she cut in. "We can worry about that later. Do go on with your story."

He sent her a stare full of suspicion, but to her relief, continued his tale. "Yes, well, when I woke up, I was deep in the woods, alone, and with a thundering headache. I started walking in what I hoped was the right direction, but then I fell down a gully and hurt my ankle. I couldn't even stand on it, much less walk. I thought the blasted thing was broken."

"Oh, my dear." Cecily grasped his hand, which now felt cold. "You must have been so worried and fearful."

"Bloody angry, more like it." He shook his head. "I wanted to kill whoever had left me there to die. It was dark, bitterly cold and snowing so hard it blanketed the ground around me. I knew if anyone was looking for me they'd never find a trail."

"We did look for you. For hours." Cecily held his hand to her cheek.

The answering look in his eyes warmed her heart. "My dear, I'm so very sorry. That must have been difficult for you."

"For us all." Cecily swallowed hard. "So that's when the gypsies found you?"

"Yes. I was amazed when, without warning, I was surrounded by a dozen or so silent men. At first I thought they'd come to kill me, though I couldn't imagine why. It was a relief, I can tell you, when I realized they had come to rescue me. How they knew I was there I can't imagine, but I'm jolly glad they found me."

She waited a moment to steady her voice. "What I don't understand, is why the gypsies didn't simply bring you back to the Pennyfoot."

"I requested, commanded, and finally begged them to take me back. Pedro told me later that they were scared to go into town. As I told you, they'd heard about the murder and thought they might be arrested and the camp raided by the constables."

"What did they intend to do with you, then? Keep you as a prisoner forever?"

Baxter smiled. "No. Only until I could walk back on my own."

"But that could have been weeks!"

"Good Lord, I hope not!" Baxter stared at his bound foot in dismay. "Bad enough I have to hobble through Christmas. I certainly hope I'm walking again by the end of the year."

"Well, Kevin should be here soon. Madeline said she'd have him here as soon as he could leave his surgery."

Baxter rolled his eyes. "I don't see why I have to put up with that pompous ass. It's merely a sprained ankle, and Miranda assured me it will heal in a week or two, providing I don't try to walk on it." He shook his head in disgust. "Dashed inconvenient time to be disabled, I must say. It will put rather a damper on our Christmas, I'm afraid."

Cecily barely heard the latter part. "And just who, may I ask, is Miranda?"

A gleam appeared in his eyes. "I'm flattered, my dear, but you have nothing to fear. Miranda is Pedro's daughter. Very capable, quite charming, and much too young to be a threat. As you know, I vastly prefer my women mature in years and experience."

Cecily pretended to be offended. "Your women? How many women, exactly, are we talking about?"

Baxter reached for her and pulled her into his arms. "Only one, my dearest love. Only one."

"In that case, I shall forgive your lascivious rambling." She leaned into him and deposited a kiss on his mouth.

He was returning it rather satisfactorily when a tap on the door drew them apart. Upon opening it, Cecily was surprised to see Mrs. Chubb had brought up the tray herself.

"I had to come and see for myself, m'm," the housekeeper said, as she carried the tray into the boudoir. Catching sight of Baxter, her face lit up with delight. "There you are, sir. It is such a pleasure to see you sitting there, I'm sure. You have no idea how worried we all were. Thought you were dead, we did."

Cecily made a small sound of protest, but Mrs. Chubb rattled on without hearing her. "What with that poor dead man in the trap, and madam gone all the time, we didn't know if we were coming or going, that we didn't."

Baxter sent Cecily a meaningful look before answering the housekeeper. "Please thank everyone for their concern, Mrs. Chubb, but as you can see, I am quite well except for a slightly sprained ankle. Had it not been for that, I could have walked home from the woods."

157

"Well, what I'd like to know, is how you got lost in the first place." She laid the tray down on the table at his elbow, then dug her fists into her hips. "I don't know how Samuel could just go off and leave you like that, I'm sure I don't. He doesn't remember a thing about it, or I'd give him a piece of my mind. Box his ears, I would, if I thought he had just abandoned you."

"He didn't abandon me," Baxter began, but Cecily interrupted, cutting off his words.

"That will be all, Mrs. Chubb. I don't want to excite Mr. Baxter. He needs his rest."

"Oh, of course, m'm. I do beg your pardon." Mrs. Chubb scurried to the door. "It's just that I was so pleased to see him and everything. Thank you, m'm. Thank you, sir."

The door closed behind her, and Cecily let out a breath of relief. "Goodness, I was afraid you were going to tell her everything before I'd had a chance to hear it all."

Baxter eyed her with suspicion. "What did she mean about you being absent all the time?"

Cecily took her seat by his side again. "She exaggerated. I was here a good deal of the time."

"And when you weren't?"

"I paid Mr. Thorpe a visit at Whitfield Manor. Just to pay my respects, of course." She lifted the cover from the plate Mrs. Chubb had brought up. "Oh, look, your favorite. Pork pie and pickled onions. Do have a bite. I'm sure it's every bit as good as your gypsy rabbit stew."

Ignoring the food, Baxter frowned. "I wasn't aware you were familiar with the Hargrove family."

"I'm not." Cecily wrestled with her conscience for a moment or two, then burst out, "All right. I went there to find out who killed Gavin Hargrove and why. I thought it might lead me to your whereabouts, since you were obviously involved."

Baxter groaned. "I thought as much. I suppose there's no point in reminding you that the constables are responsible for apprehending criminals?"

Cecily shrugged. "Sam Northcott has handed the case over to Scotland Yard. He's convinced a gambling syndicate killed Mr. Hargrove over some gambling debts. But that couldn't be so."

"Why do you say that?"

She told him about her conversation with Naomi Kendall. "At first we thought it might be Naomi," she said, "because whoever attacked Samuel was wearing her scarf. If she was telling me the truth, however, someone else took that scarf to disguise his face. Someone at Whitfield Manor killed Mr. Hargrove. I'm sure of it. The question is, who?"

Baxter's scowl warned her to end the discussion. "Well, I'm home now, so you can stop interfering in police affairs and get back to your own vocation, which is providing our guests with a memorable Christmas. And by memorable, I sincerely hope that will be both pleasurable and free from any more nefarious acts of violence."

"No, I can't," Cecily said unhappily.

Her husband's face darkened. "You can't what?"

"I can't leave it to the constables. I'm sorry, Bax, but someone tried to kill you and Samuel. He was attacked again in the woods when we went looking for you. Madeline and I were attacked in the woods as well. Someone is willing to go great lengths to see that we don't discover who was responsible for Gavin Hargrove's death."

"All the more reason for you to stay out of it." He reached for her hand again. "We were almost parted forever, my beloved. Promise me you will leave this investigation to the police. Now that Northcott has turned the case over to Scotland Yard, I'm sure they will find the killer in short order, and until then you and Samuel must stay indoors, where you'll be safe."

She knew better than to argue. When Baxter made up his mind about something, he was as rigid as a stone wall, and she had no desire to row with him so soon after his ordeal. "Perhaps you're right," she murmured. "Though I should dearly like to know how the body ended up in our trap and in our courtyard. I suppose it will have to wait. After all, tomorrow is Christmas Eve, and I shall be busy enough with all the festivities downstairs, as well as taking care of you."

"I can take care of myself," Baxter said stubbornly. "A good night's rest and I should be able to hop around the place without too much trouble."

"Absolutely not." She set her jaw. "You will stay off that ankle until it is completely healed."

"If you think I'm going to spend Christmas shut up in this room, you are badly mistaken." His expression was mutinous, but his eyes pleaded with her. "I've been a virtual prisoner for two miserable days. I deserve to enjoy the festivities."

Against her will, she softened. "Of course you do, my love. We shall see what the doctor has to say."

If she thought that would placate him, she was disappointed. Baxter merely grunted, but his face warned her that he would take no advice from Kevin Prestwick, no matter how well intended.

And she was right. The moment Kevin walked into the boudoir, she could tell Baxter proposed to be difficult. He never could seem to forget that once upon a time Dr. Kevin Prestwick's pursuit of Cecily had been quite persistent, in spite of her resistance to his charms.

No matter how many times Cecily had assured her husband she had never had the slightest romantic interest in the handsome doctor, Baxter's skepticism made his relationship with Kevin somewhat strained on occasion.

The doctor, on the other hand, seemed merely amused by Baxter's jealousy, for want of a better word, which only fueled her husband's misplaced irritation.

"Well, old boy, good to see you in one piece." Kevin's breezy manner always seemed to bring a breath of fresh air to a stuffy room, which was one of the reasons his predominately female patients adored him so. He smiled at Baxter as he pulled a stethoscope from his black bag. "Let's just listen to the old ticker, shall we?"

"There's nothing wrong with my tick . . . heart," Baxter grumbled. "It's my foot and my head that need examining."

Unable to contain her mirth, Cecily burst out laughing, earning a fierce scowl from her irate husband.

Kevin managed to keep a straight face as he peered at the spot Baxter had indicated on the back of his head. "Oh, my. That's a nasty-looking bump. The skin is broken, but it looks clean enough." He probed in Baxter's hair with his long fingers.

"Ouch." Baxter pulled his head out of reach. "That's blasted painful."

"Sorry. Just wanted to make sure there was no infection." Kevin jammed the ends of his stethoscope in his ears. "Now just hold still a minute."

Red faced, Baxter endured Kevin's examination.

"Good, good," Kevin murmured. "Strong and steady."

"I really don't know why my wife insisted on your presence." Baxter scowled at Cecily. "I shall be perfectly well in a day or two."

"Well, let me look at the ankle."

Cecily's amusement faded as she watched her husband wince in pain. It would be some time, she thought, before Baxter would be walking on two feet again.

Kevin confirmed her doubts when he straightened. "The only way that is going to heal in good time is if you avoid putting weight on it. I can bring you a pair of crutches if you absolutely insist on getting around."

Baxter screwed up his face in disgust. "I absolutely insist. It's Christmas."

"It is, indeed." Kevin dug in his bag and pulled out two small white packets. "I'll leave you something for the pain and I'll call in on you again tomorrow with the crutches. Meanwhile, stay off that foot." He glanced at Cecily. "How are you feeling? Madeline tells me you had quite a scare in the woods." His expression hardened. "I'd like to get my hands on the blighter responsible."

"Well, thankfully we are both in good health, and I'm sure Scotland Yard will catch up with the scoundrel in due course," Cecily said hurriedly, before Baxter could chime in.

"Meanwhile, I hope you will watch over Madeline, just in case someone out there wants to hurt her."

Kevin still looked grim. "I certainly intend to, though you know Madeline can be annoyingly independent."

Cecily smiled. "Then perhaps you should take matters into your own hands and make it your business to protect her permanently."

Baxter growled. "For heaven's sake, Cecily. Do stop trying to organize everyone's lives."

Kevin finished packing up his bag, picked it up, and headed for the door. "As a matter of fact, Cecily could well be right. In fact, I may have some plans in that direction for tomorrow night."

He was out the door before she could question him further. Excited, she turned to Baxter. "Do you think he plans to propose? How marvelous!"

Baxter sighed. "Trust a woman to ignore what's important."

"That *is* important."

"No, what's important is that apparently both you and Madeline are in danger. I shan't rest until this fiend is captured and imprisoned."

Cecily walked over to the bell pull and tugged on it. "Please don't concern yourself, Bax, dear. As you say, I'm perfectly safe here, and I have far too much work waiting for me to waste time chasing after Mr. Hargrove's killer."

And at the time, she meant it.

CHAPTER
❈ 14 ❈

"He looks very white around the mouth," Mrs. Chubb said, in answer to the chorus of questions flung at her the moment she entered the kitchen. "And he's got his foot all bandaged up, he has. I don't think he'll be doing much walking about this Christmas."

"Well, at least he's home." Gertie lifted her hands from the sink and dried them on her apron. "I bet madam's feeling a whole lot better now."

"I'm sure she is." Mrs. Chubb frowned at Pansy, who was on her knees over by the stove. "What on earth are you doing down there?"

Gertie tossed her head at Michel. "She's cleaning up after Michel. He threw mashed spuds on the floor."

Michel answered with a roar. "I did not throw the potatoes.

164

They fall down." He brought his hand down hard on the stove. "So!"

Pansy squealed and dropped the dustpan, scattering mashed potatoes over the floor again.

Gertie twisted her mouth at him. "Maybe if you hadn't bleeding took a swipe at the saucepan with a flipping tea towel they'd have stayed on the flipping stove instead of falling on the bloody floor."

Michel's tall white hat bobbed up and down as he yelled back, his French accent dissolving into broad Cockney. "And if Miss Nosy Bloody Parker minded her own business instead of sticking her snozzle into things wot don't concern 'er, maybe we could all get on with our work."

Mrs. Chubb raised her eyebrows at Gertie.

"He's been at the bleeding brandy, ain't he," Gertie said, with a sneer. "Always forgets he's flipping French when he's drinking, don't he."

Mrs. Chubb looked aghast at the chef. "Michel! What are you thinking!"

Gertie answered for him. "Celebrating, he says. Any bleeding excuse, I say."

"What are you celebrating?" Mrs. Chubb demanded, advancing on Michel. "I hope it's not Christmas, 'coz you're a day or two early. We've got supper for fifty-four guests to get on the table, and you'd better look sharp about it."

Michel's face turned purple. "I'm celebrating the return of Mr. Baxter, if you must know. Anyhow, I don't take orders from you, you old battle-axe."

"You do if you want a job." Mrs. Chubb reached for her

rolling pin hanging on the wall. "Maybe a bash on the head with this will sober you up."

For a moment Gertie thought the chef might stand up to her, but then he backed away, muttering a bunch of French words that fortunately nobody could understand.

"That's better." Mrs. Chubb hung the rolling pin back on the wall.

"Did Mr. Baxter say what happened to him?" Gertie asked, raising her voice to be heard above Michel's angry clashing and banging of saucepan lids.

"Not to me." Mrs. Chubb opened the oven door and peered inside. "These Yorkshire puddings are taking too long to cook. Pansy, stoke the fire and add some more coal."

"Yes, Mrs. Chubb." Abandoning her dustpan, Pansy hurried over to the coal scuttle and lifted it.

Gertie watched her struggle with it for a moment or two, then went to help her. Between them they shoveled more coal into the bottom of the cooking range and slammed the door.

Red in the face, Pansy grinned at Gertie. "Ta, ever so."

"You'd better get in the dining room and make sure the maids have the tables laid properly," Gertie told her. "I'll clean this blinking mess up."

Flashing her another smile of gratitude, Pansy dashed out of the kitchen.

"So we still don't know how the stiff'un got in the trap," Gertie said, squatting down to sit on her heels. She reached for the dustpan and brush. "That's still a bloody mystery."

"Maybe we'll never know." Mrs. Chubb opened a cupboard and took down an enormous silver tureen. "Samuel says

Scotland Yard is looking into it now, so it's not our worry anymore."

Gertie didn't say so, but she was willing to bet that if madam had her way, she'd get to the bottom of the mystery herself. Madam was really good at solving mysteries. Not like that bumbling twerp, P.C. Northcott. He never got anything right.

The only thing she hoped was that madam didn't get into any trouble. For one thing was certain, whenever madam went after a villain, she didn't look out for herself too well. She was always getting into sticky wickets. One of these days she was going to take one chance too many. Gertie was sure about that. She just hoped she wasn't around to see it.

"There's something I don't understand," Cecily said, after the maid had left with Baxter's empty plate. "If whoever attacked you was the same person who killed Mr. Hargrove, why would he go to the trouble of strangling the poor man, then hang him in a tree, presumably to make it look like an accident, and then come back later to the scene of the crime? That doesn't make any sense at all to me."

Baxter grunted from behind the newspaper he'd picked up to read.

Talking more to herself than her disinterested husband, Cecily murmured, "I suppose he could have wanted the body discovered, and was afraid no one else would see it. But then, why go to all the trouble to hang him in the tree? He could have just *said* he found him hanging from a tree."

More silence from behind the newspaper.

"I can understand why Randall Thorpe wanted me to believe it was an accident. If Scotland Yard investigates the case, they'll find out he was the one gambling with some very shady people, not his cousin. I imagine that could cause all sorts of trouble for him."

The newspaper rattled in Baxter's hands.

Deciding she'd tested her husband's patience enough, she rose to her feet. "Oh, very well, I'll leave you in peace. It's time I went down to the ballroom, anyway. Phoebe and her dance troupe are getting ready to put on the Christmas show. I should be there."

"Good Lord," Baxter muttered, "I'd forgotten about that. Haven't you had enough trouble lately without inviting disaster with those pitiful excuses for entertainers?"

Cecily, as always, rushed to the defense of her dear friend. "Come, Baxter. You know very well that our guests enjoy Phoebe's little events. Even if she has had her share of unfortunate incidents."

The newspaper lowered to reveal Baxter's furrowed brow. "Which one in particular were you thinking of? The python that escaped from its basket and terrorized the audience? Or perhaps the weapon that flew from the stage during the sword dance and just missed skewering a prominent aristocrat to her chair?"

Cecily sighed. "You're not being fair. Some of the incidents that happen are quite out of Phoebe's control. Like the magician's assistant who failed to reappear, or the ghost that haunted the balcony in the middle of the tableau. Those weren't Phoebe's fault."

"Except that no one in the audience would have seen that ghost if her troupe of dancers hadn't caused pandemonium on the stage, collapsing to the floor and revealing far more of their anatomy than was decent."

Cecily hid a smile. "Well, as I said, our guests enjoy the events, and that's all that matters."

"They may enjoy laughing at those buffoons, I'll give you that." Baxter retreated once more behind his newspaper.

Cecily wrinkled her nose at him and left him to read in peace. It was not at all surprising for him to be in a snappy mood after all he'd been through. At least he'd promised to stay in his chair for the evening. That's all she could ask from him right now.

Reaching the ballroom, which had now been transformed into a theater by her energetic maids, Cecily made straight for backstage.

Already the neatly lined up chairs were almost fully occupied. Apparently everyone was determined to enjoy the Christmas presentation. Pleased with the turnout, Cecily slipped through the door that would lead her to the dressing rooms.

A chorus of raised voices told her the cast of the show was not yet ready to take the stage. Above the babel, Cecily could clearly hear Phoebe's shrill voice.

"Is-a-*belle*! Your wig is on back to front, for heaven's sake! Take it off at *once*. It looks like a bird's nest getting ready to take flight."

"Birds' nests don't fly, Mrs. Fortescue," a voice piped up. "Only the birds inside it fly."

"You know very well what I mean. Dora, do put your

clothes on. You'll catch your death of cold prancing around in your pantaloons like that. Besides, someone might see you."

A chorus of giggles answered her.

Cecily sighed. She had to admire Phoebe's persistence. For years the poor woman had been trying to whip her dancers into shape—screaming, cajoling, threatening, pleading—anything that would get them on stage to perform a reasonably artistic activity.

So far, she had failed to achieve anything more than a herd of clumsy women's attempts at feats beyond their capabilities.

Upon opening the door, Cecily ran full tilt into the usual pandemonium before a performance. Some of the women were still in their underwear, and Isabelle, the undisputed ringleader in the war against Phoebe, stood twisting a mass of white false hair around and around on her head.

"Cecily!" Phoebe cried, and rushed toward her. Her dark red satin suit, trimmed with white fur, looked most becoming. She wore a white hat, its wide brim decorated with holly and red ribbon roses.

Pinned to her bodice was an enchanting brooch, gleaming silver under the light from the gas lamp above her head. Cecily leaned forward to examine it closer and saw it was a fox, wearing britches and a jacket.

"Isn't it adorable!" Phoebe patted it with obvious affection. "Dear Frederick gave it to me. An early Christmas present. He gave it to me today especially so I could wear it tonight. Don't you think it's too, too precious of him?"

"Indeed it is," Cecily agreed. "Extremely thoughtful."

"Well, anyway, thank heavens you're here. Isabelle needs help with her wig. Would you be an absolute angel and arrange it for her properly? Thank you!" She sailed away again without waiting for an answer, screeching at the top of her lungs. "Get your clothes on, ladies. *Now!* Unless you want to appear on stage in your unmentionables!"

"That'd make 'em sit up and take notice," Isabelle said, grinning.

"Come here." Cecily took the wig off the young woman's head and examined it. "I think this is the way it goes." She dragged it down on Isabelle's head. "There." She stood back to examine the effect.

While Isabelle was no lightweight, the Father Christmas costume she wore hung on her in dismal folds of red velvet. Her boots must have been borrowed from the same source, since they flopped up and down as she walked, making a horrible squeaking noise. "You need a pillow inside that coat," Cecily observed.

"Oh!" Isabelle's face lit up. "I knew I'd forgotten something." She flopped and squeaked her way across the room to where a pillow sat among a pile of props. After stuffing it inside her coat, she clasped a large belt around her middle. Then she looked at Cecily for approval, patting her padded stomach.

Cecily thought she looked more like a badly dressed expectant mother than Father Christmas, but kept her opinion to herself.

Instead, she nodded her approval, just as Phoebe called out, "Cecily! Can you get these pesky buttons buttoned for me? Thank you!"

At last the women were ready. Phoebe ushered them all into the wings, then went out into the lights amidst thunderous applause to announce her revue.

The string quartet had agreed to play for the presentation, and was seated in front of the stage at floor level. Phoebe was careful to stand well back so that absolutely no one would catch a glimpse of something they shouldn't.

She made her announcement and sailed back to the wings, while her troupe trudged out to face the expectant audience.

Arriving back at Cecily's side, she puffed and patted her chest. "Now all I have to do is pray they won't do something dreadful. Actually, the rehearsal went rather well, so perhaps this will be one revue that won't end in a fiasco."

"I'm sure everything will be just fine." Cecily smiled at her friend. "I'm going out to the front to enjoy the show. Will you come with me, or do you prefer to stay here in the wings?"

"Oh, goodness, I wouldn't dare to leave now. Those silly women can never remember which song comes next, and I need to be here so I can prompt them."

"Of course. Then I shall see you after the revue." With a sigh of relief, Cecily returned to the ballroom and found an empty chair at the rear of the room.

Madeline had organized the footmen to construct the scenery for the stage and they had done an excellent job. The backdrop of a winter scene, with its skaters on a pond, snow-covered cottage, and a snowman, looked quite professional.

Fake trees stood on either side of a full-size gingerbread

house with a white picket fence. All very charming. Against the snowy background, the colorful costumes brightened the whole stage.

The audience seemed to enjoy the Christmas songs, and the dancers even managed to glide rather stiffly around each other without mishap. The finale drew some murmurs of appreciation as the dancers pulled a large Christmas tree onto the stage, which had been lavishly decorated by Madeline.

Dressed in red and green, the dancers gathered in front to sing the final song. The entrance of Father Christmas drew a round of applause, and Cecily was just thinking that Isabelle really didn't look quite so bedraggled from a distance when the inevitable happened.

As Isabelle swung her sack of toys over her shoulder, the pillow under her coat slipped and fell to her feet. In her haste to grab hold of it, she dropped the sack on the foot of the dancer next to her. The irate woman let out a yell and hopped backward. Straight into the Christmas tree.

Cecily held her breath as the heavily laden tree wobbled back and forth, while everyone on stage stared at it in horror. For a breathless moment it seemed it might right itself, but then, in excruciating slow motion, it crashed to the floor.

The tinkling of broken glass mingled with the cries from the stage could be heard, while a tide of discreet titters swept through the audience.

All might have been saved if the dancers had simply ignored the tree and finished their final song. Instead, they scrambled to get off the stage, jostling each other in their haste. Someone's elbow caught one of the fake firs, and it fell into the next one. The domino effect ended with a thunderous crash as the gingerbread house toppled to the ground.

The dancers fled, all but one, who stood in the middle of the carnage and bawled. Someone in the front row of the audience began clapping, and soon everyone was on their feet, applauding and cheering with great gusto.

Knowing how devastated Phoebe would be, Cecily jumped to her feet, intent on getting backstage to console her. Before she could move, however, Phoebe rushed out to the middle of the stage, holding up her hands for silence.

Gradually the applause died down and the audience took their seats once more. With great dignity, Phoebe stepped forward.

Cecily never heard what she said. The stage lights had reflected on the silver brooch Phoebe wore, flashing bright as she gestured with her hands.

It was then that Cecily remembered where she had heard about a silver fox. Colonel Fortescue's words came back to her as clearly as if he spoke them beside her. *We're going to hunt for another silver fox, aren't we, my little pet?* And Phoebe's answer. *Dressed up in riding clothes, I suppose.*

The colonel hadn't been chasing a fox that day in the woods. He'd found one. The silver brooch that Phoebe now wore. What else was it he'd said?

She frowned, trying to remember what it was the colonel had mumbled, just before she'd left to return to her office. A moment later she was on her way backstage again. She had no idea where the colonel was now, but she intended to find him and speak to him. Just as soon as possible.

CHAPTER

❈15❈

It was some time before Cecily could corner Phoebe and discreetly ask for the whereabouts of her husband. The upheaval before the revue was minuscule compared to the chaos ensuing backstage afterward.

Dancers milled about, heatedly arguing with each other over whose fault it was that the set was ruined. Some cried, others yelled, while Phoebe rushed around soothing and chastising at the same time.

Isabelle, minus her wig and pillow, stood in the middle of the fracas, waving her arms around like a windmill. "It weren't my fault!" she screamed. "It was Elsie! She was the one what knocked over the Christmas tree. Stop blaming me for everything!" She stamped her foot in temper, and her capacious Father Christmas trousers slid to her ankles.

Phoebe shrieked and rushed to help her pull them up again, much to the amusement of her entourage, most of whom had miraculously regained their sense of humor.

While Phoebe attempted to restore order, Cecily supervised the cleanup onstage. Finally, when the last entertainers had dispersed, Cecily found Phoebe in the act of mopping her brow with a dainty lace-edged handkerchief.

She did so without removing her hat, which somewhat limited the effect. Then again, Phoebe never removed her hat in public. The speculation among the less charitable of her acquaintances was that she was bald and wore a wig. Only Cecily knew if that were true, and she wasn't about to satisfy anyone's curiosity.

"Did your husband accompany you this evening?" Cecily asked, as the two of them entered the ballroom.

Phoebe looked surprised at the question. "Yes, he did. As far as the bar, that is. He's probably still there, since I don't see him anywhere in here." She gazed around the ballroom with an annoyed frown. "He promised me he would watch the performance. Drat the man. I should have known better than to leave him alone in the bar."

"Perhaps he saw the revue then returned to the bar," Cecily murmured. It was a futile hope, of course. She wouldn't get much sense out of him if he were in his usual inebriated state. Her questioning might have to wait until tomorrow.

"I suppose I'll have to go in there and drag him out." Phoebe's tone suggested she'd give the errant colonel a rather large piece of her mind, as well.

"I should like to speak with him, if you don't mind." Cecily grasped Phoebe's elbow and guided her with unladylike speed across the floor to the doors.

"I say," Phoebe protested, when they emerged into the hallway. "You must be in a dreadful hurry. I didn't even have time to exchange comments with my audience."

Which was exactly what Cecily was hoping to avoid. Having enjoyed a fair amount of liquid refreshment before and during the review, many members of Phoebe's audience might well forget to be tactful in their appraisal of the evening's performance.

"I'm sorry, Phoebe." Cecily let go of her arm. "I would like to have a word with your husband before you leave."

"Well, it must be important, that's all I can say." Phoebe peered up at her, her face creased in concern. "He didn't do something awful while I was backstage, did he?"

"Not as far as I know."

Phoebe let out her breath. "Thank goodness. You never know with dear Frederick. He means well, of course. Don't they all? He does, however, have a tiny little problem with . . ." She paused, then leaned in closer to Cecily and whispered, "Language, if you know what I mean. Military, you know. They used a lot of colorful language while fighting in that dreadful Boer War. Some of it rubbed off on him, poor dear."

It was Cecily's considered opinion that bad language was the least of the colonel's problems, but she refrained from pointing that out. "Well, I'm sure we'll find him on his best behavior, entertaining the guests with his war stories."

"Oh, great heavens, let us sincerely hope not."

They reached the door of the bar, just as a group of men was leaving. From inside, the colonel's hearty guffaw could be heard above everyone else. "Oh, dear," Phoebe said, twisting her gloved hands together. "I can't go in there unescorted, but how am I going to catch his attention?"

"Fortunately," Cecily told her, "as manager, it is not considered improper for me to enter there alone."

Since Phoebe was well aware of this fact, Cecily didn't wait for an answer, but promptly walked into the bar, leaving her friend fluttering outside.

The colonel sat at a table with two other men, both of whom looked as if they'd like to escape but didn't quite know how. They all sprang to their feet as Cecily approached. At least, the two guests sprang. The colonel heaved himself off his chair, fell back down, grunted, then leaned his hands on the table to lever himself upward.

The table rocked back and forth, sending a snifter toppling on its side. Fortunately it was empty, but Fortescue picked it up, looked at it and muttered, "By Jove, there goes another good drop of wallop down the drain."

He peered in Cecily's direction, focused on her face for a second or two, then announced, "There you are, old bean. What have you done with the Pennyfoot? Put her out to shee? She's heaving like the deck of a shchooner in a howling gale, what? What?"

The two men gave Cecily sheepish looks. "I'm afraid he's a bit under the weather, madam," one of them said.

Recognizing the men, Cecily nodded. "Good evening, Sir Harold. Sir William, how nice to see you again."

The men in turn bowed and kissed her hand. "Do you

need a hand with this gentleman?" Sir William asked, glancing doubtfully at the colonel. "Rather a handful, I'm afraid."

The colonel beamed in response and waved the empty glass at them. "Bottoms up, old girl!" He lifted the glass to his lips, tilted it, frowned, tipped the glass upside down and shook his head. "Dashed if I remember drinking all that," he muttered.

"Thank you," Cecily assured the two anxious men. "But I'll see the colonel leaves safely. His wife is waiting for him outside."

The men left, obviously wary about leaving her to deal with the tipsy colonel.

Fortescue's gaze wandered in her direction. "Sit down, old bean. Wanna drink?" He held up his hand to catch the eye of the barman.

"Thank you, no, Colonel," Cecily said hastily. She took a seat at the table, knowing the colonel would remain on his feet, however hazardous that might be for him, until she sat down.

With a look of vast relief, Fortescue fell back down on his chair. "Hope we're putting into port soon, Mrs. B. Getting a bit nasty out there, what? What? Not good on the old tummy."

"We're already in port," Cecily assured him, hoping that might steady him a little. She felt reasonably sure she'd be wasting her time by questioning him while he was in this state, but she had to try. "I saw the brooch you gave your wife for Christmas," she added. "It's very unusual. If you don't mind me asking, where did you get it?"

The colonel swayed back and forth, his eyes red rimmed and glazed. "Brooch? What brooch was that, then?"

"The silver fox, dressed in riding clothes." She'd deliberately used the same words he'd used, hoping it would jog his memory.

Anxiously she waited, while he digested her answer. "Ah, yes! I remember! Furry little chap with a hunting jacket. Dashed adorable, I thought, what? What?"

"Quite, Colonel." Cecily paused, then added carefully, "Do you remember where you found it?"

"Found it?" He sounded scandalized, and for a moment Cecily thought he would deny it, but then he leaned forward, one finger trying valiantly to find the side of his nose. "Shecret, old girl."

Cecily leaned forward, too, trying not to breathe in the alcoholic fumes seeping from the colonel's mouth. "You can tell me, Colonel. I promise I won't tell."

He sat there staring at her for so long with that glassy expression she was afraid he'd fallen asleep with his eyes open. Then he said abruptly, "Oh, very well. If you inshisht. I found it in the woods. Didn't tell the li'l lady, though. She thinks I bought it in Harrods."

"I wouldn't dream of telling her otherwise." She sat back, before she was overcome by his brandy-laced breath. "You mentioned that you heard someone singing in the woods where you found the brooch, did you not?"

He frowned, trying to thread his way through his addled brain. "I did? Can't imagine why I'd say that, old girl. I don't remember hearing shinging. Not at all. No, sir. Oh, wait a minute!"

She waited patiently through another few seconds of glazed staring until he burped, and put his hand over his mouth. "Shorry, old girl. No, it wasn't singing. Not at all. I said I saw someone *swinging*. Up in a tree." He looked inordinately proud as he puffed out his chest. "Dashed good memory, that, what? What?"

"Very," Cecily solemnly agreed. "Who did you say was swinging in a tree?"

Wrinkles appeared in the colonel's forehead. "Blasted strange, that was. Some chappy it was, swinging from a branch. Right above where I found the fox thingy. Thought it was a monkey. Saw a lot of them in India, you know. I remember the time—"

"Fred-er-ick!" Phoebe's voice carried clearly across the room. Loud enough to hush the conversation of everyone in the room.

Fortescue looked startled. "Good Lord! Did you hear what I heard?"

Cecily rose, forcing the colonel to stagger once more to his feet. "Your wife is getting tired of waiting for you, I'm afraid."

"My *wife*?" He blinked rapidly in the direction of the door. "What on earth is she doing at sea? I don't remember bringing her aboard."

"You're not at sea." Cecily laid a hand on his arm. "I'd be honored, Colonel, if you would escort me to the door."

Her appeal to his sense of chivalry worked wonders. His eyelids stopped flapping, he straightened his shoulders and stuck out his elbow. "My pleasure. Yes, indeed, madam. My distinct pleasure." And with that, they made somewhat unsteady progress to the door.

Phoebe pounced on her husband the minute he was outside in the passageway. "Look at you, Frederick. I can't leave you alone for a moment. Why can't you simply have a drink and leave, like everyone else?"

"Drink?" The colonel swayed, then righted himself. "Who shays I've been drinking? Who's the cad shpreading ugly rumors about me? I'll challenge him to a duel, by George. Where is he?" He spun around too fast, and would have lost his footing if both Cecily and Phoebe had not grabbed hold of him.

"I think you'd better take him home," Cecily murmured. "I'll have one of the footman bring up a carriage."

"Awfully kind of you, Cecily." Phoebe took a firmer hold of her husband. "Come along, Frederick. We'll wait outside. The fresh air will do you good." With a wave of her hand, she led her stumbling husband down the hallway to the lobby.

Cecily waited until the door closed behind them before hurrying up the stairs to her own husband. Well pleased with her success with the colonel, she ran their conversation over again in her mind.

Now she understood why the killer had come back after leaving the body hanging in the woods. The brooch must have been dropped when Gavin Hargrove was murdered. The colonel found it when he went for his morning walk in the woods and picked it up, catching sight of the body at the same time.

Later, the killer, realizing the brooch was missing and that it could lead to his identity, must have come back to look for it and ran into Baxter and Samuel. Probably left them both for dead.

All she had to do now was find the owner of the brooch. One thing seemed obvious. It would appear that the person who'd strangled Gavin Hargrove, and attacked and left for dead her husband and stable manager, was either a woman, or the killer had a female companion. Either way, she knew exactly where to start asking questions.

Early the next morning Kevin Prestwick stopped by to see Baxter. He brought with him a pair of crutches, which Baxter eyed with disgust. "If you want to get out of that armchair," the doctor told him, "this is your only alternative."

Cecily watched anxiously as her husband attempted to navigate the boudoir carpet with the clumsy apparatus. When he stumbled she uttered a cry of dismay.

Kevin caught him deftly by the arm and steadied him. "Don't worry, old chap," he said cheerfully, "you'll soon get the hang of it."

Baxter's expression suggested he'd like to wrap both crutches around Kevin's neck, but he managed a halfway-civil nod. "Thank you," he muttered.

"Not at all, old boy."

Seeing Baxter's scowl, Cecily decided it was time to intervene. "Thank you, Kevin," she said, hurrying forward to take her husband's arm. "We'll practice for a little bit before venturing out into the corridor."

Kevin looked at her, doubt written all over his face. "Just don't try the stairs without help. That can be a little tricky."

"Don't worry. I'll have Samuel give us a hand to get downstairs."

"I don't need a hand." Baxter jerked the crutches out in front of him, then swung himself forward in between them.

He used a little more momentum than necessary and landed ahead of the crutches, tottered backward and again was saved from a fall by Kevin's quick action.

"Slow and steady, that's the secret," Kevin said. He took the crutches from him, helped him hop back to his chair and sat him down. "Look, it's like this." With remarkable grace he swung himself effortlessly around the room. "It's rather fun once you get the hang of it," he said, handing the crutches back to Baxter.

Baxter gritted his teeth in a sinister smile. "I appreciate the lesson, old boy, but I assure you I can manage quite well without all this tutoring."

Cecily gave Kevin a worried look. She'd heard the sarcasm in her husband's voice, even if Kevin hadn't. "I think you'd better go," she said, softening her words with an expansive smile. "I'll see that he's careful."

"Very well." Kevin picked up his hat from the sofa and headed for the door. "Let me know if he has any trouble."

Thankfully, Cecily closed the door behind him, and turned to find Baxter struggling out of his chair.

"Dratted fool," Baxter muttered, as he balanced himself on one foot. "Thinks he knows everything."

"Well, he has had experience with crutches and he is a doctor, after all. He's supposed to offer advice. That's why he was here."

"I didn't ask him to come." Baxter hopped across the room to the window and looked out.

Cecily felt a twinge of sympathy for him. Baxter was a proud and independent man. Having to suffer the indignity of relying on the help of others to get around would sorely try him. She could not, however, let him wallow in self-pity. "Do try not to be difficult, my love," she said, as she walked up behind him. "I know this is hard for you, but you must know we are only trying to help."

"I know, I know." Baxter let out a long suffering sigh. "It's just dashed bad timing, that's all. I just wish I knew who did this. I'd see he paid for it. Dearly."

"Well, perhaps we'll know more once Sam Northcott gets back. Once we tell him what's been happening, I'm sure he'll launch another investigation."

"Don't count on it. That simpleton wouldn't know where to start. Besides, didn't you say he'd handed the case over to Scotland Yard?"

"Well, yes, but—"

"Well, then, he'll simply wash his hands of the whole thing. It's Christmas. You know Northcott. He never lets anything interfere with his own enjoyment."

She was very much afraid that Baxter was right. Meanwhile Scotland Yard would be wasting time investigating the gambling syndicate. By the time they decided to examine the case more thoroughly, the killer could have already attacked someone else she cared about.

Which meant that it was up to her to find out who was responsible for all these attacks. She would have to carry on without the help of her wounded husband. More importantly, she would need to keep her activities a secret from him. For if Baxter knew she was still investigating the murder, he would do everything in his power to convince her to stop. And something told her that there was no time to waste.

CHAPTER

❁ 16 ❁

Gertie had barely finished stacking the clean breakfast dishes back in their cupboards when Pansy rushed into the kitchen, her cheeks flushed with exertion.

"I just saw Daisy upstairs," she said, flapping a hand in front of her face to cool it. "She has your twins with her. Says she's got to see you right away."

"Flipping heck." Gertie shut the cupboard door with a loud smack. "Now what's up?"

"She didn't look too happy." Pansy walked over to the sink and turned on the tap. "The kiddies were running about and she had a hard time keeping them quiet. Philip was getting really upset. You know how he is about the staff making a noise in the lobby."

"Well, the twins are not exactly staff, now are they." Gertie watched Pansy splash cold water on her face. "Here, what're you all hot and bothered about, anyway?"

Pansy dabbed her face with her apron. "I just ran all the way down the stairs from the top floor, didn't I"

"What for?"

Pansy shrugged. "I was trying to catch up with Samuel. I saw him coming across the courtyard from a window and I wanted to talk to him. By the time I got down there, though, he'd disappeared. He must be in madam's office, or something. I've looked everywhere else."

Gertie eyed her curiously. "Must be important."

Pansy turned her face away. "Not really."

"Go on. You can tell me. I won't say nothing to nobody. Honest."

Pansy's voice sounded muffled as she pretended to hunt for something in a drawer. "I just wanted to ask him what he was doing tonight, that's all. Seeing as how we all got some time off, I thought if I gave him enough hints he might ask me to go out with him."

Gertie raised her eyebrows. "Oo, like that, is it? You're sweet on Samuel?"

"Not really." She turned a defiant face to Gertie. "I just like talking to him, that's all."

"Well, I wish you luck. Samuel's a good bloke and all that, but he's fussy about who he keeps company with. I haven't seen him with a lady friend in ages."

"I know. That's why I thought—" She broke off. "Oh, never mind. He probably wouldn't want to go out with me, anyway."

Gertie grinned. "You'll never know unless you ask."

"Ladies don't ask gents to go out with them. We have to wait to be asked."

"Then you could wait forever. You could ask him without him knowing you were asking."

Pansy wrinkled her brow. "How do I do that?"

Gertie sighed. "I don't have time to talk about it now. I have to go and see what the matter is with Daisy and my kids. If I get time, I'll talk to you later about it."

Pansy didn't look too happy. "Well, all right, but don't wait too long. The day will be gone before we know it."

"Don't I know it." Gertie swung out of the door and into the hallway. She'd like to see Pansy and Samuel get together. They were both good people, and it would be nice if they ended up sweethearts. She supposed she was a silly romantic at heart. At least for other people.

Trudging up the stairs, she allowed herself to think about Ross for a moment. The gentle Scotsman had been a wonderful husband. Although a good many years older than she, he'd really cared for her and the twins, taking them back to Scotland with him and working hard at his business so that they'd all have a good life.

She still missed him at times, although thinking back over her marriage, she couldn't really say she'd been madly in love with Ross McBride. He'd come along at a time when she was feeling lonely and unloved, and he'd made her feel good about herself again.

Reaching the top of the stairs, she smiled to herself. They had some good times together, though, and she'd always be grateful for the way he'd taken the twins into his life and been a father to them for a little while. Not many men would be willing to do that.

Which, she told herself without pity, was why she'd remain unmarried for the rest of her life. Not that she regretted that for one minute. She had the twins, and they were everything to her. She wouldn't swap them for a husband if he were the richest, kindest, most handsome man in the world.

She could hear the voices of her offspring the minute she stepped into the foyer. James was the loudest, screeching like a scalded cat as he tore around and around in a circle, his coat flapping behind him like giant wings.

Lillian stood by the Christmas tree, howling at the top of her voice while angry tears ran down her face. Daisy stood over her, talking earnestly to the child who seemed determined to drown out Daisy's words with her sobs.

Cursing fiercely under her breath, Gertie rushed over to them. As she passed James she hooked her fingers in his coat and dragged him off his feet, hauling him struggling and yelling over to where Daisy now stood looking helplessly at her.

"I'm sorry, Gertie." Daisy tucked stray strands of hair from her forehead under her hat. "I've tried everything and I just can't do anything with them. I thought I'd give them a breath of fresh air, but Lillian wants to go and James refuses to go with us and I can't leave him here alone."

James uttered another loud shriek and Gertie cuffed him over the ear. His loud howl of outrage almost shattered her eardrums. Lillian stopped crying, but stood there sniffling and wiping her nose with her hand.

Gertie raised her voice. "Both of you, listen to me. You're ten years old now and should know better. One more sound out of either of you and I'll tell Father Christmas not to leave you any toys this year. Not only that, you'll spend Christmas in the bloody coalhole. Both of you."

James clamped his mouth shut but continued to struggle against the hold she had on his coat. Lillian whimpered, then fell silent under Gertie's threatening glare.

"That's better." Gertie smiled at Daisy. "They're excited about it being Christmas," she said. "Look, I've got an hour or so to spare. I'll take them out for a walk and you can have a rest. You look like you need one."

Daisy looked as if she were about to hug her. "Are you sure? I know they're being a handful but usually I can cope. It's just that I just talked to Doris on the telephone. She's found out she's having a baby and she wants me to go up to London to see her after Christmas. It put me in such a dither I can't think of anything else right now and—"

"Doris is having a baby!" Gertie's grin spread all over her face. "Wait until I tell Mrs. Chubb! Our little Doris. I can't believe it."

Daisy shook her head. "Neither can I. Which is why things got out of hand this morning." She patted Lillian's head. "I guess we're all overexcited."

"Well, just wait with them a minute while I get my coat and hat and I'll take them for a walk." Still grinning, Gertie sped away. She couldn't imagine fragile little Doris with a baby, but she couldn't be happier for her.

And if that happiness was marred by just a touch of envy, Gertie wasn't about to admit it. She had her twins, and a good home for all of them at the Pennyfoot. That was all she needed or wanted. Wasn't it?

"Hold on, Mr. Baxter," Samuel said, his words punctuated by gasping breaths, "you've got to take it a little slower down these stairs. You'll have us both tumbling to the bottom if you go too fast."

"Really, Baxter," Cecily said, following anxiously behind them, "for heaven's sake take your time. You have all day."

"I want to get to the office before anyone sees me like this." Baxter grunted as he swung down another stair.

Behind his back, Samuel rolled his eyes at Cecily. "All right, sir, but you're going to look a lot more undignified if you land on your arse."

"Watch your tongue, young man!" Grumbling and grunting, Baxter made his way down the stairs.

Cecily had to admit, he managed the crutches much better than she'd expected. It seemed he'd be able to get around on them after all. Which meant she had time to carry out her own plans.

"I have some errands to run," she said, when she had him settled in the office. "I've asked Gertie to look in on you in an hour or so in case you want something to eat or drink."

He stared at her in suspicion. "Where are you going?"

Playfully she patted his cheek. "You know better than to ask that on Christmas Eve."

"I thought we agreed that you would stay indoors until this murderer was apprehended."

"You agreed. I didn't." She headed for the door. I shall be

perfectly safe in the High Street. No one is going to attack me there in front of everyone. In any case, I shan't be too long. Just don't try to get up the stairs until Samuel and I come back. Promise me?"

"You're taking Samuel?"

"I prefer that he drive the carriage. Some of those young footmen go too fast for my taste."

To her relief he accepted that, and she left him with another assurance that she would be home again as soon as possible.

"We have to call on Phoebe," she told Samuel, as he helped her into the carriage later. "Then we're going to Whitfield Manor."

Samuel looked at her in alarm. "Are you sure you should be doing that, m'm? What did Mr. Baxter say about it?"

"What Mr. Baxter doesn't know won't hurt him." She smiled at him. "Don't worry. We'll be careful, and I doubt whoever attacked us will try again while we are on the premises of the manor."

"I certainly hope you're right, m'm." Samuel closed the door and she leaned back in her seat. Much as she hated to admit it, she had a certain amount of trepidation about the wisdom of continuing the investigation.

She was convinced that whoever killed Gavin Hargrove was someone from the manor, and every time she walked in there she was putting herself and Samuel in danger. Yet she could not ignore such a significant clue as the silver fox brooch. If she could find the owner of that, she would know the identity of the killer, and could then go to the constabulary and convince Northcott to arrest him. Or her. Or them.

The possibility that two people were involved did nothing to alleviate her apprehension. Then again, she had Samuel with her. As long as they kept their wits about them, she assured herself, no harm would become them.

She could only hope her convictions were justified.

Phoebe appeared both pleased and surprised when she opened the door to Cecily a few minutes later. Speaking softly, she drew her inside.

"The colonel's asleep upstairs. He's feeling a little under the weather this morning."

Cecily could well believe that. Also keeping her voice low, she said, "I haven't time to stay. I came to ask a favor of you."

Phoebe looked disappointed. "You have time for a cup of tea and a bun? I just brought some back from Dolly's tea shop. You know her delicious currant buns are irresistible. Surely you must have just one?"

Cecily's mouth watered at the thought, but quickly she shook her head. "No, really, Phoebe, I can't. It's Christmas Eve and I have a hundred things I have to do."

"Quite." Phoebe sighed. "Very well, then what is it you want to ask me?"

Cecily hesitated. "This is going to sound rather odd," she said at last. "But I'd like to borrow the silver fox brooch the colonel gave you. Just for a few hours," she added hastily, when she saw the doubt on her friend's face.

"Why on earth would you want to borrow that?" Phoebe looked perplexed. "You already have such wonderful jewelry to wear."

"Actually, I would like to find something similar to buy Mrs. Chubb for her Christmas present. I thought if I could show the brooch to the shopkeeper, she'd know exactly what I was looking for." She had rehearsed the lie over and over on the way to Phoebe's house, but now that she'd actually said the words they sounded utterly unconvincing.

Fortunately, Phoebe was not the most discerning person in the world. Her frown cleared at once. "Of course, Cecily dear. I'll fetch it for you. I'm flattered that you like it so much. My husband has excellent taste, does he not?"

"Impeccable," Cecily agreed, on a sigh of relief.

She waited while Phoebe crept up the stairs, then returned a minute or so later, the brooch in her hand. "I know you'll take care of it," she said, handing it over. "It means a great deal to me. Though if you ask me, it's much too good for the likes of Mrs. Chubb. I hope you find a far less expensive version."

Cecily suppressed a twinge of guilt as she took the brooch and slipped it into her pocket. If it did, indeed, belong to the killer's accomplice, or worse, the killer herself, then it was unlikely Phoebe would get the brooch back. What's more, the colonel's secret would likely be revealed.

That was something she'd have to worry about later, she decided. The important thing was to find the killer and have him arrested, before he could strike again.

She grew increasingly uneasy as they drew close to the manor. Perhaps she had been a little imprudent, taking such a risk. She wondered what Baxter would do, should something happen to her.

Who would take care of him, see that he ate proper meals

and got enough sleep? Who would chide him when he worked himself up in a temper, and soothe his brow when his business worries got the better of him?

She envisioned him standing by her grave, alone and grieving, and almost came to tears herself. Then she scolded herself for her macabre imagination. As long as she remained vigilant, nothing so drastic would happen to them. She kept telling herself that over and over, until once more the carriage rolled up the drive to Whitfield Manor.

She was both surprised and relieved when the door was opened by Mrs. Trumble. "Wilmot is indisposed," the housekeeper told her, when Cecily inquired as to his whereabouts. "Quite a nasty cold he's got."

Though Cecily would not wish an illness on anyone, she was nevertheless happy to be dealing with the housekeeper, rather than the sour-faced butler. She didn't like the way he hovered around or appeared out of nowhere like a ghost materializing out of the shadows. "I would like to speak with Miss Kendall, if I may," she said, glancing around the lobby just in case Wilmot had somehow recovered enough to investigate the visitors.

Samuel stood a little behind her, twisting his cap in his hands in a way that told Cecily he was as unsettled by this visit as she was.

"I'll see if she's accepting company," Mrs. Trumble said.

She was about to turn away when Cecily said quickly, "Before you leave, Mrs. Trumble, if you have a minute. I have something to show you." She fished the brooch out of her pocket and held it out to the housekeeper. "I was wondering if you recognize this brooch. Samuel picked it up at the end of the driveway. It's such a lovely piece, and we thought it might belong to someone at the manor."

The housekeeper took it from her and turned it over in her palm. She seemed to study it at great length before handing it back with a shake of her head. "Never seen it before, m'm. It doesn't belong to anyone here, as far as I know."

Disappointed, Cecily took it from her. "Well, thank you, Mrs. Trumble. If you wouldn't mind telling Miss Kendall I'm here to see her?"

"Of course, m'm. Right away." After one last glance at the brooch in Cecily's hand, the housekeeper shuffled off down the hallway.

"I didn't see you pick up no brooch," Samuel whispered, when the housekeeper was out of earshot.

"I didn't." Cecily laid a finger against her lips. "Colonel Fortescue found it in the woods, close to where Gavin Hargrove was hanging."

Samuel's eyes widened. "He saw the body?"

"Yes, he did. Apparently he didn't think it was worth mentioning to anyone until I asked him about it."

"Probably thought the bloke was hanging there for fun." He shook his head. "So you think the killer dropped the brooch?"

"Yes, I do." Cecily glanced down the hallway. "I'm hoping Miss Kendall will recognize it."

"Even if she does," Samuel said, following her gaze, "she's not likely to tell you, is she."

"Unless she saw it on someone else."

"Ah!" His face brightened. "So you don't think Miss Kendall killed her fiancé?"

"No, I don't. Though it's still possible she was there." She looked intently at Samuel. "I know you don't remember much about the person who attacked you, but was it possible there were two people in the trap that day?"

Samuel's forehead creased in a frown. "I . . . don't think so. I only remember one, but it's still all hazy. I do know there was only one in the trap the second time."

She was about to answer when Mrs. Trumble spoke from the hallway, making her jump.

"Miss Kendall will see you now, Mrs. Baxter."

Nodding a warning at Samuel, Cecily followed the housekeeper down the hallway to the sitting room.

As she entered the room, a tall figure unfolded himself from the armchair and walked toward her. "Mrs. Baxter, this is a most pleasant surprise."

Randall Thorpe's smile did not reflect in his eyes as he bent over Cecily's hand. "To what do we owe this unexpected visit?"

Cecily glanced at Naomi, who sat unsmiling by the fire. For a second or two Cecily thought she saw fear on the young woman's face, but then she turned away to stare into the flickering flames.

Unsettled by the unforeseen presence of Randall, Cecily did her best to subdue her misgivings. She had counted on him being occupied with business matters, but it seemed she would have to discuss the brooch in his presence.

Which would certainly alert him to the fact that she was still pursuing the identity of Gavin Hargrove's killer. Not a comforting thought, considering everything that had happened the past couple of days.

CHAPTER
✿ 17 ✿

The wind off the ocean froze Gertie's lips and brought tears
to her eyes. Although the sun filtered through fluffy white
clouds, farther out to sea a thick band of black sky heralded
another storm.

It would probably snow again, Gertie thought, as she
trudged along the Esplanade, holding a small hand in each
of hers. Lillian seemed subdued now, though James skipped
about, tugging and pulling until Gertie jerked him back
with a sharp warning.

"What did I tell you? Behave or it's the coalhole for you."

"When is Father Christmas coming?" he demanded.

Gertie sighed. "I've told you until I'm blue in the face.
He's coming tonight. But only if you're really, really good
and only after you're both fast asleep in your beds. So you'd

better do as you're told for the rest of the day if you want to see toys in your pillowcases tomorrow morning."

"Father Christmas is coming tonight, Father Christmas is coming tonight, Father Christmas is coming tonight!" Chanting happily to himself James hopped and skipped along by her side.

Gertie looked down at Lillian, who was chewing on the thumb of her mitten. Her little face looked pinched with the cold, and Gertie felt sorry for her. "We'll just go to the end of the Esplanade and back," she told her. "Then when we get back I'll ask Mrs. Chubb to make us a cup of hot cocoa."

James cheered, but Lillian just went on plodding along by her side, tugging at the mitten with her teeth.

Gertie stopped. "What's the matter now?" She bent down to look in the little girl's face. "It's Christmas Eve. You should be happy. Father Christmas is coming."

Lillian's eyes filled with tears. "I want Daddy to come, too."

Gertie felt a pang of remorse. What a terrible mother she was not to realize the children would miss their father. Well, maybe James didn't. He didn't let much bother him. But Lillian was like her mother. She got silly over things like that.

Letting go of James's hand, she put her arms around the little girl. "I know you miss Daddy, Lilly, but you know he's gone to heaven and he can't come back."

"Why not?"

"Because it's too far, that's why not." Gertie's heart ached for her. "But he can see you, and he wants you to be happy and smiling. You want Daddy to enjoy his Christmas, too, don't you?"

Lillian nodded.

"Well, then, we have to show him we're happy and excited about Christmas and then he will be, too. He—" She broke off as a loud shout was followed almost immediately by the screeching sound of a motorcar's brakes.

Gertie swung around, and let out a shriek of horror. Her son stood in the middle of the street, frozen in shock, just inches from the bonnet of a motorcar. Coming the other way at a fast clip was a horse and carriage, and she started forward, terrified James would dart out in front of those flying hooves.

As she reached the edge of the curb, a man in a dark blue coat leapt out from behind the wheel of the car, ran around to the front and scooped up James.

After a quick look each way, he strode toward Gertie, carrying the struggling boy under his arm. It wasn't until he deposited him at Gertie's feet that she recognized her son's savior.

Dan Perkins looked down at her, his face grim. "Is this yours?"

And, once again, Gertie had no answer.

"I came to have a word with Miss Kendall," Cecily said, nodding in the direction of the young lady. "I apologize if I'm intruding."

"Not at all." Randall gestured at the chair he'd vacated. "I thought perhaps you had changed your mind about attending the funeral."

Cecily cursed herself for her wayward memory. "Of course. The funeral. It is this afternoon."

"Yes, it is." Randall's dark gaze probed her face, waiting for her to continue.

Cecily glanced once more at Naomi, who now sat looking at her with an expectant air. The idea of asking her about the brooch with Randall hovering over them was unsettling. Unfortunately, there was no Madeline to help get rid of him this time.

Deciding she had no other choice, Cecily dipped into her pocket for the brooch. Carrying it over to Naomi, she repeated the story she'd given Mrs. Trumble. "I thought it might belong to someone here in the manor," she said, smiling pleasantly at Randall, who still watched her with his sharp gaze.

Naomi seemed listless as she took the brooch and examined it. After a moment or two she shook her head. "I'm sorry, I don't know who it belongs to," she said. She raised her head, and her eyes met Cecily's with a clear message in them.

Taking back the brooch, Cecily murmured, "Thank you, Miss Kendall. I'm sorry to have bothered you on such a sad day. I sincerely wish you well at the funeral this afternoon. Please accept my regrets at your loss."

Naomi bowed her head. "Thank you," she said, her voice barely above a whisper.

Withdrawing from the fire, Cecily smiled at Randall. "I won't intrude on your privacy any longer. While it seems inappropriate to wish you a happy Christmas, I trust tomorrow will bring you a measure of peace."

Randall nodded gravely. "Thank you, Mrs. Baxter. Now may I escort you to the door?"

He took her arm, and Cecily jumped violently when the door opened before they got there, revealing Wilmot standing on the threshold. Apparently he'd recovered enough to resume his duties. If Randall had summoned him with a bell, she had neither seen him do so, nor heard the sound of it.

"Good day, Mrs. Baxter." Randall nodded at Samuel. "Thank you for calling."

"Our pleasure," Cecily said graciously. She walked out into the hallway, with Samuel right behind her. Together they followed Wilmot to the front doors.

His silence was intimidating, though his red nose and watery eyes suggested that rather than sound undignified he'd prefer not to speak at all.

The door had barely closed behind them when Samuel muttered, "I don't like that Randall Thorpe. Something about him gives me the willies. Wouldn't surprise me at all if he'd bumped off his cousin to get all the money."

"It certainly is a strong motive," Cecily agreed.

"Do you think Miss Kendall was lying about the brooch?" Samuel led the way down the steps, watching her with one eye to make sure she didn't trip. "She had a funny look on her face when she looked at it."

"Yes," Cecily murmured. "I noticed that, too. I wonder—?" She broke off as the front door opened up behind her. Turning, she saw Naomi appear at the top of the stairs.

"Mrs. Baxter!" she called out, and ran lightly down the steps toward her.

Cecily waited, not in the least surprised to see her. She had known right away that Naomi had something she badly wanted to tell her, and that she did not want to say it in front of Randall Thorpe.

Now she could hardly wait to hear what it was that Naomi felt was so important.

Reaching the bottom, Naomi looked back at the door over her shoulder. "About the brooch," she said, her voice low and hurried. "I think I've seen it somewhere before, but I don't remember where. That fox design is distinctive. I remember thinking how charming it looked. I'm sure it belongs to someone I've met. I just don't remember who."

Cecily nodded. "Well, thank you, anyway, Miss Kendall. I appreciate you coming to tell me."

Naomi's smile was strained. "I don't suppose it has anything to do with Gavin's murder?"

Feigning surprise, Cecily raised her eyebrows. "Why would you think so?"

Naomi shrugged. "That's why you've been calling on us here, isn't it? To find out who killed Gavin? You didn't really find the brooch in the driveway, did you."

Samuel uttered a small sound of protest, while Cecily frowned.

Naomi sent another furtive glance up the steps behind her. "Look, all I'm saying is that it looks as if someone here in the manor killed Gavin. I won't sleep at night until he's locked up. So if there's anything I can do to help find out who he is, just tell me."

Cecily hesitated, then said quietly, "To be honest, I don't know if this brooch has anything to do with the murder or not." She took the brooch out of her pocket, watching it flash in the sunlight. "It was found near the body, and since the killer came back sometime after the murder, I assume he was looking for something that might incriminate him." She held up the brooch. "This."

It was Naomi's turn to frown. "But men don't wear brooches."

"Then either the killer was a woman, or he had an accomplice."

Naomi stared at her for long seconds. "Randall has been keeping company with a woman in the village. He denied it when I asked him about it, but I know he's lying. I've seen them together."

Trying to hide her eagerness, Cecily waited a moment before asking, "Do you know who she is?"

Once more she was disappointed when Naomi shook her head. "All I know is that she lives in the village, has dark hair, and dresses rather poorly. I'm not sure I'd even recognize her if I saw her again. Though Randall seemed to know her very well."

"Then I shall have to find her and ask if she has lost a brooch recently." Cecily slipped it back into her pocket. "Thank you for your help, Miss Kendall."

"Oh, please, do call me Naomi." She smiled at Cecily. "I feel as if we are beginning to know each other quite well." Her smile faded almost instantly. "I hope you find the killer before long, Mrs. Baxter."

"Please, try not to worry. You are quite safe as long as you don't ask too many questions."

Once more the fear appeared in Naomi's eyes. "I

shouldn't be seen talking to you. Be careful, Mrs. Baxter. I should hate to hear that something awful has happened to you." She glanced at Samuel. "You be careful, too, Samuel."

The young man blushed, and Cecily hid a smile. "I do hope your Christmas won't be too melancholy," Cecily said.

Naomi sighed. "I'll feel better once the funeral is over. Happy Christmas to both of you." She turned and ran up the steps, leaving both Samuel and Cecily staring after her.

"Come," Cecily said, as the door closed behind the young woman, "I must get back before Mr. Baxter starts worrying about me. I've been gone far too long as it is."

"Yes, m'm." Samuel opened the door of the carriage. "Right away, m'm."

Cecily climbed in and leaned back against the soft leather. She'd had such high hopes of finding out to whom the brooch belonged. She'd been so sure the owner was in the mansion. Now she had to look for a mysterious woman in the village.

One thing appeared certain. Naomi no longer seemed convinced that Randall Thorpe was innocent. In fact, if the fear in her eyes was anything to go by, Cecily sensed that Randall Thorpe was the cause. Naomi suspected Randall of killing Gavin Hargrove. It would seem, Cecily thought wryly, that she was back to square one.

"I just took my eyes off him for a flipping minute and he was gone." Gertie grabbed James to her and hugged him close. Looking up into Dan's concerned face, she felt like crying. "Thank you. He could have been killed out there."

"Yes, he could've." Dan looked down sternly into James's face. "What were you thinking, lad, running out in the street like that? Don't you know how much you frightened your mama? If I hadn't seen you coming and put on my brakes, I would have run right over you. Then there would have been no Christmas for you, my boy."

To Gertie's surprise, James looked suitably repentant. "Yes, sir," he mumbled.

"All right, then." Dan looked back at Gertie. "What about you? Are you all right, then?"

"Apart from the trembles I'll be all right." She gave James a little shake. "I could kill him, though."

Dan shook his head. "I think he's had enough fright to keep him quiet for a while." He looked back at his motorcar. "I'd better get back to it before someone runs a horse into it."

James tugged on his sleeve. "Mister? I like your motorcar."

Gertie had to agree. It was a lovely car. All blue and silver and shiny, like the pictures she'd seen in the magazines. "Is it new?"

"Two months old yesterday." Dan pulled his shoulders back in pride. "She's a beauty all right." He sent Gertie a sideways glance then smiled down at James. "How'd you like to come for a ride with me?"

James shouted his reply. "Yes! Can I, Mama? Please? Please?"

"I don't think he should—" Gertie began. But Dan interrupted.

"I've got plenty of room for all of you. Just around the town? It won't take long and they'd enjoy it."

Even Lillian looked excited, though Gertie could tell she was a little nervous. She looked back at the car. It was a nice car. She'd always wanted to ride in a nice car.

"All right," she said, setting James off again with another shout of glee. "Just around the town, then."

"I'll take you back to the Pennyfoot afterward. Come on." After making sure the road was clear, he grabbed James's hand and led him over to the car. With a quick push he helped him up onto the backseat, then turned and grabbed Lillian about the waist. With no effort at all he lifted the little girl and set her down next to James.

Then he turned to Gertie. "Your turn."

"I'll manage meself, thank you very much." She ignored his grin and walked around the bonnet to the passenger side. Before she could open the door Dan was at her side, opening it for her. With a nod of her head, she climbed up and sat down.

The car smelled of leather and lemon polish. She ran her hand over the seat. It was as soft as a baby's bum. There was a little clock on the shelf in front of the driver's seat, but she couldn't see what it said.

James was wriggling about with excitement in the backseat and she twisted her head to look at him. "Sit still or we'll get out right now."

James immediately leaned back against the soft leather.

"Where are we going, Mama?" Lillian asked.

"We're going for a jaunt around the town," Dan said, poking his head in the driver's side. He reached under the seat and pulled out a handle. "Just got to start her up."

Gertie watched him put the handle in somewhere below

the bonnet and start cranking. After a moment or two the engine coughed, then started a loud throbbing.

"We're off, we're off!" James chanted.

"Be quiet, now," Gertie warned.

Dan climbed back in, did something with a lever on the floor and they started forward.

Gertie hung on to the little handle in the door with one hand and her hat with the other. She felt like a queen, chugging down the road by the side of her king, with the engine making little popping noises now and then that startled the passersby.

They passed a horse and trap, then another, as they chugged easily up the hill. James and Lillian exclaimed with excitement over every bump in the road, and when the engine banged really loudly, both of them shrieked in delight.

Dan looked right at home behind the wheel, his hands deftly steering the motorcar past horses and bicycles and the stray pedestrian. He grinned at her when they reached the top of the high street. "So what do you think of her? Pretty natty, huh?"

"It's very nice." She didn't want to admit how wonderful it made her feel to be gliding along so smoothly. A lot different from a carriage. Almost like flying. It made her feel like the rich toffs who brought their motorcars to the Pennyfoot.

Which made her wonder just how a butcher could afford a motorcar like this one. All the butchers she'd ever known rode bicycles around town. Dan must have got a lot of money from somewhere to buy it. He didn't even look like a butcher in his smart coat and cap.

She thought about what he'd said the day before when she'd told him she was off for Christmas Eve. *I can't talk about it.* It made her uneasy, wondering what he was doing that he couldn't talk about, and owning a posh car and all. She was putting two and two together, and she didn't like what it was adding up to at all.

CHAPTER
18

The carriage had traveled halfway down the driveway when, to Cecily's surprise, it suddenly jerked to a stop. Thrown forward, she uttered a cry of dismay. Her hat, torn loose from the pins that held it, slipped forward over her eyes. As she struggled to right it, she heard a deep voice shouting words she couldn't understand.

Heart pounding, she peered out of the window, but could see nothing. She heard Samuel answer, his voice raised in outrage.

"Get out of the way, you lunatic, before I run you over."

More shouting, then without warning, the far door was flung open.

Cecily gasped when she saw Silas Gower, brandishing a rake in the air, his face white with cold rage. "You leave Mr.

Thorpe alone, you hear me? He ain't done nothing. You leave him alone!"

Cecily shrank back as the gardener leaned into the carriage. "I have no quarrel with Mr. Thorpe," she assured him. "I have no intention of causing trouble for him." *Unless he killed his cousin*, she added inwardly.

"He's a good bloke, is Mr. Thorpe." The gardener bared his teeth like a ferocious dog. "He wouldn't hurt no one. He—"

His words were cut off by the sound of pounding horse's hooves. At the same time Samuel appeared behind the gardener and closed his hands around the older man's throat.

"Get away from this carriage," he snarled, and dragged Silas away from the door.

The hooves clattered to a stop, and Cecily heard the horse snort with impatience.

A man's voice spoke, and then Randall Thorpe appeared in the doorway. "I do apologize for my gardener, Mrs. Baxter," he said smoothly. "I've sent him on his way. I do hope he didn't upset you?"

Recovering her breath, Cecily managed a smile. "I'm quite all right, Mr. Thorpe. Thank you."

"Thank goodness. Silas can be a little gruff but he wouldn't hurt a fly."

That wasn't the impression he gave me, Cecily thought, cringing at the memory of that bony hand reaching out to her. "You have quite a champion there," she murmured. "He seemed to think I was a threat to you in some way. I simply can't imagine why."

A gleam appeared in Randall's dark eyes. "Nor I, Mrs.

Baxter. I assure you, this is a gross misunderstanding on his part. I'll see that he's enlightened, I promise you. I should hate to alienate such a charming guest of Whitfield Manor. I trust we shall see more of you in the near future?"

"You can count on it, Mr. Thorpe. Happy Christmas to you."

"And you."

Randall withdrew, allowing Samuel's anxious face to reappear. "Are you all right, m'm? He didn't hurt you, did he?"

"I'm quite all right, Samuel. Let us just go home now."

"Yes, m'm. Right away."

"Oh, and Samuel?" She leaned forward as he began to close the door.

He opened it wider again. "Yes, m'm?"

"Thank you for coming to my rescue. I knew I could count on you."

His face broke into an expansive grin. "Entirely my pleasure, m'm."

He closed the door, and a moment later she heard him scramble up into his seat. The carriage jerked, then pulled forward, speeding up to a fast clip, moving toward the road.

From the window Cecily could see across the lawn. Silas Gower was just disappearing into the trees.

The incident had upset her more than she cared to admit. Loyalty was one thing. Threatening her like that was definitely another. She wondered what Randall Thorpe had done to earn such fierce devotion from a member of his staff, especially one with whom he should have had little contact.

Remembering Naomi's accusation that Gavin had betrayed her, Cecily stared thoughtfully at the trees flashing past. Could it be possible that Silas Gower was grateful to his new master for ridding him of his rival for his wife's affections?

It was certainly something worth contemplating.

She was still thinking about it several minutes later when again she heard the pounding of horse's hooves. They had reached the brow of the hill, where the road turned sharply toward the ocean. On one side the gentle slope of the downs rolled all the way down to the edge of the woods. On the other lay the cliffs, towering high above the golden sands and the sea below.

The road was narrow, but wide enough for two carriages to pass each other, as long as care was taken by both drivers. The driver coming up behind them seemed in a great hurry.

Cecily could hear the thundering hooves, but no rattling of wheels. She relaxed. There was plenty of room for a single rider to pass.

No sooner had she thought it, then a horse drew level with the carriage. From where she sat, she could not see above the rider's shoulders, but as he passed, she saw something flap in the wind. The tail end of a blue scarf, with an insignia embroidered on it.

She shouted out a warning to Samuel. As she did so, the crack of a whip rang out in the cold, still air. The horses whinnied and plunged about, sending the carriage back on its rear wheels.

Samuel's shout could be heard above the thrashing of hooves. Again the crack of a whip, and the terrified shrieks from the horses. The carriage swayed violently, sending Cecily to the floor on her knees.

Samuel kept on shouting, while the carriage spun this way and that, until she lost all sense of direction. Then, with a jerk that sent her crashing backward, the carriage leapt forward, racing behind the frenzied pounding of the horses' hooves.

The blow to her head made her dizzy. She felt awareness slipping away, and just before she lost consciousness, her last thought was to wonder in which direction the carriage was speeding. To the comparative safety of the woods, or directly toward the cliffs and the deadly plunge to the sands below?

In spite of her concerns, Gertie had to admit that Dan was very good company. Not only did he keep her amused with his jokes about the village and it residents, he made sure to include the twins, making them laugh as well. She liked that.

All too soon the ride came to an end, and Dan parked the motorcar in front of the Pennyfoot's main entrance. Gertie was hoping Samuel would come out to greet them. She was really looking forward to seeing his face when he saw her sitting there like the Queen of Sheba. He'd be so envious.

She was quite disappointed when one of the footmen came out instead. What's more, he didn't even look at her when Dan turned down his offer to park the motorcar. "I'm just dropping off my passengers," he said, and the footman nodded and ran right back up the steps.

Dan turned off the engine, then ordered the twins to stay put on the seat until he told them they could leave.

To Gertie's surprise, they didn't even argue. Just sat back and waited like little angels. "You're good with children," she said, as he helped her out of the motorcar. "They like you."

He looked perfectly serious when he answered her. "The important thing is, do *you* like me?"

Flustered, she didn't know how to answer him. She wanted to tell him she liked him a lot. Especially when he was so nice to her twins, even if they were little devils at times. She liked the way he made them all laugh, and his nice manners.

She liked the way he talked—more proper than most blokes she knew—even if he was a saucy bugger. More than anything, she liked the way he made her feel. It had been a long time since any man had made her feel all soft and warm inside. Like she was special in some way.

If it hadn't been for him being so secretive about what he was doing that night, she might even have found the nerve to say some of it. But trusting a bloke was everything to her, and something just didn't sit right with Dan Perkins.

His face broke out in a smile, though she could tell by his eyes that he was hurt by her silence. "Well," he said, reaching into the back for Lillian, "if it takes you that long to think about it, I don't think I want to know the answer."

He deposited Lillian on the pavement and held out a hand for James to grab.

Aching inside for having upset him, Gertie took hold of her children's hands. "Thank you very much for the ride. It was lovely. We've never been in a car before, and we all had a good time, didn't we, kiddies?"

"Yeah!" the twins agreed in chorus.

215

Dan smiled at them and patted Lillian on the head. "It was entirely my pleasure. Maybe we can do it again sometime. That's if your mother will allow it."

The twins let out another cheer, while Gertie tried to find her tongue. "That would be very nice," she said at last.

Dan nodded. "I wish you all a very happy Christmas." He touched the brim of his cap, then turned to leave.

Gertie held her breath for a moment, then blurted out, "I do like you, Dan. Really I do."

He paused and looked back at her. "Then prove it. Come out with me."

"I can't. I don't have another night off until after New Year's Eve."

He looked at her for a long moment, then leaned back against the motorcar's door. "How about tonight, then?"

Her heart gave a little jump. "Tonight? I thought you said you were doing something."

"I am. I thought you might like to do it with me."

Her heart had started pounding now. Hoping he wouldn't notice her cheeks growing warm, she said cautiously, "What is it?"

"I'll tell you tonight." He tilted his head to one side. "Are you game?"

She struggled for several seconds with her common sense, but then curiosity and a very strong yearning to go out with him won the battle. "All right. I'll see you tonight. What time?"

"What time are you off?"

"Eight o'clock."

"That will work out just fine." He grinned at her, turned

to go, then swung back to look at her. "Oh, it has to be on one condition."

"What condition?"

"That you swear you will never tell anyone what we were doing tonight."

That threw her off balance for a moment. "It's not something that's going to get me in trouble, is it?" she asked at last.

"Now, do I look like the kind of chap who would get a lady into trouble?"

Yes, you do, she thought uneasily. Nevertheless, she decided to give him the benefit of the doubt. "All right," she said reluctantly, "I promise."

"Cross your heart?"

"Cross my heart." She made a cross with her thumb over her chest.

"All right, then. See you at eight." Whistling, he reached into the car and pulled out the starting handle. "Don't be late!"

"I won't." Her knees had started shaking so she didn't wait to see him drive off. Instead, she pulled the twins up the steps and inside. It wasn't until the twins were safely in the care of Daisy once more and she was back in the kitchen that Gertie asked herself the question that had been hovering in her mind ever since Dan had left.

What in the bloody hell did she think she was doing?

Drifting in and out of consciousness, Cecily first felt a sharp pain in her head, then rough hands on her. Feebly she tried to push them away, but the clouds of oblivion overtook her again.

The next thing she felt was water dripping on her face, cold and irritating. She brushed at the annoying drops with her hand, then opened her eyes. Her head ached abominably and a sharp pain in her back caused her to gasp as she tried to move.

At first she couldn't imagine why she was lying half in, half out of her carriage, with grass tickling her nose and rain spitting down on her from the open sky above. Then memory flooded her mind. *Thank God.* The horses had bolted for the trees.

The pain in her back, she discovered, was the carriage step digging into her. Dragging herself upright, she carefully dislodged her legs and pulled them from the carriage.

She felt as if her head floated above her shoulders, and at first she had trouble focusing on the scene in front of her. Then a scuffling noise caused her to turn her head. Both horses stood nearby, one grazing and the other staring at her as if waiting for a command.

They seemed to be unhurt—a miracle considering the damage done to the carriage. It lay on its side, one door hanging off, and one wheel shattered. Pieces of the shafts still hung from the horses' harness, and more had been scattered over the grass.

As for Samuel, she could see no sign of him.

Scrambling to her feet, Cecily clung to the wrecked carriage for support as the ground swayed beneath her. Clouds had covered the sun since she had left the manor, and the rain that had awoken her, now fell steadily on her bared head.

Peering inside the carriage, she saw her hat lying on the floor and reached in for it. Again she had to steady herself with a hand on the carriage window.

Cramming her hat unceremoniously on her head, she looked around. Several feet away a bundle lay in the deep grass. She peered harder, her heart dropping when she realized it was her stable manager. With a great effort, she focused on the still form and staggered over to him.

Dropping on her knees beside him, she called his name. "Samuel? Please, try to answer me." Gently she shook his shoulder, then more forcibly. "Samuel? Please wake up." *Dear God, don't let him be dead.*

To her utter relief, he stirred, then moaned. Bending over him, she saw that the wound on his head had opened up again and blood now seeped through the bandage.

She had to get him home, and as soon as possible. But how? The carriage was obviously out of the question. She eyed the horses. Perhaps, if she could get Samuel up on one of them, she could lead him home on the other. It was certainly worth an attempt.

Carefully she got to her feet, pleased to find that the ground stayed relatively firm this time. Talking softly, she held out her hand to the nearest horse. He backed away from her, his eyes rolling in alarm.

"Come boy," she said, "I won't hurt you. Everything will be all right." She moved closer, and took hold of his bridle.

He danced away from her again, tossing his head. Once more she grasped his bridle, and this time managed to reach his neck. In soothing tones, she coaxed him over to where Samuel still lay on the ground.

Worried that his eyes remained closed, she nudged him gently with her foot. "Samuel? You have to get up on this horse. I can't lift you by myself, so I need you to help yourself as much as you can and I'll try to do the rest."

Samuel moaned something in reply and opened his eyes. "What happened?"

Relieved to be communicating with him, Cecily said quickly, "We had a little accident with the carriage. It's badly damaged, I'm afraid, so we'll have to ride the horses home."

"I've never seen you on a horse, m'm."

"Yes, well, it has been rather a long time since I rode one." She looked doubtfully at the other horse, who stood staring at her with a baleful gleam in its eye. "I daresay I shall manage, however. Now, do you think you can climb up on him?"

"I'll give it a try, m'm." Gamely, Samuel struggled to sit up, while she watched him with anxious eyes.

After a moment, during which she thought he might faint again, he seemed to recover, and got himself unsteadily onto his hands and knees.

She was beginning to have serious doubts about his ability to stay on the horse, even if she could manage to get him up there, which at the moment, didn't seem likely. She watched him stand, only to have his knees buckle and drop to the ground again.

She was about to suggest he hang on to the horse for leverage when she heard a sound that made her blood run cold.

The pounding of hooves and the rattling of wheels.

Samuel must have heard it at the same time. He turned a white face in her direction, his eyes wide and staring.

"Quickly!" Cecily let go of the horse's bridle and took hold of Samuel's arm. "We must hide in the woods."

Grunting, Samuel hauled himself to his feet. "What about the horses?"

"Never mind the horses. They'll have to watch out for themselves." She started dragging him toward the trees. "Hurry, Samuel. Any minute now he'll reach the top of the hill and be able to see us."

Stumbling and running, she dragged and pushed Samuel along, while the trap drew closer and closer, until it was about to burst over the brow of the hill.

At last they were inside the cover of the first few trees, though the slim trunks were much too straggly to hide them for long. "We have to go deeper," she cried, and then Samuel stumbled, falling headlong at her feet.

She crouched down next to him, prepared to shield him with her body if needs be. Perhaps, by some miracle, the driver of the trap would miss the wreckage of her carriage and go right on by.

It was a futile hope. She heard the clattering hooves leave the road and thunder across the grass. The bouncing trap rattled and creaked as it drew closer. She couldn't see the driver, but it really didn't matter. There was no doubt she'd have a close-up view of him any minute now.

Shouts back and forth. There were two of them. She froze, knowing she would stand no chance against two. This was the end for both of them. Crouching down, she whispered, "I'm so sorry, Bax, my love."

CHAPTER
❀ 19 ❀

A moment later Cecily heard the one thing she least expected: a familiar voice calling her name.

"Cecily? Where are you, Cecily?"

In disbelief she stood, while at her feet Samuel whispered, "Thank the Lord."

The voice came closer, and then there he was, leaning on crutches with a face like thunder.

"Baxter!" She hadn't realized she'd said his name until he turned his head in her direction. Then she was running, heedless of the nettles that dragged at her skirt, mindless of the hat that flew from her head.

At last she threw herself at him, putting them both in danger of toppling over. He dropped one of the crutches and wrapped his arm around her. Her head on his shoulder, she said tearfully, "I thought I would never see you again."

"Are they all right?" Kevin Prestwick appeared at Baxter's shoulder, his face taut with dread.

"Samuel is over there." Cecily gestured behind her. "I'm afraid his head has opened up again."

Kevin sent an anxious look in Samuel's direction. "What about you?"

"I'm all right." Her lips felt stiff when she smiled. "Apart from a nasty bump on the head and a really sore back, that is."

"I'll take a look at you in a moment." Kevin glanced at Baxter, who nodded his approval, then strode over to where Samuel was struggling to get to his feet.

"What happened?" Baxter held her away from him to get a better look at her face. "What in blazes are you doing out here?"

His voice betrayed the anxiety he'd suffered, and she felt guilty for causing him so much pain after all he'd been through. Avoiding a direct answer to his last question, she said hesitantly, "We were attacked by a horseman, and the horses bolted. I'm afraid the carriage is in ruins."

He pulled her closer. "I shall be in ruins if you continue to disregard my wishes. I begged you not to expose yourself to danger. Did you not tell me you intended to shop in the High Street?"

"I did." She gulped, and kept her face averted from his angry gaze. "I'm sorry, Bax, but I simply had to find out who this brooch belonged to and—" She broke off as her probing fingers encountered an empty pocket. "It's gone!"

"What brooch? What are you talking about?"

Quickly she told him about the colonel finding the brooch at the spot where Gavin had hung from the tree. "I couldn't imagine why the killer returned for the body, but then I realized he came back for something that could incriminate him."

"But what would he be doing with a woman's brooch?"

"That's something we have to find out. My assumption is that either the killer is a woman or he had an accomplice. I really must find that brooch, Bax." She attempted to pull away from him. "It could be the only clue we have to the killer's identity."

"Then let Northcott find it," Baxter said, his hold on her arm preventing her from leaving. "I think you've done more than enough sleuthing for one day."

"Please, Bax. This is important. I promise I will ring Sam Northcott and tell him everything I know just as soon as I get back to the Pennyfoot. But I must find that brooch." She gave him her most earnest smile. "It could well be a matter of life or death."

His jaw jutted at an uncompromising angle, but after a moment of staring into her eyes, he relented. "Oh, very well. I'll help you look."

"No, you really shouldn't be out here on that ankle. Go back to the trap and wait for me there." She glanced over to where Kevin was bandaging Samuel's head again. Assuring herself her stable manager was in good hands, she turned back to Baxter. "Please?"

"I am not leaving you again until we are safely home." He started swinging himself toward the wrecked carriage. "I've spent enough hours today worrying about you."

Knowing how useless it would be to argue further, she followed him.

Upon reaching the carriage she knelt down to peer inside. After patting the seats and searching the floor, she had to accept that the brooch was not in the carriage.

"It must have fallen out," she said, as she got carefully to her feet.

A few yards away, Baxter moved slowly on his crutches, peering at the ground around him. "I can't see it anywhere around here."

"I shall have to retrace the path the horses took from the road—" She broke off, as a sharp memory returned. Rough hands on her, turning her over . . . She gasped.

Immediately Baxter turned his head. "What is it?"

"I remember now." She lifted her hands in a hopeless gesture and let them fall. "The man who attacked us. That's what he wanted. He knew it would lead me to his identity. I remember his hands on me. He must have taken the brooch right out of my pocket." She stared at Baxter in horror. "Dear God, he could have killed us both."

"Damn the bastard!" Baxter swung toward her. "If he hurt you, I'll—"

She shook her head at him. "It's all right, Bax. Really. He just took the brooch. Nothing else. I would know."

He stared at her for a long moment, his face mirroring the doubts that plagued him. Then he nodded. "Very well. Let's get home so we can ring that fool Northcott and be done with this business."

Right at that moment, with her head aching and her back breaking, Cecily was only too happy to agree. She'd had enough excitement for one day. As for Gavin Hargrove's killer, apparently his attacks were meant merely to scare them off, not finish them off, or he would have surely done so while he had the chance. He must feel confident that his crime would remain unresolved.

The thought that he might well get away with murder depressed her. She could only hope that either P.C. Northcott or Scotland Yard would be able to solve the puzzle, since it seemed to be beyond her capabilities to do so.

After much heaving and grunting, both Baxter and Samuel finally got settled beside Cecily in the trap. Kevin took up the reins and soon they were bowling along the Esplanade, where the clouds were once more receding to leave a clear sky.

Cecily shivered as the cold wind whipped her face. She was more than ready to take up her duties once more as manager of the Pennyfoot, and leave the murder investigation to those who were more experienced pursuers of criminals.

It irked her to no end, however, that she had been unable to solve this particular puzzle. If it hadn't been the Christmas season, with a full house at the country club, she told herself, she might have pursued the chase a little longer.

Having such a valid excuse for accepting defeat made it a little easier to swallow. But only a little. She would have to work hard to put it all out of her mind. Concentrating on the job at hand and ensuring that the guests of the Pennyfoot Country Club had a Christmas they would remember with pleasure for many years to come would help.

Back in her boudoir, she shrieked aloud at her appearance. Baxter, who had sunk onto a chair the moment they entered, looked up in alarm.

"What is it now? Not your head? I thought you told Prestwick it didn't hurt that badly."

"It's not my head." She held out both hands to him. "Look at me." She made a dismal picture for him to observe, she thought, doing her best to smooth back the stray wisps of hair that hung about her face. Her coat was torn, as was the hem of her skirt. Mud streaked her face, and her gloves looked as if they had been fished out of Deep Willow Pond.

Baxter didn't help matters when he ran a critical gaze over her from head to toe. She relaxed, however, when she saw the gleam in his eyes.

"After spending most of the day thinking I might not see you again," he murmured, "I can assure you, I have never seen you look more appetizing."

His words warmed her as no fire could. She pulled off her gloves, then walked over to him to touch his dear face. "Now you can understand how devastated I felt when you were missing for two days."

"I can." He reached for her and pulled her down beside him. "I sincerely hope that neither of us have to go through that again."

She sealed her agreement with a kiss. It was good to be safe at home with her love by her side. Though she did wish she knew who had killed Gavin Hargrove. And why.

Cecily rang P.C. Northcott early that evening, only to be told by the operator that the constabulary was closed until after Boxing Day, and that if it was an emergency she was to call Inspector Cranshaw.

Since she had no wish to talk to that gentleman, she called Sam Northcott at home. He sounded irritated at being disturbed, though he did his best to hide it.

Cecily recounted everything that had happened, and when she was finished the constable waited some time before answering her. Finally he said gruffly, "Well, Mrs. Baxter, it do seem as how you've 'ad your share of h'adventures lately. I have warned you in the past about interfering in police business. Not at all a suitable place for a lady, as I've said many times."

"Yes, yes." Cecily grasped the telephone a little more tightly. "Never mind all that now. What I want to know is what you are going to do about it."

"Do about what?"

Cecily gritted her teeth. "About Gavin Hargrove's murder, of course. Now that we have all this new evidence, it's clearly not a gambling syndicate who's responsible, since it wasn't Mr. Hargrove who owed them money. That means it's most likely someone at Whitfield Manor who killed him. Isn't it your job to hunt down the killer and put him in prison where he can't hurt anyone else?"

"Well, that's exactly what I am doing." Northcott indulged in an infuriating pause before continuing. "The truth is, Mrs. Baxter, Scotland Yard decided there wasn't enough evidence for them to investigate the case, so they put it back into my lap, so to speak."

"Well, why didn't you say so. It's my firm belief that one of the occupants of Whitfield Manor is responsible, and might well kill again if he finds himself in danger of being identified."

"Well, I can't really say as how anything you've told me points to the murderer." Northcott smacked his lips, as if he were enjoying a tasty snack. "All this talk about a man with his face covered up and driving a trap. All that could be is someone driving too fast. That trail through the woods is dark. Makes it hard to see anyone until you're on top of him and then it's too late to stop."

"Driving too *fast*?" Cecily was almost speechless with disbelief at the man's stupidity. "Was he driving too fast when he hit Baxter over the head? Or when he was throwing rocks at Madeline and me in the woods? I can assure you—"

She broke off as a clear picture popped into her mind. She and Madeline running from a shower of rocks. White rocks. She saw again Silas Gower brandishing shears above his head while he stood with one foot on the rockery—a rockery filled with white rocks. And later, Silas's bony hand stretching out to her through the door of the carriage.

"That were probably the gypsies," Northcott said brusquely. "Unruly lot, they are. Never know what they'll be up to next. Throwing rocks and hitting people is right up their alley. They should be run right out of the country, that's what I say."

"Well, what about the brooch the colonel found? Surely you want to know to whom it belongs?"

"Could belong to anyone, m'm, couldn't it. Probably a gypsy what dropped it. Now that I think about it, from what you've told me, it seems clear to me that the gypsies had a hand in the murder. I intend to suggest as much to Inspector Cranshaw. I'm sure he'll want a thorough investigation, and we'll find the perpetrators of this crime, never you fear."

Cecily made one last effort to convince the stubborn constable. "What about the driver with a scarf wrapped around his face? Doesn't that seem as if he had a strong desire to disguise himself for fear of being recognized?"

"Probably covered his face up against the cold wind. I do it meself sometimes."

Suppressing a strong urge to scream, Cecily let out her breath. "I just hope you find the killer before he kills again. If not, Sam Northcott, you will surely have a death on your conscience."

He sounded put out when he answered. "Now, now, Mrs. B., no need to get worked up about it. I'm sure Inspector Cranshaw will soon find out what really happened, and then we can all forget about it. It's Christmas—and you should be enjoying yourself now that you have your husband back safe and sound."

And letting him enjoy his Christmas in peace, his tone implied.

Giving up, Cecily hung the telephone back on its hook. There wasn't much she could do about it now, but the minute she could get away she would pay one more visit to Whitfield Manor. To ask Emily Gower if she owned a silver fox brooch.

"I don't think I shall attend the ball tonight," Baxter announced. He sat in his rocking chair in the boudoir, watching Cecily sift through her wardrobe in search of a gown to wear. "I won't be able to dance and I shall only get in the way."

"Piffle." Cecily drew a shell pink gown from the rail and held it up in front of her. Turning to the dressing table mirror to see her reflection, she murmured, "What do you think?"

"Enchanting." Baxter leaned forward. "That gown is one of my favorites."

"I know. Which is why you must escort me to the ball. I wouldn't dream of wearing this anywhere without you."

"I won't be able to dance."

"You won't need to dance."

"You'll spend all evening fussing over me instead of conversing with our guests. I can't deprive them of your charming company."

She glanced at him out of the corner of her eye. "But you would deprive me of yours."

"I shall make it up to you when you return."

"I will not leave you here all alone on Christmas Eve." She carried the gown over to the bed and laid it down. "I would not enjoy a single second I am away from you. In fact, I should be so consumed with misery I would not be pleasant company for any of our guests."

Baxter sighed. "You give a good argument."

"Of course. I learned from a master." She leaned down and dropped a kiss on his forehead. "Now stop being such a bear and get dressed. Our guests would be sorely disappointed were you not there to joke with them. The ladies, especially, enjoy your sense of humor."

"I'm not sure my sense of humor will be all that evident since I'm restricted by this dratted ankle."

"Then just do your best, Bax, darling. After all, your worst is better than most people's best."

"Flattery becomes you." He grinned at her. "Very well, but don't expect me to enjoy being trapped in a chair all night long, forced to watch you glide around the floor in another man's arms."

"Trust me, my love, I will not be gliding anywhere."

"In that gown no man will be able to resist you."

"Then I shall do the resisting." She walked over to the wardrobe and removed his dinner suit. "Now put this on and stop trying to get out of it with all this sweet talk."

"I suppose Prestwick will be there."

She almost laughed at the disgust in his voice. "Of course. Have no fear, he'll have eyes only for Madeline." She clasped her hands at her bosom in a little thrill of excitement. "I really do think he's going to propose to her tonight."

Baxter grunted. "Those two deserve each other."

Cecily smiled serenely at her reflection in the mirror. "They do indeed," she said softly.

She remembered Baxter's words later that evening as she watched Madeline float across the floor in the arms of her beloved doctor. Their courtship had not been a smooth one. Madeline's sorcery with plants and herbs had clashed horribly with Kevin's scientific approach to medicine.

Many times Cecily had sat in Dolly's tea shop listening to her friend's account of her latest row with the good doctor. It was a miracle they still kept company, much less considered taking marriage vows.

Madeline had insisted over and over that a union between the two of them was impossible, yet there she was, radiant in a white lawn frock sprinkled with yellow and orange marigolds, gazing up into her partner's eyes with all the adoration of a woman madly in love.

It would be interesting indeed to see if Kevin could sum up the courage to ask for her hand, and even more fascinating to know just what Madeline's answer would be.

Sighing, Cecily turned away. She would know soon enough. All she could do was wait, and hope that things worked out the way she would like. A wedding to look forward to would be a marvelous way to start the new year.

CHAPTER

❊ 20 ❊

For the rest of the day Gertie was in such a fever of worry and indecision she could hardly concentrate at all. When she filled all the gravy boats with custard instead of gravy, Mrs. Chubb let her have it.

"What the devil has got into you today, Gertie McBride? You're all fingers and thumbs, and your head must be full of cotton wool. Are you ill?"

Gertie miserably emptied the custard from each gravy boat back into the cauldron on the stove. "I'm sorry, Chubby. Me mind is bloody miles away, I know."

"Yes, it is. And don't call me Chubby." Mrs. Chubb folded her arms across her bosom. "Something's bothering you, Gertie. You might as well tell me what it is because I'll find out eventually."

Dan's voice echoed in Gertie's head. *Swear you will never tell anyone what we were doing tonight.* "Oh, it's nothing. It's just that I'm going out tonight and I'm feeling a bit guilty about leaving the twins on Christmas Eve."

Well, it was half the truth, anyway. She *was* feeling a bit guilty. Especially since she didn't know what the bloody hell she was letting herself in for.

"Go on." Mrs. Chubb looked at her in surprise. "Well, you don't have to feel guilty. They'll be in bed fast asleep before you even go out. Where are you going, then?"

"I'm not sure." Gertie could have cut out her tongue. Now she was in for some awkward questions, none of which she could answer.

"What do you mean you're not sure? You haven't made up your mind yet?"

"Yeah, that's it." Gertie managed a tight smile. "I haven't made up me mind. It's me night off, and it's Christmas Eve, and I just want to do something different for a change."

Mrs. Chubb narrowed her eyes. "You're not doing anything that could land you in hot water, I hope?"

"Course not." *Bloody hope not.* "What do you think I am?" She stacked the messy gravy boats on a tray and carried them over to the sink. "Anyway, I won't be going anywhere if I don't get these dishes washed and filled with gravy."

"Well, just don't let Michel catch you making mistakes like that again tonight. You know how he gets at Christmas. Everything has to be perfect or there's the devil to pay."

Nodding in relief, Gertie rinsed out the gravy boats. From now on she'd better pay attention, or Chubby would be watching her every move.

At long last the dinner rush was over and she could go back to her room to get ready. She didn't have many clothes to choose from, and she really hoped they weren't going anywhere posh. Pulling out a dark green suit from her wardrobe, she held it up in front of her. The long skirt and fitted jacket was trimmed with braided velvet, a shade darker than the fabric. If she wore her white frilly waist with it, she'd look festive enough for anything.

Even prison. The unbidden thought unnerved her, and she collapsed on the side of her bed. Why couldn't he tell her what he was doing tonight? Surely he wouldn't get her in trouble? When she'd asked, he hadn't given her a straight answer. What if he was stealing jewels or something, and selling them to buy a nice fancy motorcar and posh clothes?

She'd be as bad as he was, if she was with him. She'd be carted off to prison, too, if they got caught. She felt sick. What a bloody daft twerp she was to say she'd go with him. Perhaps he wouldn't come. Perhaps he'd forget.

Seconds later a tap on the door made her jump out of her skin. It opened, and Pansy stuck her head in. "You've got a visitor," she announced, her eyes sparkling with delight. "It's that Dan Perkins. He looks different without his white butcher coat."

"Bloody hell." Gertie shot to her feet. "Ask him to wait, will you? Tell him I won't be a minute."

"Yes, madam. Of course, madam." Polly gave her a sly grin. "I told you he fancied you. Thought you weren't a bit interested in him."

"I'm not." Gertie walked over and started closing the door in Pansy's face. "I'm interested in his motorcar, that's all."

"Oo, he's got a motorcar? What—" The rest of her sentence was cut off by the door snapping shut.

Gertie shook her head, then dressed as quickly as she could. A quick comb through her hair, then a few pins to hold her hat and she was ready. Trying her best to calm what felt like squirrels chasing around in her stomach, she pulled on her coat, then rushed out into the hallway.

A minute or two later she entered the lobby and spotted Dan immediately. He stood over by the Christmas tree, fingering one of the lace angels. He had his back to her, and she couldn't help looking at his shoulders. He was so strong. She'd never have a chance if he should turn on her.

Cursing herself for her silly nerves, she walked over to him, her feet making no sound on the soft carpet. "I hope I didn't keep you waiting too long," she said, when she reached him.

He swung around, his smile already making her warm inside. "I was just admiring the Christmas decorations. They're pretty. Just like you, Gertie McBride."

She felt her cheeks growing hot. "Go on with you. So where are we going, then?"

"Ah." He held a finger to his mouth. "A secret. You'll see when we get there."

She followed him down the steps, and made up her mind she was going to forget her worries and have a good time. He seemed like a nice bloke. And if he was up to no good she could always just walk away.

Hugging that somewhat fragile assurance, she climbed once more into the front seat of the motorcar. Dan cranked the handle and the engine coughed. She loved the way it sort of rumbled while they were standing still. She loved the smell of the leather, the shiny clock in the shelf, the polished handle on the gear lever.

In fact, she loved everything about the motorcar. One day, she promised herself, she'd have a motorcar of her own, and she'd learn to drive it. What power to hold in her hands! Dan had told her it would go fourteen miles an hour, and even faster downhill. That seemed really fast to her. A lot faster than riding a bicycle.

This time, instead of going into town, Dan took the road going across the downs. That scared her a little. It was so dark and lonely up there on the cliffs, and the thought of gypsies floating around the woods didn't help.

"Are you warm enough?" Dan asked, as the wind buffeted the motorcar and made it rattle.

"Yes, thank you." She hugged the collar of her coat around the back of her neck. It was a bit chilly, but at least the windows kept the worst of the cold outside. She looked through the glass and saw they'd turned onto the Wellercombe road.

"We're going into Wellercombe?" Her anxiety came flooding back. What if she had to run away from him? She'd never find her way home from Wellercombe. She'd be stuck there on Christmas Eve and she wouldn't see her babies on Christmas morning.

She should never have come. What was she thinking?

"Not all the way. We'll be stopping just before we get to the town."

"Are we going to a pub?" She remembered he'd asked her to play darts with him.

"No, no pub."

"The music hall?" That was something else she'd never seen. The closest she'd been to a music hall was Phoebe Fortescue's events at the Pennyfoot, and they always ended up in a right mess.

"Not the music hall." He laughed. "You'll just have to wait until we get there."

It was time, she decided, to ask him a few questions. "How long have you lived in Badgers End?"

"Not long." He sent her a quick glance. "Why?"

"I was just wondering." She made herself sound indifferent. "I don't remember seeing you around, that's all."

"Well, until about a month or so ago, I lived in London."

She looked at him in surprise. "What made you come down here to live, then?"

"I liked the idea of living by the sea. I got tired of living in The Smoke. Too noisy, too crowded, too dirty."

"I know. I used to live there myself when I was little. But there's a lot more to do there. All those theaters and clubs and things. They've even got cinemas in London. I've never been in a cinema."

"You've led a sheltered life, haven't you."

She wasn't sure if she should take offense at that. "I wouldn't call being married twice a sheltered life," she said primly.

"You've been married twice?"

He sounded shocked and now she did get defensive. "Well, I wasn't really married to my first husband because he was already married, but I didn't know that when I married him and by the time I did know I was having the twins."

"Ouch. That must have been painful."

"I survived." This time he'd sounded as if he really understood, and she felt better. "I threw the bugger out. It was hard being on my own, but Mrs. Baxter and Mrs. Chubb took good care of me. They're the best people in the world. They looked after me and the twins after Ross, my second husband, died. I don't have no family left so they're my family now."

"I don't have any family, either. I know how that feels."

She felt a pang of sympathy, and a warm sense of sharing a bond. While she was still trying to think of something nice to say the motorcar slowed to a jerky halt.

Startled, she looked out the window and saw they were in front of large iron gates in a high brick wall. "Where are we?" She peered at the name written on the gates but couldn't see it in the dark.

"We're at our destination." Dan turned off the engine. "It's showtime."

Nervously she peered at him, trying to read his expression. "Are we going to visit someone?"

"Not really." She saw a flash of white teeth as he grinned at her. "We're going to break in."

She knew it. All along she'd had the feeling he was up to something and now she knew. He was a burglar, and she was right there breaking the law with him. "There's no bloody *we* about it." She reached for the door handle. "If you think I'm going to help you steal from those people you're flipping bonkers." She stifled a shriek when he grabbed hold of her arm.

"Wait a minute! Where are you going?"

"I'm going to bloody walk home, that's where I'm going." She turned on him with a fierce glare. "And don't you try to stop me or I'll kick you where it hurts the most."

"Ouch." She actually saw him wince. "Calm down, Gertie. I'm not going to steal anything. Just the opposite. I'm taking stuff in. Toys, to be exact."

She stared at him, wondering if she'd heard him right. "Toys?"

"Toys." He leaned over and reached into the backseat. When he pulled his hand back, he held up a red cap trimmed in white fur. "Father Christmas? Christmas Eve? Down the chimney and all that rot?"

She still couldn't seem to grasp what he was telling her. "You're playing Father Christmas?"

"That's right." He jerked a thumb over his shoulder. "Look back there. You'll see my red coat and two very heavy sacks of toys."

Following the gesture, she saw two large bulky mounds on the backseat. She looked back at the gates. "But why are you . . . ?"

"This is an orphanage, Gertie. I had arrangements made with the people who run it. They're leaving the door open for me so I can get in there and leave toys for the orphans without anyone seeing me. I only do this on the condition that I remain anonymous." He smiled at her. "Until now."

She shook her head as understanding dawned. "You've done this before?"

"A few years now, yes."

"In London?"

He nodded. "This is my first Christmas in Badgers End.

241

I wanted it to be a good one. So I got the name of the orphanage and had the arrangements made. From what I hear it took a bit of persuading before they'd allow me to do it. Once they talked to the orphanages in London, though, they were pretty quick to agree."

"That's a very generous thing to do. What got you started on it?"

He paused before answering her. "I grew up in a London orphanage. I know what it's like to go to sleep on Christmas Eve, knowing that Father Christmas wasn't going to come and that no one out there cared whether I lived or died. I swore that when I grew up and could leave that place I'd do my best to make Christmas happier for as many orphans as I could."

Gertie felt rare tears pricking her eyelids. "Blimey. That's the best Christmas story I ever heard."

He laughed. "Well, I got lucky when I grew up, so I've been able to pass some of it along."

"But why don't you want anyone to know who you are?"

He reached into the back again and pulled the coat onto his lap. "I want to be sure I'm doing it for them and not for myself. The best way to do that is to keep it all a big secret." He started pulling on the coat. "You promised, remember?"

"I won't tell no one."

"Thank you." Taking her by surprise, he leaned forward and planted a quick kiss on her cheek. "Now, do you want to come with me or would you rather wait here until I get back?"

For a moment she couldn't speak, conscious of the tingling where his lips had met her cheek. Then she said loudly, "I'm coming with you." She reached for the door handle. "I wouldn't want to miss this for all the bloody money in the world."

The frosty air stung her nose and ears as she waited for him to haul the sack out from the back of the motorcar. Shivering from the cold and a delicious sense of excitement, she watched him push open the gates. "Can I carry one of them sacks for you?" she asked, rather hoping he'd refuse. They looked flipping heavy.

He shook his head. "But, you can close the gates for me," he said, as he swung through them.

She waited until he was clear then closed the heavy iron gates. They creaked and groaned, and any minute she expected vicious dogs to come howling out of the darkness to tear them to bits.

Beckoning to her, Dan strode up the driveway, and she trotted along behind, glancing over her shoulder at the silent trees every now and then to make sure they were alone.

She actually felt like a burglar when he opened the massive door of the orphanage and slipped inside. Stepping in after him, she saw a darkened entranceway with hallways leading off in three different directions.

Dan seemed to know where he was going, as he crept straight ahead, then turned a corner. Right in front of them was a staircase. The dim light from the gas lamps kept the top of the stairs in darkness as they started to climb up.

Reaching the landing, Dan turned to his left, and she kept close behind him as they crept down another long hallway. Finally he stopped at a pair of double doors. After putting down the sacks, he carefully opened the doors and looked in.

She held her breath until he opened one of them wider and signaled for her to go in ahead of him. She slipped past him and found herself in a long, wide room with dozens of narrow beds lined up on each side. In each bed a small body huddled under the covers.

The gas lamps on the wall had been turned way down, and it took her eyes a moment to adjust enough to see the stockings hanging on the bottom bedposts.

Dan moved quietly for a big man, stuffing toys into each stocking and leaving others at the foot of each bed. She waited by the door for him, hoping none of the little ones would wake up.

It gave her such a good feeling, watching him do his work. As the minutes ticked by she felt herself liking him more and more. He was a good man, after all.

Finally he was finished, and hurried back to her, the empty sacks tucked under his arm. They quietly closed the doors behind them, and a minute or so later they were once more outside in the frosty cold night.

Gertie didn't speak until they were settled inside the motorcar with the engine rumbling. "No matter what happens to me in the future," she said unsteadily, "I'll always remember this night. It's the best Christmas Eve I ever spent."

Dan moved the gear lever and the motorcar rolled forward. "Remember you can't tell anyone about it."

"I won't. But it's a shame." She glanced at him. "Those kiddies should know what a kind man you are. I'd love to be able to see their faces in the morning."

"Well, you have two little faces of your own to see in the morning."

"Yes, I do." She wrapped her arms around herself in an effort to stop shivering. "I feel a bit ashamed now, thinking how lucky my two are, when there are so many little ones without a family to love them." She felt like crying again. "You must have been so lonely. At least I had me dad when I was growing up. Even if he wasn't much of a father."

"I'm not lonely now." His voice softened, giving her shivers down her back. "Not now I've met you."

She wanted to believe he really liked her. She really did. But she'd been hurt before by a charmer, and Dan Perkins was all of that and more. Better not to let all this go to her head, she told herself. For all she knew he could have a wife somewhere, just like Ian did.

The thought refused to let her alone, and in the end she asked him as they drove back down the Esplanade. "Didn't you ever get married? Most men your age would have been married years ago."

"Wait a minute. I'm not that old. I'm only thirty-six. Not that much older than you, I'll wager."

"And you never got married?"

"No, I never did."

"Why not?"

"I was too busy working." He glanced at her. "Why do you want to know?"

"Because I'm not the sort of girl who goes for rides in a motorcar and lets a bloke kiss her if he's bloody married, that's why."

"I haven't kissed you yet."

She couldn't tell if he was joking or not. "You kissed me just before we went into the orphanage."

"That was a peck on the cheek. When I kiss you for real, Gertie McBride, you'll know you've been kissed."

She felt as if all the air had suddenly left her body. Now she knew what a fish must feel like when it's pulled out of the water. Frantically she sought for a proper response, but all she could come up with was, "Saucy bugger."

CHAPTER
❧ 21 ❧

Christmas Day flew by for Cecily in a whirl of excitement, laughter, and intense attention to every detail. Baxter presented her with a fabulous diamond pendant, and a white fox cape that she absolutely adored. He seemed equally pleased with his new pocket watch, while the green velvet smoking jacket she'd bought for him fitted his broad shoulders to perfection.

After a leisurely breakfast in the boudoir, she visited the kitchen, where Mrs. Chubb and Michel bickered in their usual harried manner. Maids scurried about loading up trays of silverware, dishes, and festive table decorations to be carried to the ballroom where the enormous feast would be held that afternoon.

This was Cecily's favorite day in the kitchen. The divine

aroma never failed to give her the Christmas spirit. Herb encrusted turkey, goose and duck roasting in the huge oven, exotic spices in the plum puddings warming by the fire, brandy sauce simmering on the hot plate, fresh baked mince pies cooling on the shelves—they chased away the memory of breakfast and made her hungry again.

After ensuring that all was well, she went to join Baxter in the library. Upon arriving there she was informed by several of the woman guests that he had joined the men in the bar for midmorning sherry.

She was debating whether or not to join him when Pansy arrived to inform her that Madeline was in the lobby and wished to see her.

Excusing herself, she hurried down the passageway, hoping fervently that Madeline had good news for her. The moment she saw her friend's face, she knew.

Madeline was positively glowing. Hands outstretched, she floated toward Cecily, her beautiful smile lighting up her entire face. "Kevin proposed last night," she said, her breathy voice even more husky than usual.

"Madeline! How wonderful!" Excited for her friend, Cecily grasped her hands.

"I wanted to tell you last night, but I couldn't see you anywhere in the ballroom, and Kevin had the carriage waiting outside to take me home."

"I retired early last night." Cecily let go of her hands. "I had rather a trying day yesterday. But enough about me. We must have an engagement party for you and Kevin! Did he give you a ring?"

"Not yet." Madeline shook back her long, flowing hair

from her shoulders. "I'm not one for wearing jewelry, as you know. Kevin wanted me to go with him to pick one out, but I told him I don't need a ring to hold him to his promise."

Cecily laughed. "Indeed you don't. So when is the happy day to be?"

"I really don't know." Madeline gazed up at the ceiling. "Summer, I think. I'd like to be married in the meadow by Deep Willow Pond. Don't you think that would be so romantic?"

Cecily could think of a dozen reasons why she disliked the idea, but she kept her council. There would be time enough to persuade Madeline to have a proper wedding in St. Bartholomew's, where there would be less chance of Reverend Algernon Holmes falling into the pond, or causing some other equally devastating disaster, as he was wont to do on occasion.

"Well, you and I must celebrate right this moment." She took Madeline's arm. "Come upstairs with me and we shall share a glass of sherry in my boudoir."

"Well, I don't usually indulge," Madeline began doubtfully, but Cecily would not hear of her refusing.

"This is a special occasion," she said firmly, "and we are going to commemorate in the usual way, by toasting your health and your future together."

Catching sight of a footman about to enter the hallway, she called out to him. "Have a decanter of sherry and two glasses brought up to my suite right away," she ordered, and then led her unprotesting friend up the stairs.

"This is turning out to be an excellent Christmas Day," she said, as Madeline seated herself by the window of the boudoir. "I have waited so long to hear this wonderful news."

"I just hope I did the right thing by accepting Kevin's proposal." Madeline turned a worried face toward her. "You know how he feels about my herbs and potions. I simply will not give that up."

"I'm sure he's taken that into account." Cecily seated herself in Baxter's rocking chair. "It isn't as if he doesn't know about them."

"I think he believes I'll forget all about them once we are married."

"Did you tell him you have no intention of giving up your practices?"

Madeline looked down at her hands. "I didn't want to spoil the evening. He was being so terribly romantic, and I hated to introduce an argument at that point."

"Well, it's something you'll have to get settled before you actually marry him." Cecily smiled at her. "Don't look so glum, Madeline, dear. Kevin adores you. He'll accept you for everything you are, potions and all."

"I just hope you're right." Madeline let out her breath in a long sigh. "Now, what about you? How is Baxter? I saw him last night in the ballroom, but he was seated all night. Is his ankle still troubling him?"

"It will be for a while I'm afraid." Cecily got to her feet as a light tap sounded on the door. "I'm afraid he's not being too patient about it." She opened the door and took the tray from Pansy.

Thanking her, she was about to close the door again when Pansy blurted out, "Mrs. Fortescue is downstairs, asking to see you."

"Oh, please bring her right up, and bring another glass

with you." Cecily closed the door and carried the tray over to the small square table. "Phoebe's here." She put the tray down on the table. "I told Pansy to bring her up. She might as well share a glass of sherry and help us celebrate."

Madeline sighed. "Do we really have to include her? I mean, if we don't tell her the news and hide the sherry, she might not stay so long."

Cecily shook her head in mock rebuke. "Now, Madeline, you know very well you don't mean that."

"I suppose not. It's just that Phoebe can be so infuriating with her little digs at times."

"She will be as overjoyed as I am at the news." Cecily sat down to wait for her friend. "You know she will. Everyone loves a wedding."

"Well, before she gets up here, do tell me if you've managed to find out who killed Gavin Hargrove?"

It was Cecily's turn to sigh. "No, I haven't. I'm no closer to that now than I was at the beginning. It's all so confusing."

"But that means Baxter and Samuel could very well be in danger still!"

"I don't think so." She recounted the events of the day before, accompanied by gasps and exclamations of dismay from Madeline. "Anyway, all's well that ends well," she finished. "Our assailant could quite easily have disposed of us, but he didn't, which makes me think he feels confident he won't be recognized."

Madeline shook her head. "As long as that man is allowed to go free you are all in danger. I hope you will tell P.C. Northcott about the brooch. Surely he will want to find out to whom it belongs?"

"He thinks it could have been dropped by one of the gypsies. I was hoping to hand everything over to him, but though I told him everything I knew he insists now that the gypsies were responsible for the murder. Most frustrating, after all the effort Samuel and I have expended on it. As well as you, of course."

Madeline's breath came out in an explosion of wrath. "Numskull! That is exactly what Pedro was afraid of, that he and his people would be suspected of murder. Cecily, you simply have to find out who did this. Otherwise Pedro and perhaps many more of them could end up in jail for something they had absolutely no hand in at all."

"You're right." Cecily rocked back in the chair. "What I need to do is find out to whom that brooch belongs. In fact, I intend to pay another visit to Whitfield Manor tomorrow. I want to talk to Silas Gower's wife."

"The gardener's wife?" Madeline frowned. "You think the brooch might belong to her? But what would she be doing in the woods? Surely you don't suspect her of throttling Gavin Hargrove and hanging him in a tree?"

Cecily sighed. "I don't know what to think. I do think that the white rocks thrown at us in the woods came from the rockery."

"But anyone at the manor could have taken those rocks from the rockery."

"Yes, but then Silas stopped by the carriage as we were leaving the manor yesterday and became quite belligerent. He seemed to be upset about us questioning Mr. Thorpe, but then he reached into the carriage, and I wonder now if he was trying to retrieve the brooch in my pocket."

Madeline frowned. "But how would he know you were in possession of the brooch?"

Cecily told her about her conversation with Naomi on the steps. "Silas could have been working in the bushes on the other side of the steps. He could easily have overheard Naomi mention the fox design, and realize we had his wife's brooch. Thankfully Samuel knew how to handle him and pulled him away from the carriage. And then Randall Thorpe arrived and sent him on his way."

Madeline was about to answer when another tap on the door announced Phoebe's arrival.

"Please don't mention any of this to Phoebe," Cecily warned Madeline. "I shall have a hard enough time explaining why I don't have the brooch to give back to her."

Madeline covered her mouth with her hand, though her eyes were sparkling with anticipation. "What are you going to tell her?"

"I don't know," Cecily said grimly. "But I shall have to think of something. If I don't satisfy her, she'll keep pestering me until I tell her the truth, and then there'll be no keeping it a secret from anyone."

Madeline gave her a sly look. "By anyone, I assume you refer to your overprotective husband. When will men realize that we women have minds of our own and are quite capable of using them for pursuits other than housekeeping and child rearing?"

"I'm afraid that day is a long way off." Cecily headed for the door. "I do know that if Baxter finds out I'm still pursuing this investigation there'll be more trouble than I want to think about."

"Dear Frederick decided to join the gentlemen in the bar this morning," Phoebe announced as she walked into the boudoir. "So I thought I'd have a little chat with you and . . . oh!" She halted, having caught sight of Madeline by the window.

"Happy Christmas, Phoebe," Madeline murmured.

"Yes, er, happy Christmas, Madeline." Phoebe marched across the room and deposited herself on the winged armchair. "I must say, I'm rather surprised to see you here. After the way you were clinging so shamelessly to Dr. Prestwick last night in the ballroom, I rather thought you would be spending the day with him."

"I am." Madeline's smile was deceptively sweet. "But at the moment he's in the bar with the rest of the men who can't seem to get through a Christmas morning without some sort of spirits warming their stomachs. But you should know all about that, dear Phoebe. After all, that's a daily occurrence for your husband, is it not?"

Phoebe bristled visibly. "Frederick has a condition that requires the medicinal value of a small daily brandy, yes. The war, you know. All those horrendous experiences left him with a severe affliction."

"So we've noticed." Madeline leaned back in her chair. "Though I must say, the brandy seems to worsen the condition, rather than help it. The colonel tends to think he's back on the war front after he's indulged in a snifter or two. On more than one occasion I've seen him brandishing an imaginary sword with the intent of doing serious bodily harm to the grandfather clock."

Cecily hastily sat down between the two of them. "Madeline, do tell Phoebe your wonderful news! I know she'll be delighted to hear it."

Phoebe gave Madeline a lethal smile. "You are leaving Badgers End for good? How utterly wonderful!"

Madeline rolled her eyes. "Careful, Phoebe dear. The last thing the colonel needs today is to carry you home in his pocket. Especially if you're croaking like a frog all the way. That would quite spoil his Christmas spirit, don't you think?"

There was absolutely no evidence that Madeline had the ability to turn people into frogs, but her reputation for extraordinary powers was enough to make Phoebe pale at the threat.

"Madeline," Cecily said, with just a hint of rebuke, "stop teasing poor Phoebe and tell her your news."

"Oh, very well." Madeline sat up. "I'm to marry Kevin Prestwick. He asked for my hand last night."

Phoebe's eyes lit up, but she managed to sound unaffected by this announcement. "Really. Well, I wish you both well. I hope the good doctor never upsets you enough to turn him into a frog, or anything else for that matter. It would certainly make your sleeping arrangements rather uncomfortable."

Madeline's laughter pealed out. "Phoebe, dear, it's Christmas. What do you say we bury the hatchet, at least for this day, and enjoy a nice glass of sherry together?"

Phoebe set her hat more firmly on her head and smoothed down her elbow length gloves. "Very well. I've never said no to a good glass of sherry."

Relieved, Cecily reached for the decanter. "Then let's celebrate this happy occasion for a dear friend." She leaned forward to pour the sherry into the glasses.

"That's a beautiful pendant you are wearing, Cecily." Phoebe peered at it as Cecily straightened. "Diamonds, aren't they?"

"So I'm told. Tell me, Madeline, have you given any thought to what you might wear to your wedding?"

If Madeline was surprised by Cecily's swift change of subject, she showed no sign of it. "Oh, I suppose I shall wear white," she said, reaching for her glass. "Perhaps we can go shopping together."

"I'd like that. We should go to Harrods. They have the most beautiful gowns there."

"Oh, I couldn't possibly afford the gowns at Harrods. I was thinking of going into Wellercombe."

"Piffle." Cecily sipped her sherry. "I shall buy you a Harrods gown for a wedding present."

"Oh, I couldn't possibly let you do that."

"Speaking of presents," Phoebe said loudly, "Frederick has been asking about the brooch he gave me. I didn't like to tell him I'd loaned it to you, Cecily, so I told him I was saving it to wear on Christmas Day. I should like it back now, before he notices I'm not wearing it."

"Of course, Phoebe." Cecily smiled at her over the rim of her glass. "I'll fetch it for you before you leave."

"Thank you, Cecily." Phoebe seemed satisfied with that and Cecily let out her breath. She had no idea what she would say when Phoebe was ready to leave. The best she could hope for was that the sherry might lull her friend into such a pleasant state she would forget all about the brooch.

She just needed another day or two, and then, with any luck at all, she could tell Phoebe the truth. Unfortunately, the colonel would have some explaining to do, but by then Christmas would be over.

Until then, it seemed more charitable to let Phoebe enjoy the thought that her husband had gone to all the trouble of buying her a lovely gift. Thus Cecily was able to ease her conscience. At least for the time being.

As it was, she was saved from having to create a story to explain the absence of the brooch. Just as they were all enjoying their second glass of sherry, Gertie arrived at the door.

"It's the colonel, m'm," she explained when Cecily opened it. "I think he needs to go home."

"Is he ill?" Cecily glanced anxiously at Phoebe, who was explaining to Madeline the importance of marrying in a proper church.

"Nothing a good sleep won't take care of," Gertie said, keeping her voice at a discreet level. "Too much brandy, m'm. Went to his bloody head as usual."

"Oh, dear. How bad is it?"

"Well, the last I saw of him, he was galloping around the lobby, waving an umbrella over his head and shouting to everyone to keep their heads down if they didn't want it blasted shot off."

"Goodness. I hope there weren't any guests around to see that."

"Well, he scared a couple of ladies half to death, I can tell you." Gertie glanced down the corridor. "I think they retired to their rooms now. Anyhow, Philip tried to calm the colonel down and take the umbrella away, but he called Philip a perishing heathen and hit him over the head with the brolly."

"Where is Mr. Baxter? Can he do something?"

"Not while he's hobbling around on them crutches, he can't. You have to move fast to get anywhere near the colonel when he's like this. Mr. Baxter said to send Mrs. Fortescue down. She's the only one what can get through to him."

Cecily sighed. "Very well. We'll all come down. Thank you, Gertie."

"Yes, m'm."

Gertie sped away, and Cecily turned to her friends. "I'm afraid we have to cut our celebration short," she announced. "It seems that we have a crisis in the lobby involving Colonel Fortescue."

Phoebe rose at once. "I knew it. Those beastly men in the bar must have egged on my Frederick. He never overindulges when he's alone."

Madeline rolled her eyes at Cecily, but thankfully held her tongue.

Cecily led the way down the stairs, wincing as the colonel's voice could be heard echoing up from the lobby.

"Charge, you blighters! Charge, I say! What are you blasted waiting for? We'll be overrun if we don't mow them down. Every dashed last one of them! *Charge!*"

She felt sorry for Phoebe, having to face the embarrassment of placating her husband in such a public place, though it certainly wasn't the first time. Even so, Cecily had to admit, the intrusion couldn't have come at a more opportune time.

Phoebe was so agitated by her dilemma, she had completely forgotten about asking for her brooch. Cecily had gained a reprieve, and now she would have to make the most of it.

CHAPTER

❀ 22 ❀

Although Baxter was disgruntled about Cecily leaving him alone the next day, he accepted her excuse that she needed to pay her annual Boxing Day visits to the local merchants. Normally he would have accompanied her, but since his ankle still pained him, he agreed to stay home and rest.

Cecily enlisted Samuel to drive the carriage, and the two of them set out immediately after breakfast. Cecily's plan was to get through her obligatory visits as quickly as possible, thus leaving her time to visit Whitfield Manor and return to the Pennyfoot without arousing Baxter's suspicions.

Unfortunately, the butcher's wife kept her talking far too long. Standing in the shop, with its unsavory smell of sawdust and dried blood, Cecily gave her little speech and handed over the basket Mrs. Chubb had made up for the merchants.

Mrs. Abbitson exclaimed in delight over the mince pies, sausage rolls, and lemon tarts, and then proceeded to inform Cecily of the latest goings-on in the village.

Despite Cecily's attempts to cut off the flow of gossip, Mrs. Abbitson seemed determined to recount every minute detail of everybody else's business.

Cecily was at the point of being rude when the voluble woman surprised her by saying, "I'm really glad we had the chance to talk, Mrs. Baxter. My husband and I are moving to Brighton next month, so we shan't be seeing each other again. Unless you pay a visit to Brighton, and we happen to bump into each other, that is."

"I had no idea you were leaving Badgers End." Cecily looked at her in concern. "I don't know what we'll do without you. Abbitson's has been serving the Pennyfoot ever since my late husband bought the place."

"Ah yes, I remember Mr. Sinclair well. Such a shame when he died so suddenly. Hard for a woman to take over such a responsibility."

"But so rewarding." Cecily smiled. "I suppose we shall have to find a new butcher."

"Oh, no need for that. We sold the shop to Daniel Perkins. He bought it two months ago."

Cecily wrinkled her brow. "Why does that name sound familiar?"

"Well, he's been to the Pennyfoot. He helped out with the deliveries before Christmas since we were shorthanded, what with the colds everyone had. Perhaps you met him?"

"Oh, now I remember. Mrs. Chubb mentioned his name. I had no idea he owned Abbitson's, though."

"Oh, yes, m'm. Got money, he has. He was an orphan, you know, then when he left there he got a job in a butcher's shop. When the owner died, he didn't have anyone to leave the shop to, so he left it to Dan. Must have thought a lot of him."

"Indeed," Cecily agreed. "Well, I must be off—"

"Anyway," Mrs. Abbitson said, ignoring Cecily's attempts to leave, "Dan worked his fingers to the bone building up that shop and before long he had two, and then three. He did so well he didn't have to cut meat no more. Then one day last year he came down to the coast for a holiday with some friends and they stopped in Badgers End for lunch at the George and Dragon. Dan loved the place so much he decided he wanted to live here."

"How nice." Cecily deliberately walked to the door and opened it. "I'm happy he likes the village as much as we do."

Mrs. Abbitson followed her to the door, still talking. "Strange, it was. He happened to see our notice in the newspaper that we were selling the shop and he came down to see us. Bought it on the spot, he did. He's quite rich, you know."

"I shall certainly look forward to meeting him." Cecily stepped out into the street. "Please tell him to call on me when he has the time."

"I'll certainly do that, Mrs. Baxter."

A few more pleasantries later, Cecily was at last on her way.

It was past midday by the time she and Samuel were finally on the road to the manor. She had given him orders to park outside the grounds, in the hopes that she could talk to Emily Gower without being noticed by anyone else. She had no wish to engage in another bout of wits with Randall Thorpe. The man was a little too suave for her taste, and made her quite uncomfortable.

Samuel halted the carriage a few yards from the driveway. Instead of walking up to the house, Cecily cut across the lawn to the trees with a worried Samuel close behind.

"I wish you had told Mr. Baxter where we were going," he said, as they emerged at the back of the manor. "He won't like it when he finds out."

"Don't worry," Cecily assured him. "I'll tell him it was all my doing."

Samuel's expression told her that he wasn't convinced that would be of much help when faced with Baxter's wrath. She could only hope the visit would be worth the risk.

The gardener's cottage lay on the far side of the back lawns, next to a large pond where several ducks had made their home. Their annoyed quacking must have alerted Emily Gower, since she came down the path to the gate as Cecily approached.

She was a small woman, both in height and build, with gray hair dragged back from a face creased with worry lines. There was no doubt in Cecily's mind that the woman was incapable of strangling a man and hauling him up in a tree.

On the other hand, if Gavin Hargrove had pursued Emily, perhaps having given her the brooch, and Silas found out, the gardener could well have had the brooch with him when he went after Gavin in a jealous rage.

Emily's agitation when she greeted her visitors suggested she didn't have too many of them. "My husband isn't here," she called out before Cecily had reached the gate. "You'll have to come back tonight."

Relieved she wouldn't have to deal with the surly Silas, Cecily smiled at the nervous woman. "Actually I came to see you, Mrs. Gower. I'm Mrs. Baxter, from the Pennyfoot Country Club."

"I know who you are." Emily looked over at the trees, as if expecting her husband to come striding out of them. "Silas told me you've been around asking questions. I don't know nothing. If you want to know anything you'll have to ask him."

"Perhaps we'd better come back another time," Samuel said, standing close by Cecily's side.

"I won't keep you but a minute." She did her best to ignore his fidgeting. "On my last visit to the manor I found a brooch lying on the ground. I asked everyone at the manor, but since no one appeared to recognize it, I was wondering if it belonged to you."

"I don't wear brooches." Emily turned away and started up the path. "My Silas don't like jewelry. He says it makes a woman look cheap."

Cecily wondered what Baxter would say to that. "It's a silver fox," she called out to Emily's retreating back. "Dressed as a huntsman."

"Come on, m'm." Samuel sounded nervous. "We'd better get out of here before that gardener comes back here and causes more trouble."

Disappointed, Cecily was about to agree when Emily halted, then slowly turned around. "A silver fox?"

"Yes!" In her eagerness, Cecily pushed open the gate. "Do you know to whom it belongs?"

"I've seen something like that . . ." Emily began, then broke off, her eyes wide on a spot behind Cecily.

A quick glance over her shoulder confirmed Cecily's fears. Silas Gower was striding toward them, an angry scowl smoldering on his face.

"I can't remember for sure," Emily said quickly. "It was a long time ago, but I think I saw Mrs. Trumble with a brooch like that." With one last look in her husband's direction, she muttered, "I must go," then turned and fled up the path.

At the same moment, Silas's gruff voice demanded, "Here, what do you think you're doing, pestering my wife?"

Samuel muttered, "Flipping heck," while Cecily turned to meet the newcomer.

"Mr. Gower! How nice to see you again! I was just asking your wife if she'd lost a silver fox brooch. I found one the other day and thought it might belong to her."

Silas glowered at her, and shifted the heavy spade he carried to his shoulder. "My wife don't wear no brooches. Nothing like that. A wedding ring, that's all she wears."

"Yes, so she told me." Cecily smiled at him. "Well, in that case, I'll be off. I'm sorry for the intrusion."

Silas grunted, but stood aside to let her pass.

Hurrying along beside her, Samuel said breathlessly, "Whew, that was close. I thought he was going to hit us over the head with that spade."

"I don't think we have anything to worry about as far as Silas Gower is concerned."

"You think Mrs. Trumble is the killer?" Samuel laughed.

"She couldn't even hang a cat up in a tree, leave alone a grown man."

"These wiry women are stronger than they look." Cecily headed toward the manor. "In any case, I'd really like to know why she lied about not having seen the brooch before."

"But Mrs. Gower could have been wrong about seeing her with it. After all, she did say it were a long time ago, didn't she. She could have it all wrong." He shook his head. "I just can't see that skinny old woman murdering anyone. In any case, if the brooch is hers, and she lied about it, she's not likely to tell you the truth now."

"Which is why we have to search her room to see if she has it."

Samuel stared at her. "I do know one thing," he said at last. "It weren't the housekeeper that whipped our horses and nearly sent us over the cliff. I know a bloke when I sees one, even if he did have a scarf wrapped around his face."

"It's all right, Samuel. I think I know what happened, but if we are going to prove anything, we have to find that brooch. It's the only way P.C. Northcott will believe us."

"What do you think happened, then?"

"I'd rather not say until I'm sure."

"Well, how are you going to search Mrs. Trumble's room, anyway?"

"I'll find a way. What I need you to do is keep Mrs. Trumble busy while I hunt for the brooch."

Samuel groaned. "How am I supposed to do that?"

Cecily paused at the foot of the manor steps. "By being your charming self, of course. Now come along, Samuel, put a pleasant smile on your face. We don't want to arouse suspicion from anyone, do we."

"I've got a nasty feeling we're walking into a whole load of trouble," Samuel muttered.

Ignoring him, Cecily led the way up the steps and tugged on the bell rope.

Wilmot opened the door, his blotchy face and red-rimmed eyes suggesting he still suffered from his cold. "I'm sorry, madam, but Miss Kendall is not at home," he informed Cecily, when she asked for the young lady.

"Well, then, I should like to speak to Mr. Thorpe."

"Mr. Thorpe is not at home, either. I am not expecting them back anytime soon, so I suggest you return at a later, and more convenient, date."

Crushed, Cecily took a moment to gather her senses. Wilmot was in the act of closing the door when she said, "Please tell them I called and give them both my regards."

The butler gave no sign he'd heard her as the door closed with a thud.

"Well, that's that," Samuel said, his voice light with relief. "We'd better get home, before Mr. Baxter starts wondering what happened to you."

"Not yet." Cecily walked to the edge of the steps, frowning in concentration.

"He's not going to let you in there without a good excuse, m'm."

"I'm well aware of that." She smiled encouragingly at him. "Which means we shall have to find another way in without being observed."

Samuel's eyebrows almost disappeared into his hair.

"We're *what*?" He struggled with his breath for a moment, then added a belated, "M'm?"

"Come along, Samuel." Cecily marched briskly down the stairs. "There has to be a pair of French windows somewhere on the ground floor. All we have to do is find them."

"But . . ." Samuel clattered down the steps behind her. "What if someone sees us?"

"Neither Miss Kendall nor Mr. Thorpe are at home. The servants will all be busy with their chores, and if any of them do see us we shall merely explain that we are waiting for Mr. Thorpe to return home. They won't know that Wilmot didn't let us in the house to wait."

"Wilmot will know," Samuel said grimly.

"Well, yes. That is the one person we should avoid at all cost."

"Look, m'm"—Samuel moved ahead of her and barred her path—"wouldn't it be better to let the constable take care of this? You can tell him about the brooch and he can search Mrs. Trumble's room with the proper authority to do it, then no one gets into any trouble. Right?"

He stumbled backward as Cecily took a determined step toward him. "Not right at all, Samuel. P.C. Northcott will simply ignore the whole thing. He'll say that Emily Gower was mistaken, that the brooch was dropped by a gypsy and more than likely won't even mention the brooch to Inspector Cranshaw, since it holds so little significance for him."

"But—"

"The only way we can convince anyone to listen to us is to find that brooch and hand it to the police ourselves."

"Then let's wait until Miss Kendall is here so we at least

have a good excuse to be in the house." Samuel sent a nervous glance at the windows. "I don't like this breaking and entering business at all."

"You've done it before," Cecily pointed out.

"Yes, I have." Samuel puffed out his breath in exasperation. "When you've ordered me to do it. That didn't mean I liked doing it. M'm."

"But doing it usually meant a break in the case, did it not?"

When he didn't answer, she added quietly, "Once the case is handed to Cranshaw, it's very likely the gypsies will be hounded without mercy. There's a very good chance that they will be blamed for Gavin Hargrove's death. Especially if Sam Northcott has any say in the matter."

"But—"

"I can't let that happen, Samuel. Not after the way they took care of Mr. Baxter. He could have died that night in the woods if they hadn't taken him in and attended to him. I owe it to them to at least try to find out the truth."

Samuel's mouth twisted. "I hope they'll appreciate it when we're locked up for burglary."

"You worry far too much, Samuel. Now come along. We're wasting time arguing about this, and as you say, Mr. Baxter will be gnashing his teeth if we don't arrive home shortly."

"Yes, m'm. Very well, m'm."

Noticing the sarcasm in his voice, Cecily hid a smile. Not that she felt like smiling. Samuel was right. They would be taking a huge risk in breaking into the manor. If they were caught, the only justification they would have would be the discovery of the brooch and exposing Gavin Hargrove's killer.

If she couldn't find the brooch, or prove it was dropped

by the killer, they would most likely be at the mercy of Inspector Cranshaw.

It was one thing to meddle in police business when one had a fool like Sam Northcott handling the case. Incurring the wrath of the formidable inspector would undoubtedly spell trouble for both her and Samuel.

She had to find that brooch, and somehow prove it belonged to a killer. Unfortunately, she had no idea at all how she would manage that.

"There they are!" She paused, her gaze fixed on the wall that jutted out at a right angle from the main building. At the far end French windows led out onto a terrace. Heavily pruned rose bushes clung to wide trellises on either side, and large earthenware pots guarded the glass doors.

In the summer the pots would be crammed with brightly colored annuals, and the roses would fill the air with their scent. Cecily closed her eyes as she imagined the scene. How she adored roses. Her rose garden on the roof of the Pennyfoot was her favorite place in the summer.

"M'm? Are you all right? If you've changed your mind—"

Samuel's hopeful voice snatched her out of her reverie. "Of course I haven't changed my mind. I was simply collecting my thoughts, that's all."

She studied the wall leading up to the terrace. Several tall windows presented quite an obstacle. She would have to crouch very low and stay close to the wall. She hesitated for a moment, fighting her doubts, then pulled herself together. "Follow me." Without waiting to see if Samuel obeyed, she flitted across the flower beds and crouched down behind a large shrub.

She could see no sign of Silas, or anyone else for that matter. The earth beneath her feet smelled of horse manure. Silas must have put down some early fertilizer.

Anxious to get away from that unpleasant odor, she bent double and moved along the wall to the first window. Flapping a hand behind her to signal Samuel to crouch low, she crept past, making sure to keep her head below the windowsill.

It was quite an effort to stay doubled up for that long, and she straightened with a sigh of relief. Only five more windows to go.

One by one she crept past them, squishing down as far as she could go while enabling her feet to propel her forward. By the time she reached the end of the wall she felt like a crab crawling across a mile of sand.

Thankfully she straightened for the last time. The terrace was now only a few feet away from her. She turned to see how close Samuel was behind her. To her utter dismay she saw him still standing at the first corner.

She waved a frantic hand at him, then held her breath as he came at a run, skimming below the windows with far more ease than she had managed.

"What were you waiting for?" she demanded in a fierce whisper as he reached her.

He looked uncomfortable, his face red, his breathing labored. "Sorry, m'm. I just didn't think it was proper to follow too close with you bent over like that."

Cecily huffed out her breath. "I appreciate your attention to protocol, Samuel, but under the circumstances, I think we can dispense with the niceties for now."

"Yes, m'm." Samuel coughed. "What do we do now, then?"

Cecily eyed the white railings surrounding the terrace. "I suppose we shall have to climb up over those."

Samuel's expression would have been comical had it not been for the seriousness of the situation. "Wouldn't it be simpler just to go back to the house and insist on Old Poker Face letting us in to wait for Miss Kendall?"

"I considered that." Cecily walked up to the railings and ran her gloved hand up them. "But once Wilmot knew we were in the house he'd make sure to keep an eye on us. I'm quite sure he'd never let me near Mrs. Trumble's room." She turned to Samuel. "I feel quite hesitant about asking you to do this, Samuel. If you're not up to it, please tell me now."

Samuel raised his chin. " 'Course I'm up to it. I'm just not sure it's the right thing to do, that's all."

"Well, if you're sure you're well enough." She eyed the railings again. "Perhaps if you climb up there first, you can help pull me up?"

Samuel rolled his eyes at the sky. "If Mr. Baxter ever finds out, he'll run me right out of the Pennyfoot and never let me back."

"What Mr. Baxter doesn't know won't hurt him. We should hurry, though. It will be dark before we get back on the road if we take too much longer."

With one more beseeching look at the sky, Samuel pulled off his cap, tucked it in his pocket, then grasped the railings. With a couple of grunts, some heaving and tugging, he hauled himself over the top and landed with a resounding thud on the other side.

CHAPTER
✿ 23 ✿

"Shh!" Cecily hissed through the railings. "For heaven's sake. They'll hear you!"

"Sorry, m'm. It was higher than I thought." He leaned over the top of the rail and looked down at her.

His feet, she noticed, were just about level with her shoulders.

"I don't see how you're going to climb up here, m'm," he said, with a worried frown.

The same thought had occurred to her, though she wasn't about to admit it. "I'll manage," she said firmly.

"Better let me look for the brooch."

"No, it will take two of us. I need you to stand guard while I search the room." She took a firm hold of the railings with one hand and raised the other up in the air. "Grasp my hand, Samuel, and pull like the devil."

"I bloody feel like the devil," Samuel mumbled. "If you'll excuse my language."

"Quite understandable under these circumstances." Cecily gasped as he tugged on her arm and almost pulled it from the socket. Scrabbling with her feet for a hold, she clung to the railings with her free hand and helped drag herself up.

For a terrifying moment she sprawled across the top of the rail, certain she would fall back.

At her muffled shriek, Samuel abandoned all attempts at propriety. He grasped her about the waist and dragged her over. The two of them crashed to the floor with a shuddering thud.

"Oh, blimey, that did it," Samuel muttered.

Panting from exertion, it was several seconds before Cecily could answer him. "Let us just hope that no one is in that room," she said, nodding at the windows.

"If they are, they'll be out here any second." He kept his gaze averted as Cecily scrambled to her feet. "Are you all right, m'm? Not hurt, are you?"

"Only my dignity." She brushed the dust from her skirt. "Though I daresay I'll have a bruise or two to show for my efforts. Obviously I'm not quite as sprightly as I once used to be."

"Sorry, m'm." He jumped up. "I tried to hold on, but I lost me balance."

"Quite all right, Samuel." Cecily straightened her hat,

which had somehow miraculously stayed attached to her head with the help of her hatpins. "Now, since no one has come rushing out brandishing a broom at us, we can assume the room is empty. Let us go in, and remember, if anyone asks, we are simply waiting for Mr. Thorpe or Miss Kendall to return. As long as we act perfectly innocent there should be no reason for anyone to suspect us of trespassing."

"Unless Wilmot catches us."

"Well, we'll have to cross that bridge when we come to it."

"More likely fall off it and drown."

"Really, Samuel, you do have an unfortunate habit of anticipating the worst." She tiptoed over to the doors and grasped the handle.

"That's because the worst usually happens when we're on one of these escapades." Samuel glanced over his shoulder.

Cecily tugged at the handle. With a loud squeak the door swung open. "Oh, dear. This door needs a drop of oil," she murmured, then stepped through into the room. A quick look around confirmed her guess. They were in the library.

Floor to ceiling shelves lined the walls, crammed with dusty tomes of all shapes and sizes. Consumed with her passion for books, Cecily would have dearly loved to peruse the shelves. Time, however, was their enemy, and she could not afford to dally.

"Take a peek in the hallway," she ordered Samuel, "and tell me what you see. Be careful, and try not to let anyone catch sight of you."

"Yes, m'm. I'll do my best to render myself invisible right away."

Cecily frowned at Samuel's back as he sped across the room to the door. It wasn't like him to be so sardonic. Though under the circumstances, she supposed she could make an allowance.

Actually, she was feeling more than a little guilty. She had asked a lot of Samuel these past few days, especially considering he had not yet recovered from the blows he'd taken to his head. She sincerely hoped he would feel no lasting effects from all the trauma he'd been through. But if he did, she would be responsible. It was a sobering thought.

She had to remind herself again of the huge debt she owed the gypsies. There was no doubt in her mind that Sam Northcott would pounce on them as suspects just to save face in front of Inspector Cranshaw. Sam would do just about anything to avoid a confrontation with his domineering superior.

While she was still struggling with her conscience, Samuel crept back to her. "Can't see no one out there," he said, in a hoarse whisper.

"Good. Now I have to find the housekeeper's room. Most likely on the top floor in the attic rooms." She glanced around for a clock and spied one above the massive fireplace. Moving closer, she saw it was half past three. "We must hurry. There's less than hour before darkness will fall."

"What do you want me to do?"

"Keep an eye out for Mrs. Trumble and make sure she doesn't go to her room. It should take me no more than half an hour to search it."

"What'll I say if she decides to go up to her room?"

Cecily sighed. "Think of something, Samuel. Ask for her

advice on something—anything. Most people like to be asked for advice." Seeing his worried frown, she patted his arm. "Don't worry, dear. I'm sure you will manage just fine. Just be sure you don't run into Wilmot. I have a feeling he could be dangerous."

Samuel looked startled. "What do you mean?"

"Just what I say. Stay out of his sight. Now come on, I have to find that room."

Outside in the hall, Cecily paused to listen for any possible movement. She could hear nothing, not even the rumbling of a carpet sweeper. The maids were most likely taking a rest.

The thought that the housekeeper might also be resting in her room gave her qualms, but she decided to worry about that if and when it happened. Right then, she needed to find the room.

Creeping up the stairs with Samuel behind her, she had to admit to a certain thrill of excitement. She was close to the end of this particular chase, and it had been a long and frustrating one.

She reached the landing on the first floor, just as a maid hurried past. Fortunately the stairs were in shadow just there, and the maid seemed not to notice her.

Cecily held her breath until the slim figure in the black dress disappeared into one of the rooms. Turning to Samuel, she beckoned with her finger, then scooted around the landing and up the next flight of stairs.

All seemed quiet on the top floor, and she signaled to Samuel to wait by the stairs. Quietly she turned the door handle of the first room and pushed it open. The room was empty, and she spied a maid's uniform hanging from the bed post. This wasn't the room.

The second room was also empty, but there were three beds crammed in there, which told her this could not be the housekeeper's quarters.

At the end of the hallway, she finally found a door hidden away in a corner. Upon opening it she saw at once that the room was more spacious than the others. A large trunk sat in one corner with a label attached. A quick glance brought a smile of triumph to her face. She'd found Mrs. Trumble's room.

It took her a while to find the brooch. After searching the drawers in the chest and dresser, she looked under the mattress, inside the pillow cases and behind the curtains on the windowsill. After moving around several large boxes in the wardrobe, she finally found the brooch tucked away in a tiny box on the back shelf. Mrs. Trumble had gone to a great deal of trouble to hide it.

Turning it over in her palm, Cecily felt a deep sense of satisfaction. Mrs. Trumble might not have killed Gavin Hargrove, but she certainly knew who did. The very fact that the killer had gone to all that trouble to steal back the brooch proved that it was an important clue to his identity. Since it obviously belonged to Mrs. Trumble, she must have been with him when he committed the crime.

She started for the door, hoping to find Samuel still waiting at the head of the stairs. About to step out into the hallway, she gasped when a figure loomed up in front of her.

It wasn't Mrs. Trumble staring down at her with glittering cold eyes. It was the housekeeper's accomplice.

"I had an idea you might attempt something like this," Wilmot said, holding out his hand. "Now give me the brooch."

Cecily closed her fingers around the brooch. "Where is Samuel?"

"He'll be nursing a sore head when he wakes up." Wilson's teeth bared in a nasty smile. "*If* he wakes up."

Cold dread filled Cecily's chest. "If you've hurt him again I'll—"

"I don't think it will do you any good to threaten me," Wilmot said calmly. "In any case, I can't have either of you running around talking about things that don't concern you. Now give me the brooch."

"He was going to sack you, wasn't he." Cecily put her hands behind her back. "Miss Kendall told me Mr. Hargrove was going to get rid of some of the servants. She meant you and Mrs. Trumble."

Wilmot's face darkened. "More than thirty years of excellent service we gave to that man's father. Not only did he fail to provide for us in his will, he left us at the mercy of his odious son, who planned to throw us out without so much as a decent reference. This is our home. I couldn't let that happen."

"So you strangled him, and tried to make it look like an accident."

"He deserved that and more. He would have brought shame on the manor and everyone in it. His father would have rolled over in his grave if he knew half of what that man planned to do. I knew Mr. Thorpe would be far more generous and allow us to stay. So I simply arranged for him to inherit the family fortune."

Cecily shook her head. "How did Mrs. Trumble get involved in all this?"

"That doesn't concern you. Enough of this chitchat. Hand me the brooch this minute, or do I have to take it from you?"

"Here." Cecily thrust it at him.

He answered with a howl of pain and jumped back.

With her hands behind her back, Cecily had opened the brooch and used the long pin as a weapon. At the same moment she darted past him and out into the hallway.

There was no sign of Samuel as she fled to the stairs, and her heart hammered in anxiety. She had barely reached the top of the stairs when rough hands grabbed her from behind.

"You got away from me once," Wilmot snarled. "You will not do so again. I'll hide both your bodies where they'll never be found."

Cecily cried out as his fingers closed cruelly around her throat. She thrashed about, kicking and elbowing, but Wilmot's fingers tightened, cutting off the air.

Tears sprang to her eyes, and once more she pictured Baxter grieving by her grave. The shadows in the hallway grew darker and she struggled to breathe. She could feel herself growing weaker, her legs felt as if they had irons clamped to them.

Vaguely she thought she heard a shout, but the dark clouds gathered about her, and she knew no more.

"Where are they, for God's sake? They should have been back hours ago." Baxter swept an angry arm in the air, narrowly missing the tray that Gertie held.

She clutched it more tightly, rattling the cups in their

saucers. "I'm sorry, sir. Do you want Philip to ring the constabulary?"

"Fat lot of good that will do. The man's an idiot."

"Yes, sir." She stared at him, wondering anxiously what she could do to help.

"Have a carriage brought to the door," Baxter demanded. "I'll go into town and see if I can find them."

"Will you be all right to go outside, Mr. Baxter?" Gertie looked pointedly at his bandaged ankle. "Mrs. Baxter won't like it if you go out too soon and hurt yourself some more."

"Mrs. Baxter," he said, casting a baleful eye on Gertie, "should have thought of that when she disregarded my wishes and failed to come home at a reasonable hour."

"Yes, sir." Gertie backed out of the door. "I'll get the carriage right away."

Once outside, she hurried, as fast as the loaded tray would allow, along the hallway to the lobby. Philip gave her a worried look as she approached the desk. "No sign of them yet," he said.

Gertie didn't like the feeling she was getting in her stomach. "I hope nothing's bloody happened to them," she said, with an anxious glance at the grandfather clock. "It's not like Mrs. Baxter to stay out this late. Especially with Mr. Baxter laid up with that bad ankle."

"He don't look too laid up to me," Philip observed, nodding at the hallway behind her.

Gertie turned in time to see Baxter hobbling toward the stairs with remarkable speed considering he'd discarded his crutches. "He's going to look for them." She turned back to

Philip. "He wants a carriage at the door. He's going into town after them."

"His missus won't like that," Philip muttered. He gave the bell rope a tug. "Going out without his crutches. She'll be proper cross with him, she will."

"Not half as bloody cross as he is with her." Gertie stared gloomily at the stairs. "He's always saying he'll take her away from the Pennyfoot if she keeps getting into trouble. I hope this isn't the last straw for him. This could be the end of her days here if it is. Then what would we do?"

"We'd be working for a new manager, that's what." Philip started as the telephone jangled behind him. Lifting the receiver from its hook on the wall, he spoke into the mouthpiece. "Yes? Yes. Very well. Yes, I will. Thank you."

He hung up and turned a pale face toward Gertie. "That was the constabulary. You'd better inform Mr. Baxter. There's been some trouble at Whitfield Manor. P.C. Northcott wants Mr. Baxter to meet him there immediately. He sounded really upset."

Gertie felt her entire body go cold. "Did he say what kind of trouble?"

Philip shook his head. "No, but I think it had to do with Mrs. Baxter."

"Dear Lord," Gertie whispered. "I hope and pray nothing's happened to her."

"Nothing's happened to who?" A voice demanded behind her.

Gertie swung around to face Baxter. "P.C. Northcott just rang, sir. He wants you to meet him at Whitfield Manor right away."

Baxter stared at her, his eyes questioning, his jaw tense.

"I'm sorry, sir," Gertie mumbled.

He gave her a curt nod, swung around and hobbled to the door.

She watched him go, her heart aching with anxiety. Madam had to be all right. She just had to be all right. For if she wasn't, it would be the end of everything for Mr. Baxter. And for them all.

Cecily felt a terrible thirst, her throat ached and her eyelids felt as if something heavy rested on them. What kind of illness had overtaken her? She couldn't remember.

The bed she lay on was not her own. No bed she'd ever slept on could be as uncomfortable as this one. For one thing it was too short. She could feel the end of it cutting into her calves.

Voices. Vaguely familiar. A deep, gruff voice, and a timid woman's answering him. My, how her throat ached. She lifted a hand, surprised to find it so heavy and unwieldy. Giving up the effort, she let the darkness claim her again.

Voices aroused her once more. Louder, more urgent. Someone calling her name. A tender hand stroking her brow. A deep voice, harsh with anxiety.

"Cecily. For God's sake, wake up. Please, if you love me, answer me."

Obediently she opened her eyes, and smiled at Baxter's ravaged face. Great heavens! Surely that could not be tears she saw glistening on his cheeks? She tried to say his name, but the most ugly sound erupted from her mouth.

Like a toad in pain. Fire ripped through her throat and she moaned.

"Thank God. Oh, thank God." Baxter's arms lifted her, crushed her against his shoulder until she had to struggle for breath.

She couldn't breathe. Then she remembered. Weakly she thrust him back. "Wilmot." It felt as if she'd shouted the name, yet the awful harsh whisper barely left her lips.

"Hush, my love. Dr. Prestwick will be with you in a moment or two. Just lie still."

She could hear voices in the background. Sam Northcott. Who was he talking to? She knew the voice but couldn't place it. A man, and then a woman. The woman was crying. Of course. Mrs. Trumble.

She struggled to sit up, but Baxter's hands on her shoulders pressed her to the hard bed. "Lie still, Cecily. You are not to move until the doctor has examined you. Those were his orders and I'm here to see you obey them."

She swallowed, wincing as the action lit more fires in her throat. "Where am I? Where is Wilmot?"

"Wilmot is dead." Baxter's face looked grim. "If he hadn't died before I got here I would have killed him myself."

"H—" She swallowed and tried again. "How?"

"You can thank Silas Gower for saving your life." Baxter paused, as if gathering his composure. "I don't know the whole story, but somehow he knew you were walking into trouble. He followed you and Samuel. He found Samuel first. Then he heard you and the butler scuffling at the top of the stairs. He charged up there and attacked Wilmot, who fell down the stairs. He broke his neck in the fall."

Cecily closed her eyes. One more question, then she could sleep. "Samuel?" she whispered. "Is he—"

"He's alive. That young man must have the hardest head in the county. Prestwick is with him now."

Once more she let the shadows take her.

When she woke up again Kevin Prestwick was bending over her. "Drink this, Cecily," he urged. "It will help the pain in your throat."

She sipped the dark liquid, shuddering at the taste. Swallowing felt a little easier, and she tested her voice. "Thank you." She still sounded like a damaged foghorn, but the words had come out a little stronger.

Glancing around, she saw that her bed was actually a davenport in the living room of Whitfield Manor. Sam Northcott stood on the other side of the room, talking to Mrs. Trumble, who seemed even more agitated than usual. Not really surprising under the circumstances.

Carefully she moved her head to peer around the rest of the room. Apparently neither Naomi Kendall nor Randall Thorpe had returned home as yet. They would certainly receive a surprise when they did.

"I want you to refrain from talking for at least the rest of today." Kevin frowned as Baxter's chuckle followed his words.

"Sorry, old boy," Baxter murmured, "but if you know my wife, that's practically an impossibility."

"Nevertheless, you must do your best to comply." Kevin gave her a stern look. "You have a badly bruised throat and barely escaped a crushed larynx. You need to rest your vocal cords for the next twenty-four hours or you could well do some permanent damage to them."

"Don't worry, Prestwick." Baxter's expression said he would brook no argument. "I'll make sure she keeps her mouth closed."

Cecily raised an eyebrow at him in protest, but resisted the urge to retort. It hurt her to talk anyway, and she was quite content to remain quiet for the time being. Tomorrow would be soon enough to take her husband to task for his unseemly comments. Right now she just wanted to go home.

She tugged at Baxter's sleeve and mouthed a word. *Samuel?*

"He's going to be all right," Baxter assured her. "The doctor wants to move him to the hospital in Wellercombe for a few days."

"He'll be fine, Cecily." Kevin patted her hand. "I just want them to keep an eye on him for the next day or two, that's all. His head has taken quite some punishment over the last few days."

She would have to find a way to make it up to him, Cecily thought, racked with guilt. Poor Samuel. It was all her fault. He'd nearly died because of her. Perhaps Baxter was right. Perhaps it was time she stopped sticking her nose into business better left to the constables. Even if it did break her heart to do so.

CHAPTER
❧ 24 ❧

Mrs. Chubb could hardly contain herself as she waited for Gertie to get back to the kitchen. She kept looking at the clock, wondering how much longer it would take for the maids to finish setting the tables for dinner.

True, the extra staff they'd taken on for Christmas were no longer with them, but still, they'd had plenty of time to get the tables ready for the New Year's Eve feast.

At last the door flew open, and Gertie rushed in, close on her heels was Pansy. "Sorry we're late," Gertie said, "but Samuel was in the dining room talking to Pansy and that held us up a bit."

"Samuel had no business keeping you girls talking during our busy time," Mrs. Chubb grumbled.

For answer, Pansy threw her arms around the housekeeper and gave her a hug, then skipped over to the sink.

Startled, Mrs. Chubb looked at Gertie. "What's got into her?"

"Samuel asked her out," Gertie said. She laid the tray of leftover silverware on the table. "She's been waiting for that for a long time. Gawd knows why."

"Samuel's a nice man," Mrs. Chubb said, with a glance at Pansy. "You treat him right, my girl. Don't you go breaking his heart."

"Seems to me it's usually the bloke what does that." Gertie started laying the knives back in their slot in the drawer.

"Speaking of which," Mrs. Chubb said, "I heard something interesting about that Dan Perkins this morning." She almost bit her tongue to keep a straight face as Gertie gave an elaborate shrug.

"So, what was it?"

"I'm surprised he didn't tell you when you went out with him on Christmas Eve."

To her surprise, Gertie actually looked guilty as her chin shot up. "Tell me what?"

"That he's rich." She was disappointed when Gertie merely looked relieved. She'd waited for an hour or more to tell her the big news, anticipating the look on her face when she heard. "You don't seem very surprised," she added.

" 'Cos I know it's not true." Gertie closed the drawer and carried the tray over to the cupboard.

"But it *is* true." Mrs. Chubb walked up behind her. "Madam told me herself this afternoon. He doesn't work for the Abbitsons, he bought the shop from them. Not only that, he has three more shops in London."

Anxious to convince her, she told her everything that madam had told her. "That's how he came to live down here now," she finished. "He's got pots of money."

Gertie had stood with her back to her throughout her whole speech, but now she turned around, slowly, like she was in a trance.

And there was the look on her face Mrs. Chubb had waited over an hour to see.

Gertie opened her mouth, shut it again, then said feebly, "Bloody hell."

"We have a lot to celebrate this New Year's Eve." Cecily looked with satisfaction at the tables that Madeline had decorated with red, white, and blue ribbons. Above them, enormous paper balls hung from the ceilings, slowly rotating every time the ballroom doors opened.

Madeline gazed up at them with a critical eye. "I think I should have added streamers," she murmured. "They would have added more color."

Cecily laughed. "We have more than enough color. Just look at all this." She swept her hand in an expansive arc. "It looks marvelous."

This would be the last night of the Christmas season, and as always, the Pennyfoot staff had outdone themselves. The tables were loaded with delectable tidbits—everything from sausage rolls and cheese twists to iced coconut squares and lemon tarts. Huge bowls of cider punch and spiced eggnog sat amid a sea of crystal glasses, while on another table a pyramid of glasses rose four feet high, waiting for a footman to pour the champagne in a cascading waterfall to fill them.

Phoebe had hired a full orchestra to play for the dancing, and balloons waited in a huge net across the ceiling, ready to float down at the stroke of twelve.

"It does look rather festive," Madeline agreed. "So what are we celebrating, besides the beginning of a new year and your narrow escape from death, of course?"

"Your engagement, my dear." Cecily smiled fondly at her. "And Samuel's homecoming from the hospital. He arrived this afternoon. Just the fact that we're both alive and well. Even Baxter is getting around without his crutches."

Madeline's beautiful smile seemed to light up the room, as always. "We do have a lot to celebrate."

"Have you set a date for your wedding yet?"

Madeline reached for a couple of glasses and set them closer to the bowl. "Not yet. You will be the first to know when we do."

Cecily peered anxiously at her. "All is well with you and Kevin, I hope?"

"Very well." Madeline patted her arm. "Don't fret so, Cecily. Kevin and I are content to wait until the time is right. We'll know when that is, and that's when we'll plan the wedding. It will be a simple affair, so it won't take long to make arrangements."

"You will have the reception here, though, won't you?"

"I wouldn't dream of having it anywhere else."

Cecily let out her breath on a sigh of relief. "Well, thank

goodness. I would have been most upset if you'd decided to hold it in the woods or someplace."

Madeline laughed. "Speaking of woods, have you heard what happened to that housekeeper at Whitfield Manor? We haven't had a chance to talk about it since your throat healed. Kevin refuses to discuss the matter—some professional taboo or something—and I'm dying to know the whole story."

Cecily took her arm. "Come, we'll go to my suite where we can talk in peace. I have an hour or so to spare before I have to get ready for the ball tonight."

She led the way and a few minutes later they were settled in front of the fireplace in the boudoir.

"Now tell me," Madeline said, her eyes glistening with excitement as she leaned forward, "how did that scrawny little woman get mixed up in a murder?"

Cecily cleared her throat. She still sounded a little husky, and it was a constant reminder of how close she had come to disaster. "Well, it was all Wilmot's doing, of course. He was determined not to be thrown out of his home, and the only way he could ensure that was to get rid of Gavin Hargrove. So he picked a morning when Gavin had gone riding in the woods, and offered to drive Mrs. Trumble into town to pick up supplies."

"Wasn't that rather unusual for a butler? Don't they have footmen to drive the traps?"

Cecily sighed. "Yes, it was. Had I not been so intent on finding Baxter, I might have pounced on that in the very beginning. As it was, I didn't pay any attention to the fact when Randall mentioned it during our first visit to Whitfield

Manor. You see, Wilmot needed an excuse to leave the manor yet give himself an alibi. He told Mrs. Trumble the two footmen were sick, and offered to drive her himself."

"How terribly devious."

"Apparently he convinced Mrs. Trumble that killing Mr. Hargrove was the only way both of them could keep their positions. She must have been either too frightened to oppose him, or too desperate over losing her position and everything that went along with it."

"It had to be a terrible shock to her to find out she no longer had a home and a living."

"Exactly." Cecily held out her hands to warm them by the fire. "She told Sam Northcott she wasn't thinking straight or she never would have agreed to help Wilmot. Of course, once she did, there was no going back. Wilmot terrified her with tales of what could happen to her if anyone found out. She only agreed because he'd assured her it would look like an accident."

Madeline shook her head in disbelief. "Did she say what actually happened out there?"

"Yes. Apparently Wilmot sawed part way through a heavy bough right above the trail and waited for Gavin to come along. Just as he reached the tree, Wilmot leaned on the branch, intending to knock Gavin off his horse. Randall Thorpe told me that Gavin had been hit by a branch before, which probably gave Wilmot the idea."

"Rather ingenious when you think about it."

"I suppose so. It didn't work, though. Instead, Wilmot fell with the branch, and the two of them crashed to the ground. Wilmot must have been badly bruised in the fall, which was why he walked so stiffly. Something else I should have seized upon."

"Well, that could have been anything. I thought it was simply a matter of old age."

"So did I." Cecily leaned back in her chair. "Do you remember what Pedro said when he talked about finding Baxter?"

"He said a lot of things."

"I mean about the hunter being wounded like the hunted. He said it was a fair exchange. I think he was trying to give me a hint that they were both limping. I should have realized that. If only I'd put everything together earlier, poor Samuel would not have ended up in hospital."

Madeline laughed. "You're being too hard on yourself, Cecily. After all, you tracked the killer down with the brooch. That was clever of you. So it was Wilmot who threw those rocks at us?"

"I suppose it was. He must have realized I was going to keep digging until I learned the truth. Most likely he wanted to frighten me into giving up."

"Obviously he didn't know you at all. There's just one thing I don't understand. How did Gavin Hargrove's body end up in your trap?"

"Well, Wilmot had expected the fall to either kill Gavin or at least knock him out. He planned to finish him off with the branch and everyone would think that was the cause of his death. When they fell, however, Gavin was still conscious and Wilmot was forced to strangle him." She shuddered, remembering those strong hands closing around her throat.

"I'm sorry, Cecily," Madeline said quickly. "I know this must be upsetting for you."

"No, it's all right. It's good to talk about it and then I can put it behind me." She cleared her throat again. "Anyway, Wilmot had to come up with another plan, and quickly. He decided to hang Gavin by his collar in the tree and hope that everyone would think he'd choked to death. It might have worked, if Mrs. Trumble hadn't dropped her brooch when she was helping Wilmot lift the body up in the tree."

"So they came back for the brooch."

"Wilmot came back alone. It was several hours later when Mrs. Trumble realized it was missing. He took Naomi Kendall's scarf to cover his face. When we went back to the manor to confront Naomi about the second attack on Samuel, she said she'd lost her scarf *again*. Which meant it had disappeared before."

"So Wilmot borrowed it more than once to hide his face."

"Perhaps he meant to implicate Naomi. That's something we'll never know. Anyway, in between the time Wilmot killed Mr. Hargrove and then returned to look for the brooch, Baxter and Samuel had taken the body down. We don't know for sure what happened, of course, but Wilmot must have seen Baxter and hit him over the head, then run down Samuel with the trap. We're assuming he dragged them both deeper into the woods, perhaps hoping they'd get lost and perish in the cold."

Madeline shuddered. "How diabolical."

"Indeed," Cecily said, with feeling. "Of course, he never found the brooch because Colonel Fortescue had picked it up earlier. It must have been a nasty shock for him when Mrs. Trumble told him I'd arrived at the manor with it in my hand."

"But you still haven't explained how the body ended up in your trap."

"Mrs. Trumble told Sam Northcott that they stood in the trap to lift the body up into the trees. We think that when Wilmot saw the body lying on the ground after he'd attacked Samuel and Baxter, he must have tried to hang the body up again, and used our trap to stand in. Perhaps he'd left his own trap out of sight down the trail. He'd hurt his knee, so it must have been difficult for him. He might have dropped the body, overbalanced, and fallen out of the trap."

"At which the horse was spooked and bolted for home."

"Precisely. At least, that's the best theory we can imagine. I suppose we'll never know for certain."

"How frustrating. So many unanswered questions." Madeline stared into the flames. "Still, it all ended all right. Things could have turned out so much more tragically than they did. You all had an angel watching over you."

"We did, indeed." Cecily smiled at her friend. "You didn't have anything to do with that, by any chance?"

Before Madeline could answer, the door opened and Baxter limped in, his face registering surprise when he saw her. "Prestwick is down in the ballroom looking for you," he informed her.

"Oh, heavens." Madeline rose. "I promised him I would meet him there and I'm late, as usual." She waved an elegant hand at Cecily. "I shall see you both in the ballroom later?"

"Of course." Cecily rose to her feet and accompanied her

friend to the door. "Don't wait too long to set the wedding date, Madeline. Kevin won't wait forever."

"Before next New Year's Eve. I promise you." With another wave she was gone.

"It's usually the man who drags his feet with regards to wedded bliss," Baxter commented, as he drew closer to the fire.

"I am amazed that Madeline actually agreed to marry him." Cecily walked over to her husband and linked her arm through his. "How is the ankle, my love? Still hurting you?"

"Enough that I still won't be able to dance with you."

"That's quite all right. I'm quite content to sit by your side."

"Are you?" He looked uncommonly serious. "I wish I could provide enough excitement for you so that you wouldn't look for it in such dangerous environments."

"Poor Bax. I do give you such a trying time, don't I." She drew closer to him. "I must admit, this latest adventure gave me reason to doubt the wisdom of my ways. Though to be fair, had it not been for your disappearance, I might not have pursued Gavin Hargrove's killer with such persistence. After the way the gypsies cared for you, I could not stand by and allow the constables to hound them as suspects."

"That is the problem, Cecily. You can always find an excuse to get yourself involved in these misadventures. If you had any regard for my sanity, you would swear as your resolution for the new year to abstain from such nefarious activities."

"You know I can't give you such a promise, Bax, my love." She smiled up at him. "What I will promise is to at least think twice and maybe a third time before embarking on any new adventures."

"And that, I suppose," Baxter said gloomily, "is all I can expect from you."

"Indubitably." She tugged at his hand. "Come let us prepare for the ball tonight. We should look our very best to welcome in the new year." *And may it be kind to us all*, she added silently.

Here's a special preview of the next
Holiday Pennyfoot Hotel Mystery
by Kate Kingsbury . . .

RINGING IN MURDER

Coming November 2008
from Berkley Prime Crime!

"I still find it hard to believe that your wedding is only a few days away." Cecily Sinclair Baxter examined a crystal bell for cracks before handing it to the slender woman perched on a stool in front of the Christmas tree. "I truly did not think the day would ever dawn."

Madeline Pengrath's tinkling laugh seemed to echo in the high ceiling of the library. "You have to agree, I am well past the age of a blushing young bride. I can imagine what people are saying—what is a respected doctor like Kevin Prestwick thinking, marrying that old witch? She must have cast one of her dastardly spells on him."

Cecily would have laughed, too, except Madeline was closer to the truth than she cared to acknowledge. "Piffle," she said briskly. "I'm quite sure the people of Badgers End are happy that the doctor has found not only a good wife, but a beautiful one, no less."

"Why thank you kindly, my friend, but I think it's more likely they are plotting how to get rid of me."

In spite of the leaping flames in the fireplace, Cecily shivered. The Pennyfoot Country Club had dealt with more than its share of misfortunes over the past Christmas seasons. So much so that she couldn't find humor in any hint of disaster, no matter how remote.

To change the subject, she murmured, "Yet another year has flown by. It really doesn't seem that long since we were celebrating the turn of the century."

"Well, things have certainly changed since King Edward took over the throne."

"They certainly have. I often wonder if the late queen is turning over in her grave. She was such a stickler for protocol. Her son has no such restraint, I'm afraid."

Madeline grinned. "And the country is much happier for it. Come Cecily, surely you don't begrudge people some levity in their lives? You must admit, Queen Victoria was a priggish tyrant who frowned upon the slightest hint of revelry. No wonder Edward is such a libertine."

"Levity is one thing. Promiscuity is something else entirely."

"But so much fun!"

Madeline's eyes twinkled with mischief, and sensing she was deliberately trying to shock her, Cecily changed the subject again. "How is your friend Miss Danbury enjoying our little seaside town? It was good of her to come in for your wedding, though it's quite a change from London, I'm afraid. I trust she's not finding it too cold and damp for comfort?"

Madeline stretched an arm to hang the bell near the top of the tree. Her long black hair, which she refused to bind up, reached almost to her waist, and swung back and forth as she moved. "Not at all. Grace is quite enjoying the recent snowfall. It doesn't snow that often in the city."

"It does make everything seem more festive." Cecily dug into the large box on the floor and came up with a bag of white lace angels. "I noticed she wasn't at the midday meal yesterday. I do hope she's not under the weather?"

"She's perfectly well." Madeline took an angel from her and examined it with a frown. "She met a friend from London. I believe they planned to go gift shopping in Wellercombe."

Cecily stared up at her friend. "Goodness. I would have thought shopping in London would have been far more productive. After all, the choice is somewhat limited in a small town like Wellercombe."

"But the prices are a good deal more reasonable. Grace loves to find bargains, and she said her friend was delighted to spend a day at the seaside."

"Ah." Cecily nodded. "A man friend, I presume."

"Not at all. Grace doesn't much care for male companionship."

"Well, I hope she will attend the banquet this evening."

"I'm sure she will. She's looking forward to it. As am I." Madeline handed her back the ornament. "I think I'll put these angels on the tree in the foyer. They looked very nice there last year."

"They did indeed." Cecily smiled, remembering how

lovely the tree looked. "Will you make those pretty little sugar bells again?"

"I already have." Madeline waited while Cecily dug deeper into the box. "Did Phoebe manage to finish your gown for the wedding?"

Cecily paused. Phoebe Carter-Holmes Fortescue was an excellent seamstress who, before her marriage to Colonel Fortescue, out of financial necessity had sewn her entire wardrobe. She had offered to make the bridesmaids dresses as a wedding present for Madeline.

Phoebe and Madeline were Cecily's very best friends, but both could be somewhat unpredictable. "Phoebe assures me the dresses will be ready for the wedding on New Year's Eve," Cecily said, praying that was true. "She plans to do the final fitting right after Christmas."

"Well, I hope she doesn't let us down. I would hate to see my maid of honor walking down the aisle in a tea gown."

Cecily laughed. "This will be my first time attending a wedding as maid of honor. I promise you, I will make sure that Phoebe has us all properly attired."

"Yes, much as I dislike the idea of being married in a church, I am happy that you and Grace will be my attendants. I can't say as much for the other bridesmaid. I've never met Emily Winchester, but from what Kevin tells me about her, I have a feeling I won't like her."

Since Madeline's predictions tended to be remarkably accurate, Cecily felt a small qualm. She had been the one to persuade Madeline to marry her handsome doctor in the sanctity of the Lord's house, and in deference to her friend and her future husband, Madeline had reluctantly agreed.

Knowing quite well that her friend would much rather have been married privately in the woods with only the birds and woodland creatures in attendance, Cecily wanted so much for the wedding to be perfect in every way.

Picking out a green glass ball inlaid with gold filigree, she murmured, "I happened to bump into Mrs. Winchester yesterday morning. She seems pleasant enough, though a little put out. Her husband had to return to London for the day. An emergency with a patient, I believe she said. He's Kevin's best man, isn't he?"

"Yes. Dr. Winchester studied with Kevin in London. They have remained best friends, even though they haven't seen much of each other since then."

"Well, I'm sure you and the doctor's wife will become the best of friends, too." She handed the ball to Madeline. "You have such a sweet nature, Madeline. Everyone who knows you loves you."

"Not everyone. Phoebe, for instance. She will never forgive me for not inviting her to be a bridesmaid."

"On the contrary, I do believe she was quite relieved. I know she was most pleased that you had accepted her offer to sew the dresses."

"Well, I felt obligated to allow her to be part of all this fuss. After all, her son will be performing the ceremony." Madeline sighed. "I suppose her cuckoo husband will have to be there."

Cecily hid a grin. "I can't imagine Phoebe being there without him."

"Well, we can only hope that he behaves himself and refrains from attacking imaginary enemies or I'll be forced to turn him into a toad."

Cecily's grin vanished. As well as she knew Madeline, she could never be quite sure that her friend wasn't actually capable of carrying out her outlandish threats.

"At least we shall have one dependable member of the wedding party," Madeline murmured. "It was so very gallant of Baxter to agree to give me away." She raised herself on her toes to reach an upper branch, her floral skirt swirling around her bare ankles.

Madeline often declined to wear shoes or stockings while indoors, which has raised more than one aristocratic eyebrow in the halls of the Pennyfoot.

As for the local residents of Badgers End, they were well used to Madeline's odd habits. Though the women tended to fear her and kept out of her way, unknown to most of them their husbands flocked to Madeline's house for a supply of her special potions. Many of them owed their continuing virility to Madeline's magic touch with herbs and flowers.

"I do think that's enough on the tree for now." Cecily gazed in admiration at her friend's handiwork. "It looks quite dazzling. Besides, I'm becoming quite nervous watching you dance around on that narrow stool."

Madeline laughed, and leapt lightly down from her perch. "Dear Cecily. You know you worry entirely too much."

"Perhaps." Cecily closed the lid of the box. "Then again, while running an establishment as popular as the Pennyfoot, I have a lot to worry about."

"You should insist that Baxter help you more. After all, he used to be manager of the Pennyfoot before he married you."

"Baxter has his own business to worry about. Though he

does help me a great deal when we are busy. Which reminds me. He should be home from the city by now. I need to talk to him about the Christmas Eve ceremonies."

"And I must finish the decorating if I am to attend the banquet tonight." Madeline bent down and with surprising ease hoisted the heavy box in her arms. "Christmas is only two days away. There is still so much to do before the wedding." She hurried over to the door. "We will see you at the banquet, then. It was good of you to invite Kevin and me."

"It will be your last Christmas as a single woman." Cecily followed her to the door. "I want all of us to share at least part of it."

Madeline made a face. "Including that insufferable Phoebe and her deranged husband?"

"Of course." Cecily gave her a gentle poke. "You can complain about Phoebe all you like, Madeline, but I know quite well that you are fond of her."

"As a horse is fond of flies," Madeline muttered. She waited for Cecily to open the door for her then squeezed through with the box in her arms. "Ah well, beggars can't be choosers, as they say."

She drifted off down the hallway, her breathless "Good-bye" floating behind her.

Gertie McBride stomped down the hallway to the kitchen, muttering to herself under her breath. *Christmas.* Nothing but a big fuss and a lot of hard work. She slapped open the kitchen door so hard it swung back, bounced off the wall and smacked into her as she barged through.

"Bloody hell!" Rubbing her nose, she glared at Mrs. Chubb as if it were her fault.

The housekeeper dug her fists into her ample hips and shook her head at her chief housemaid. "Gertie Brown McBride! What's got into you lately? You're like an elephant loose at a vicarage tea party, crashing and banging around like that."

"I bumped me nose, didn't I." Gertie stalked over to the sink and turned on the tap. "I think it's bleeding."

"Here, let me look." Mrs. Chubb peered at her face. "No, it's not bleeding. Now you'd better tell me what's got you in such a dither."

"It's that Lady Clara on the top floor. Blinking miserable, she is. She's been complaining ever since she got here two days ago. Her window doesn't have a view of the ocean, and the fireplace isn't big enough, and the bedclothes aren't silk and she wants fresh roses on her dresser."

Mrs. Chubb raised her eyebrows. "Roses?"

"Yeah." Filling her palm with the ice cold water, Gertie splashed some on her sore nose. "She says as how she heard about the rose gardens here and was expecting roses in her room. Talk about potty. Who ever heard of roses growing in the winter?"

Mrs. Chubb dusted flour from the bib of her apron and went back to her table. Picking up her rolling pin, she began flattening out the lump of pastry on the large wooden board. "Maybe you should have a word with madam. She'd want to know if one of her guests isn't happy. Especially the wife of an important member of parliament like Sir Walter Hetherton."

Gertie sniffed, dug in the pocket of her apron for a hand-kerchief and dabbed her wet nose. "What's so blinking important about him, anyway? He makes me sick, strut-ting around like he's Lord Almighty. Not like he's royalty, is it."

"He might as well be, seeing as how he's the speaker in the House of Lords."

"So what?"

"So he's blue-blooded, that's what."

"I bet if he nicks his chin with a razor his blood is as red as yours or mine."

"You know what I mean."

Gertie tossed her head. "Well, hoity-toity Lady Clara ain't the only wife of an MP. What about that Mrs. Crossley in room twelve? She's the wife of an MP, too."

"Roland Crossley might be an MP, but he's in the House of Commons. There's a world of difference." The housekeeper reached for a pie plate and slapped the pastry onto it. Taking a knife, she deftly trimmed the edges, leaving strips of the dough lying all around the plate.

"They both work for the government, don't they?" Gertie walked over to the massive dresser and pulled out a drawer. Taking out a tray of silverware, she closed the drawer again with a nudge of her hip. "Anyhow, he ain't no bleeding saint, neither. Went off hunting yesterday, he did, and left his wife all alone. What was she supposed to do all day all by herself?" Carrying the tray over to the table, she muttered, "All a bunch of gormless twerps if you ask me."

"Nobody's asking you, my girl, so hold your tongue." Mrs. Chubb gathered up the strips of pastry and squeezed them into a ball. "Talking like that about our guests will get you into trouble with madam, if you don't watch out."

"Madam would agree with me." Gertie picked up a fork and started rubbing it with a soft cloth. "She don't have no time for the government, seeing as how they treat women. Throwing them into jail and doing horrible things to them when all we want is the right to vote like the men."

Mrs. Chubb sighed. "Don't get started on that again, Gertie McBride. Once you get on your high horse over women's rights it takes a stick of dynamite to get you off."

"What ees this I hear about dynamite?"

Gertie looked up as a wiry man in a white chef's cap strode into the kitchen. "Nothing to do with you, Michel," she said sharply, "so you can keep your blinking nose out of it."

"It is to do with me if you blow up my kitchen, *non?*" The chef marched over to the stove and started rattling the saucepan lids—a sure sign he was upset about something.

Wisely, Gertie kept quiet. She loved to get Michel going in a good fight and usually got the best of him, but she knew when to leave him alone and judging by the way he was throwing stuff around on the stove, this was one of those times.

Instead, she caught Mrs. Chubb's eye and silently mouthed at her. *What's up with him?*

The housekeeper lifted her shoulders and let them fall. Shaking her head in warning, she said sharply, "Stop arguing and finish polishing that silverware. We'll be serving supper in less than two hours and the tables aren't even laid yet."

Gertie raised her chin in protest. "The banquet's being held in the ballroom, remember? The tables have been laid since the crack of dawn this morning."

"Not with the silverware they haven't. Before you do that, though, find madam and let her know that Lady Clara isn't satisfied with her room. She wouldn't want anything to spoil a guest's Christmas visit."

"I don't know what's so bloody special about Christmas, anyway." Gertie rubbed the cloth viciously on a dessert spoon. "Work ourselves to death, we do."

Mrs. Chubb frowned. "You love Christmas. You know you do. You get as excited about it as those twins of yours."

"Yeah, well, sometimes I get tired of all the fuss."

Michel slammed a saucepan down on the stove. "I know what is making her so meeserable. She misses her sweetheart, *non*?"

Gertie sent him a ferocious glare. "Just goes to show what you know, Mr. Bleeding Know-It-All. I don't miss him at all, so there."

She barely resisted the urge to stick out her tongue at him. Nothing was going to make her admit that she missed Dan Perkins dreadfully. It was about this time last year when she first met him, and all the Christmas preparations reminded her of those exciting days.

Mrs. Chubb looked worried. "You're not pining after Dan still, are you, Gertie? I don't know why you turned him down, I really don't. He's got money. Lots of it. He could have given you and the twins a wonderful life."

"In London," Gertie said sharply. "I told you all this before. He wanted us all to go and live with him in the city.

Can you see the likes of me trying to fit in with the people he mixes with every day? All those toffs sticking their noses in the air because of the way me and my little ones talk? No bleeding thank you."

"You could have learned to talk better," Michel offered.

Gertie turned on him. "Why should I bloody talk better? It's not how I talk but how I bleeding behave that makes me what I am."

"Exactly," Mrs. Chubb said, shaking her head at Michel. "Dan knew that."

"Well, his friends wouldn't." Gertie threw down the last fork in disgust. "Sooner or later they would have turned him against me. I've been through enough bloody heartache with men. I'm not going to let another one break my heart, so there."

"Just because the twins' father didn't let on he was married when he got you pregnant doesn't mean all men are like that." Mrs. Chubb dusted more flour from her apron and slapped her hands together to dislodge it from her fingers. "Look at Ross McBride. He loved you enough to marry you and take on another man's children, didn't he. Not many men like that."

"Yeah, and then he went and died on me, didn't he. Left me all alone and broke my children's hearts."

"He couldn't help dying, Gertie."

"Yeah, well, I'm through with men. As far as I'm concerned, me and my twins are better off without them." Gertie headed for the door.

"You say that all the time," Michel called after her. "Until the next one, *oui*?"

"Bugger off," Gertie said rudely, and swept out into the hallway.

By the time she'd climbed the stairs to madam's suite she was feeling a little less cranky. The gorgeous fragrance of pine from the Christmas tree followed her, and in spite of her bad mood she felt a tug of excitement at the thought of the twins on Christmas morning when they saw what Father Christmas had brought them.

James and Lillian were her life, and she'd move heaven and earth to make them happy. They had been through so much, losing Ross—the man they'd adored and looked upon as a father.

Thank heavens they'd never known their real father. Gertie pulled a face as she reached madam's door and raised her hand to knock on it. Ian Rossiter was never no good and never would be.

Hearing madam's voice from within the room, Gertie squared her shoulders, pushed open the door and went inside.